POWER

Dark Anomaly, book 2

Marina Simcoe

To My Captain

Power

Marina Simcoe

Marina.Simcoe@Yahoo.com

Facebook/Marina Simcoe Author

This book is a work of fiction. Names, characters, places and incidents are a product of the author's imagination. Locales and public names are used for atmospheric purposes. Any resemblance to actual people, living or dead, or to businesses, companies, events, institutions or locales is completely coincidental.

Cover Design by Naomi Lucas and Marina Simcoe

First Edition

Spelling: English (American)

Editing and Proofreading by Cissell Ink

Power is a Science-Fiction romance. It contains graphic descriptions of intimacy, violence, and discussion on topics that may be triggering for some. Intended for mature readers.

Chapter 1

THE IMPACT WAS ENORMOUS. Much harder than I'd expected. The hull of our spaceship groaned and screeched. The walls warped and bulged. The panel closest to Val, one of our pilots, caved in, somehow breaking through the protective energy barrier around her chair. She screamed in pain as the armrest snapped, digging into her side.

Jose, the captain, had lost control during the landing, which turned into a crash. I'd caught the moment it happened. His eyes grew larger as he frantically ran his fingers over the control panel. His skin paled, and perspiration beaded on his forehead. No matter how hard he worked, he couldn't prevent our ship from slamming into the edge of the anomaly harder than even the worst of the landings during our training sessions.

Then, all went still and dark.

A moment later, the auxiliary system kicked in, flicking on the lights.

"Val!" Jose climbed out of his seat and rushed to his second-in-command who doubled over in her seat. "Are you okay?"

"I'm pretty sure I broke my rib," she groaned, pressing her hand to her side. "And I think I'm bleeding."

Like all of us, Val was wearing a pale-blue suit, covered with colorful logos from the collar to the boots. I saw no tearing in the material and no blood. It didn't mean she wasn't bleeding underneath it.

Lee, the scientist on board, clicked his seat belt off and jumped out of his chair. "We need to get her into the medical capsule."

Val groaned softly as Lee led her to the wall with the medical bed concealed inside.

"How is everyone else doing?" Jose rose to his feet, surveying the rest of us—two on-board engineers and me, the movie producer.

Yes, that was what I was—the movie producer. My sole purpose on the team was to record everything that could later be assembled into a movie, a documentary, or a series to air for profit. The footage would also provide visual evidence of whatever we discovered here.

The Earth Space Coalition had stopped exploration of the Anomaly GR-A8502 shortly after the disappearance of the scientist Svetlana Kostyk. She had been part of the team studying the mysterious anomaly from a station that orbited the nearby water world Omphi. She'd gone missing during a solo mission a little over fifty years ago. Her ship had lost all communications with the station, and neither the ship nor Svetlana Kostyk had ever been found.

Passionate about her work and new discoveries, it was believed that Svetlana might have come too close to the Anomaly and had been sucked in along with her ship.

Instead of shedding some light on the mysterious Anomaly, Svetlana had only added more mystery to this celestial body. Her disappearance sparked a number of speculations on what might be inside of it.

Five years ago, it had been proven that a solid core lay at the center of the unpredictable force field, renewing keen interest in exploring it further. The mission was deemed too risky by the Earth governments who refused to finance it. Luckily, several private corporations had stepped in, outfitting our expedition.

"Nadia? Are you okay?" Jose glanced my way, not leaving Val's side.

I climbed out of my chair, unsteadily. "I'm fine, I think—"

A screeching noise cut me off, then a fountain of sparks shot from the wall. Another malfunction? Were we not done crashing yet?

Both engineers rushed to the wall but were forced to keep their distance as the spray of sparks fanned in a wide circle. The melting paneling material dripped to the floor.

"Get in the suits, everyone!" Jose ordered. "We have a hull breach."

Lee quickly turned Val toward the hatch where our suits were kept. I ran after them.

With a slamming sound, an uneven oval cut-out of the wall fell in, followed by a smoky cloud with a chemical smell.

"What the—" I heard the confused voice of one of the engineers who was fully enveloped into the smoke. His voice was cut off by a wet crunching sound that I couldn't place at first.

A tall, dark figure emerged from the dissipating smoke that rolled off his shoulders like a cloak.

Then the motionless body of the engineer came into view. He lay on the floor, his neck twisted at an unnatural angle. My stomach roiled when it dawned on me what that wet-snappy sound had been. The monster that had just barged onto our ship had snapped my teammate's neck.

I stepped back, frozen in shock and horror. I'd never witnessed a murder before. Heck, I'd never seen any crime being committed right in front of me. Crime, in general, had been all but eliminated on all the main planets of the Federation, including Earth.

I kept staring at the motionless body on the floor, unable to move a muscle. The man who'd been a living, breathing, thinking individual just moments ago, was nothing but a corpse with its neck snapped.

Jose recovered first.

"We are a peaceful delegation!" He faced the newcomer—the *errock*, I recognized his species.

His yellow eyes narrowed as he gave each of us an assessing glare.

At least a few inches taller than the biggest man of my crew, the *errock* seemed twice as broad. His reddish skin darkened to gray on the hard ridges running along his arms and bald head. Wearing black pants, dark boots, and a wide utility belt, the male was topless.

Errocks were a civilized nation. Yet this individual's behavior was that of a feral, murderous animal.

The second engineer suddenly leaped on the newcomer's back with a laser knife clutched in his hand.

With a grunt, the *errock* grabbed the engineer's head and yanked it, twisting it with his hands. The human's neck snapped with the same wet cracking noise I'd heard earlier. I swayed on my feet, ready to barf.

"Oh, my God..." Val whimpered. She staggered backwards to the wall while pressing an arm to her side. Her face as white as the wall behind her, she slid to the floor.

"Run!" Jose shoved me aside, grabbing a long, heavy tool from the shelf in the suit storage.

Run! But where?

According to the glowing sign over the airlock by the control panel, outer space lay behind it. I had no time to get into my spacesuit. We were trapped on the ship, with the huge, murderous *errock* blocking the only exit he'd created. Where did he come from? Why was he killing everyone unprovoked?

I had no idea, but it was clear he wasn't going to stop. A murderous glimmer in his eyes, lips curved in a menacing smile, he faced Jose.

I anxiously darted my gaze along the walls and the ceiling around me, searching for an escape route, a place to hide, anything. Running to our sleeping cabin would only make it easier for the *errock* to corner me there.

My body shook. Everything inside me vibrated with horror and the need to escape.

The escape capsule!

Tripping over my feet, I dashed for the round door next to the suit storage.

From the corner of my eye, I caught the sight of Jose being hurled against the wall by the monstrous *errock*. Our captain's head dangled awkwardly, only attached to his body with muscles and skin.

Lee ran for the opening the *errock* had cut out, probably hoping to escape that way.

Val was lying on the floor next to the round table in our common area in the middle of the ship.

"Val!" I yelled. "Here!"

Curled into a ball, she didn't move. Was she dead, too? The monster must've gotten her already.

"Lee!" I screamed, stabbing my fingers into the control panel next to the entrance of the escape capsule. The door slid open, and I climbed in.

I poked my head out, searching for Lee. The *errock* held him over his head. He slammed our scientist over his knee, snapping the man's spine in half.

My head spun, terror lodging tight in my throat. I hit the panel on the other side of the door, locking myself inside.

The capsule was designed to take us off the Anomaly upon completion of our mission if the ship failed.

My entire team had been annihilated in seconds. Screw the mission, the documentary I was supposed to make, and the astronomical reward I'd been promised.

With trembling fingers, I strapped myself into one of the six seats inside the capsule and initiated the take-off sequence on the on-board computer.

I was the last survivor of our ill-fated expedition, and I was getting out of here.

A red warning flashed on the control panel in front of me.

"Not enough power to complete the take-off sequence."

What exactly did it mean? I feverishly searched my brain for any mention of this message during my year-long training for this mission.

The capsule was much smaller than the spaceship. Its engines, however, were many times more powerful than the ship's. The sole purpose of this thing was to take us off the Anomaly. Why wouldn't it do just that?

Had something been damaged during our crash landing? I punched more buttons on the control panel, trying to troubleshoot the problem.

The dreadfully familiar sound scraped against the capsule door from the outside.

The *errock*!

He had murdered my crew and was now cutting through the door of the capsule to get to me, too.

Again and again, I re-started the launch sequence, getting the same message.

"Not enough power."

The shower of hot sparks blew into the capsule. The *errock* was cutting through the door, and I was trapped here, like a mouse in a jar, with nowhere left to run.

Panic shot through me.

"How much power do you need? To lift off a capsule the size of a bus?" I yelled at the control panel. Shaking with anger and fear, I punched it with my fists.

I heard a loud thud behind me. The fine hairs on the back of my neck stood up as I sensed *his* presence inside the capsule. His heavy breathing reached my ear.

I didn't want to turn around and face him. Everything inside me urged me to curl into a ball and make myself invisible. Only, there was no place to hide in the capsule.

I'd been cornered.

"Where do you think you're going?" the *errock* growled, mockingly.

Hearing him speak somehow made him even more monstrous. He obviously was a self-aware, intelligent being, not an enraged animal. Yet, he had killed my entire team in cold blood.

His words spurred me into action. I scrambled to the wall, avoiding his hands as he reached for me, then scurried for the opening he'd just made.

If I made it past him, I could get off the ship the way he had come. Fingers crossed, there were no more creatures like him out there.

Tripping over my hands and feet in panic, I climbed out of the opening and back into the spaceship.

"Not so fast." The *errock's* heavy hand swiped me off my feet.

I fell face down. Then the enormous weight of the *errock* crashed on top of me.

Nearly crushed under him, I could barely breathe. Clawing at the floor tiles with my fingers, I attempted to crawl from under him, but that was like trying to shift a tank off me.

"I'll fuck you fast before anyone gets here," he growled in my ear, yanking at my suit. "But I *will* fuck you, even if it's the last thing I do."

He hooked his fingers into the neckline of my suit from behind, and tugged it down, almost choking me. The material held, frustrating him. Painfully grabbing on to my shoulder and hip, he flipped me over.

I came face to face with my attacker. The look in his yellow eyes terrified me even more than his actions. There was no thought in them, no emotion other than the unhinged, feral lust.

Pinning my hips under his pelvis, he straddled me.

The moment his chest lifted off mine, I greedily sucked some air into my oxygen starved lungs.

"Female," he smirked, pawing at my breasts through the suit. Leaning closer, he sniffed my neck. "Smell good, too. Good enough to eat." He dragged his tongue down my throat.

"No. Please..." I whimpered, already knowing that my pleas would make no difference to him. He acted as if he didn't even hear them, sniffing down my body.

Hooking his arms under my knees, he yanked them open and dropped his head between my thighs.

Around my core, I felt the heat of his mouth through the suit. Then a sharp pain blinded me as he bit down.

Anger cut through the terror from the pain. I thrashed in his arms, slamming my fists at his bald head. The three hard ridges running along his skull hurt my hands, but I didn't care. I didn't care about anything other than getting as far away from this monster as possible.

"Yeah, fight me." Satisfaction was thick in his growl as he effortlessly caught my both hands in one of his and fisted his other hand in my hair.

Tears sprang to my eyes at the pain on my scalp as he yanked.

"You didn't wait for me, Nocc," a new deep voice suddenly sounded from above us. "It's against the rules to board a new ship on your own."

Through the blurry film of tears, I saw another *errock* standing by. His arms folded across his chest, he seemed unaffected by the horrors that one of his species had inflicted on my spaceship and my person.

Did he come to join my attacker?

The thought made me wish I'd been killed along with Lee, Val, and the rest of my crew.

"Fuck off, Wyck," the one called Nocc gritted through his teeth. His hand in my hair, he yanked my head back, grinding his crotch against me.

I screamed again at the sudden pain in my neck. It felt like it would snap any minute. Maybe he would kill me sooner than later?

Wyck, the second *errock*, grabbed Nocc around his throat and shoved him off me. I was able to draw a full breath once again.

"What the fuck!" Nocc leaped to his feet with a speed shocking for his size.

Wyck shifted from foot to foot, as if confused by his own action.

"You're killing her," he muttered.

"Not yet. First, I'm going to fuck her!" Nocc bellowed, lunging for me again. "You can stay and watch, but don't you dare get in my way."

I rolled on the floor, scrambling away from him. Nocc tripped over my foot with a long, filthy curse.

Wyck quickly stepped over my legs, placing himself between Nocc and me.

"Kill those who are aggressive," he said. "Let the captain deal with the rest. Those are the rules for each new ship's arrival."

"Since when do you care about *his* rules?"

"There is no need to kill her." It sounded more like a suggestion than a call to action. My defender wasn't that passionate about defending me.

"I'm not killing her," Nocc snarled. "I'm fucking her. Just as soon as I get her out of that damn suit."

"Fucking and killing is the same in your case," Wyck observed calmly.

"In *our* case, Wyck." Nocc shoved at the other *errock's* shoulder. "Don't you forget that. *Errocks* are one and the same around here." He threw a lustful look down at me. "Help me strip her. I'll let you have what's left of her after me."

Thankfully, Wyck didn't seem convinced.

"Vrateus will need to see her first."

"*Him?* You know what will happen once he gets here. Nothing!" Nocc spat through his teeth. "I want my fun. Now."

He licked his lips, glancing down at me again.

"I think you should wait." That came as just another suggestion, though there was a certain power in Wyck's voice.

"Why? Is it because he's made you the leader of his guard?" Nocc scoffed. "Maybe you think he'll give *you* the female?"

Both of them appeared too absorbed by their arguing to pay me much attention. Pulling my legs up, I crab-walked away from them.

A hissing growl behind me sent a chill of dread down my spine. Swinging my head around, I came face to face with a creature that could've only come from a nightmare. All of it felt like a horrible dream.

A three-headed animal the size of a large dog scowled and hissed at me. Each of its mouths possessed several rows of sharp translucent teeth. A wet roar vibrated in all three of its throats.

I choked on my next breath as the monster lunged for me. With a clank, the chain around its middle neck stretched, yanking the beast backwards. It was chained to the railing on the wall I realized with relief as I scurried out of its reach.

Now, I was trapped between the three-headed hissing monstrosity and the two giant *errocks*.

"Get out of my way!" Nocc roared, sending a powerful blow at Wyck's jaw. The other *errock* staggered back, shaking his head.

"Fuck you, Nocc!" he yelled, lunging into a counterattack a moment later.

The two collided like giant boulders crashing into each other with the aftershock of the impact reverberating through the entire ship.

"You're not getting her, boy," Nocc squeezed through his clenched teeth, punching Wyck in the ribs.

"I am your fucking leader, Nocc!" Wyck pummeled Nocc's head, landing one blow after another. How the other *errock* remained conscious and upright after that beating was beyond me.

Frantically, I searched for a way around them. With the escape capsule proven useless, I needed to sneak past them to the cut-out that Nocc had made in the hull of the ship. I had no idea what lay beyond it, but it couldn't be much worse than what threatened me in here.

Stifling my whimpers of horror, I crawled over to Lee's broken body. Jose was lying just a short distance away from him. Both dead. Val was gone, though. Did Nocc move her? Or was she still alive? The hope that she might've survived this nightmare and gotten away rose inside me.

Maybe I could get out of here, too?

My hope was quickly squashed as someone blocked the exit—a group of aliens, it appeared. Though, I had no chance to see who exactly or how many.

"What is going on here?" A tall male entered.

I quickly retreated to the animal on the chain. Ironically, the horrible beast seemed to be less threatening than the men. At least the animal would just kill me quickly. A shudder of fear and misery rolled through me at my utter lack of options.

Hardly sparing me a glance, the newcomer moved toward the *errocks*. He was dressed better than them in a white voluminous shirt, tall boots, and dark brown pants. He had a white stripe of fur on his head and a long, fluffy tail. His species seemed familiar, like I'd seen them in a picture somewhere.

Themul.

I remembered the name for his kind. They came from a small, obscure planet on the fringes of the Federation. I'd never met one in person before.

Brought down to his knees, Nocc smeared blood on his face with the back of his hand. He spoke to the newcomer, "This does not concern you. You already have a female. You can't have them all."

Wyck had pummeled him hard enough to break skin on his lip and possibly the cartilage in his nose. The two had fought like savage beasts. Over me, "the female?" Did I somehow land in pre-historic times? Unfortunately for me, the lives of women weren't great back then.

I searched the floor for anything I could use as a weapon.

"So, you have fought, I see," the newcomer said to the *errocks.* "Wyck won?"

Nocc leaped to his feet. "He is not getting her!"

Other aliens started to climb in through the opening. There were several different species. I recognized a *dimo*, his tall bulky body covered in hard plates similar to a rhinoceros, a few *yourlus* with clusters of pale-blue tentacles instead of arms and legs, and at least one black-and-beige *ognat,* with eight pairs of skinny limbs all along his oblong body.

"He did best you," the *themul* said to Nocc.

My gaze fell on the handle of the laser knife under Lee's foot. One of the engineers had dropped it. Keeping an eye on the males debating who "deserved" to rape me first, I scooted closer to Lee's dead body.

The arguing grew louder.

"No one is getting the female!" the *themul* shouted fiercely over the noise. "No one!"

He lifted his hand, holding a gun. The sight of the weapon sent a new shiver of dread down my spine.

Sliding my hand under Lee's foot, I swiped the knife handle quickly and hid it inside the long sleeve of my bodysuit. The laser utility knife was a tool, not a real weapon. Still, having something to defend myself with made me feel a little better.

"She will be brought to the mess hall, weekly." The *themul* said, making me snap to attention. "You'll be getting your entertainment back."

This man appeared to have authority over the rest of them. The *errocks* had stopped fighting in his presence. Those who had come later kept their distance, remaining close to the opening in the wall.

"As the leader of my personal guard, Wyck will have the honor of taking care of the female," the *themul* announced.

What possibly could "taking care" mean in this place? I nervously balled my hands into fists, expecting Wyck to attack me any minute.

Nocc growled. Spitting on the floor, he threw a heated glare at the *themul* then stormed out, shoving everyone out of his way.

The man in the white shirt definitely was in charge here. Now, he was giving instructions to Wyck.

"What about the second female?" Wyck asked.

"What second female?" the *themul* replied sharply.

"When I got here, there were two females, at first."

Two?

Wyck had seen Val, then. Where did she go? I hoped for her sake that she'd managed to hide on the ship somewhere.

One of the aliens called the *themul* "captain," confirming my assumption that he must be the figure of authority here.

I took a bracing breath.

"You're the leader here," I addressed the captain.

"Was there another human female on the ship?" he asked me. "Where did she go?"

"Another?" I stared at him. There was no way I would tell him about Val. If she had managed to hide, she'd be better off staying hidden. "No. Just me. I'm the only one left alive," I said quickly. "Listen, I'm appealing to you as the leader—"

"No," the captain cut me off. "Wyck is in charge of you. Tell him what you need. Wyck, take her out of here, the rest of you..." he faced the males filling in the space. "You all will have to help me remove the equipment tonight."

Everyone seemed to be moving on, leaving Wyck, the *errock* who had just fought for the right to rape me, "in charge" of me.

Panic spiked hot inside me. "Captain!" I scrambled to my feet.

"Listen," Wyck spoke to me. "What's your name?"

"I'm not talking to *you*," I dismissed him quickly, moving after the captain who had already started to organize his crew.

Wyck strode to me. I'd never realized how massive *errocks* really were. Maybe because I'd never stood next to one this close before. Or maybe this one was especially huge, even for his kind.

Much taller than an average human male, Wyck towered over me. His chest was above my eye level, his bulging muscles partially concealed by a short leather vest that was open in the middle.

"Fine," he said. "Don't talk to me, then. I don't care about anything you have to say, anyway."

He wrapped his enormous hand around my arm, dragging me toward the opening in the wall as if I were nothing more than a fly.

Chapter 2

"Let me go!" The female thrashed in his grip as he took her out into the corridor.

Her scent, maddeningly tantalizing, assaulted his senses. Warm and feminine, she smelled...sweet, like the pollen sugar Svetlana used in her baking. Suddenly, he wondered if the female's skin would also taste sweet if he licked it...

"Get your filthy paws off me!" She made another attempt to yank her arm out of his hand.

The males, crowding the corridor, snickered and leered. Some laughed openly.

Wyck closed his eyes for a moment and quickly exhaled the air rich with her enticing sweetness. Reining in the wild urges her presence had caused wasn't easy, but he needed to focus. He was the newly appointed leader of the captain's personal guard, and he would be damned if he'd let this woman humiliate him in front of the crew.

"Move it." He clenched his jaw, shoving her ahead of him.

The crew parted as he walked her down the corridor, but he lacked the authority of Vrateus to command their respect. They didn't remain quiet.

"Hey, Wyck, are you going to have fun with her?" Someone shouted from the back of the crowd.

"Can I get in on it, too?" Another one chuckled eagerly.

"Listen, you lost a bet three days ago. I want her to pay for you." Krakhil, the *dimo*, unceremoniously reached out and grabbed her thigh, making the female squeal and jump.

"Out of the way," Wyck growled low, shoving the *dimo* aside with his shoulder.

He didn't ask for the female to be placed in his care. Now that this task had been assigned to him, however, he couldn't fail. He already sensed that looking after her would bring its share of trouble.

The female made another attempt to twist out of his grip.

"Let me go, I said." She even stomped her foot. Cute. But useless, nevertheless.

He didn't waste words on her, dragging her along, past the crowd.

"Do you hear me at all?" she raised her voice. "Are you too dumb to understand? I'm not going anywhere with you, or with anyone of your kind. Not after what happened on the ship."

She shoved her elbow into his ribs, hitting the flashlight in the pocket of his vest. The pointy end of the flashlight's handle painfully jammed into his side, sending a flash of irritation through him.

"Stop this." He yanked her arm sharply.

She cried out. The high-pitched sound brought him to a stop.

"You dislocated my shoulder!" she yelled, grabbing onto her arm with her other hand. "It hurts like hell!"

Was she really *that* fragile?

He let go of her, just in case, then stared, unsure what to do next.

She stopped screaming abruptly. Spinning on her heel, she bolted down the corridor, away from him.

A sly, little liar.

He stalked after her, being in no particular hurry. She disappeared out of sight, running around a bend in the corridor, but there was nowhere for her to run. She wouldn't get far.

The corridor lay inside the outer layer of the Dark Anomaly's disk, stretching along the entire habitable sector. It was long but not endless. The female wasn't familiar with the layout of the Anomaly.

She'd never find a place to hide where he wouldn't find her. Besides, her scent trailed in a strong alluring tendril behind her, guiding him.

The female's sharp cry made him move faster, though. It seemed she hadn't made it far after all.

As he turned around the corner, the female came into view. Lying on the floor, she kicked her feet at Kex and Tezul who both tried to climb on top of her.

Instead of rushing to her rescue, Wyck slowed his pace.

Kex was a *yourlu*. The purple, four-armed Tezul was a *bretoin*. Both were horny but not hungry. Had she been attacked by one of the inherently cannibalistic types like *ognats* or *kreers,* he'd be worried about her being bitten and—depending on the location of the bite—seriously injured or even killed.

These two would simply try to get into her pants. Since Nocc's actions hadn't taught her to be cautious, Wyck decided to fall back and let these two teach her another lesson.

He was far less articulate than Vrateus, the captain, to eloquently explain to this female the dangers of running around the Dark Anomaly on her own. He also lacked the captain's patience. *Showing* her what awaited her was much more efficient than telling, in his opinion.

He sauntered toward the trio rolling on the floor. Tezul used his six limbs to catch and immobilize the legs of the female, while Kex slithered his tentacles into the opening of her neckline, yanking the closure of her suit down. The two sides of it fell open.

The sight of the delicate globes of her partially exposed breasts momentarily stopped Wyck in his tracks. The impact of rushing desire felt like a physical blow to his groin. He swallowed a groan as both his cocks throbbed in the tight confines of his pants. Her sweet scent seemed to have permeated his entire being.

With a grunt, the female arched her back, freeing her arm. Something bright flashed in her hand, then half of one of Kex's tentacles dropped to the floor with a wet, sloppy sound.

The female had a weapon!

And she'd sliced Kex's tentacle off.

Alarm jolted him out of the stupor that his raging lust had plunged him into.

Kex wailed in pain. Tezul didn't seem to notice anything at all, busy with fitting himself between her legs while ignoring her suit.

Grabbing Kex by the scruff of the short, tattered shirt he wore, Wyck tossed him aside. Next, he kicked Tezul off her. Whimpering and glaring at him, both scurried away.

"Come." He reached for the female's upper arm again, but she kept brandishing the knife in her hand.

Sitting up jerkily, she suddenly stabbed the blade into his side.

The pain zigzagged through him, all the more acute as it was unexpected.

"What the fuck!" he roared, shock and anger rolling through him in swells. To his relief, however, at least his desire had subsided. "Why me?"

"Why not?" she bit out, her breathing ragged, her expression startled, as though her jamming the laser between his ribs surprised her as well. "Are you any better than them?"

She yanked the closure of her suit back up.

He certainly didn't believe himself to be *better*—or worse—than anyone else on the Dark Anomaly. He was simply a part of the crew. One of them.

"Give it to me!" He wrestled her back to the ground.

Stradling her thighs, he pressed her arm to the floor then forced her fingers open to release the knife handle.

"No!" She slammed her free fist into the side of his head.

The blow was more infuriating than painful. The wriggling of her lithe body under him rushed blood to his groin, all over again.

"Will you stop!" He leaped off her, shoving the laser handle into a pocket on his vest.

"Give me back my knife." Propped on her elbows, she glowered at him from the floor.

Her suit was primly closed all the way up to her throat now. But there was something about her position—her bent legs open, her breasts thrust upward—that made him momentarily lose focus.

She jumped up to her feet, going for the pocket where he'd put her knife. "I need it back!"

"And I need you to listen to me!" He caught her arms and gave her a shake.

This was not going well. His ability to concentrate around her was severely impaired, and he needed all his mental power to keep her safe. It didn't help that she seemed to be dead set on getting herself in trouble.

Immobilized in his grip, she glared at him, her eyes wide open, wild and...green, like the plants in Malahki's garden. Fear shone vividly through her expression. He sensed her body vibrating with it. Fear often made people make irrational decisions and act rashly, didn't it?

Maybe he should try to calm her down first before attempting to talk any sense into her.

"You *need* to listen to me," he said again, softer this time. Closing his eyes for a moment, he inhaled deeply. Her scent rushed in, filling his lungs, but he ignored it the best he could and loosened his grip on her arms somewhat. "What's your name?" He asked again, keeping his voice low and calm.

She blinked, releasing a shuddered breath.

"Nadia." Her voice trembled.

"My job is to keep you safe, Nadia. Don't make me fail at it."

Chapter 3

"MY JOB IS TO KEEP YOU safe."

It took a moment for his words to register. "Safe" should mean I was in no immediate danger, shouldn't it? Of course, it largely depended on Wyck's definition of danger. It didn't escape me that he hadn't been in a rush to help me fight off my assailants.

It felt like from the moment I landed in this place, someone had been trying to assault me. Wyck ended up helping me, every time. Unhurriedly, almost reluctantly, but he had stopped them. Other than manhandling me and taking my weapon away, he hadn't tried to harm or assault me himself.

"What do you mean by 'safe?'" I had to clarify.

"I need to keep you alive." He shrugged. "Not eaten."

"Eaten?" Surely, I didn't hear him right. Sentient beings—humans or aliens—didn't eat each other.

"A few of us here might eat you if you're not careful."

His casual tone must mean he was joking. Wasn't he?

The individuals in this place appeared crude and rough, less civilized than any species I'd ever encountered. I got the impression, though, they were after my body to satisfy their carnal needs, not their hunger. Their actions had been despicable. However, cannibalism would be a whole new level of savagery.

"Would *you*...be one of those few?" I watched him closely.

He made a face, giving me a once-over, as if accessing a supermarket package of meat.

"No. I don't eat humans," he finally said to my relief. Though the fact that he'd taken some time for deliberation before giving me his answer unnerved me.

"Would you do anything else to me?" I asked carefully.

"Right now," he wrapped his huge paw around my upper arm once again, "I will deliver you to your room and keep you there."

"What for?"

He tugged me along the corridor once again. The movement made him wince. He pressed his other hand to his side, over the wound I'd inflicted.

"Come," he bit out sharply.

I moved promptly alongside him. Dark blood welled between his fingers. The knife's blade would have cauterized the edges of the wound. However, I must have made the gash long enough or deep enough or both for the blood to seep through.

"You'll need to get someone to look at that." I gestured at his side.

"Who?" He gave me an incredulous glance, as if I'd suggested something utterly ridiculous, like he'd hop on one foot around me.

"Don't you have a doctor here? Or something like a medical capsule?"

I could tell him about the one we had on our ship. It was meant for humans, but it might have a program to assess and treat other species as well.

Thinking about the medical capsule brought the memory of Lee and Val who never got to use it. The thought of my entire crew left lying dead on the floor stabbed through my heart with pain. Over the year of training, I'd gotten to know those people well. We hadn't been close friends, but we'd gotten along well. I knew they all had dreams they'd hoped to fulfill after completing this mission. Now, most of them were dead. Their dreams gone.

"No. There're no doctors here." Wyck let go of his side, wiping the blood from his hand on his pants. "I'll be fine."

Fine.

Why should I care about his wounds if he didn't? I had other things to worry about. Things that concerned me, personally. Scary things.

"What's going to happen to me, now?"

"You'll stay here." He stopped in front of a set of dark-gray double doors and shoved one side open.

"For how long?" I didn't go through the doors, didn't even so much as glance inside. I had the feeling that walking in would signal my acceptance of my fate before I even knew what it was.

Letting go of me, Wyck crossed his arms over his massive chest, staring at me expectantly with the most bizarre yellow eyes.

"For as long as you shall live," he replied.

For the rest of my life? It didn't even matter how long or short it was going to be. If I were to spend it all here, in this place, it meant my life might as well be over already. I stared at him in a stupor as the seconds ticked by.

"I...I can't," I muttered finally. "I need to get back."

"Back where?" He sounded confused.

"Back to Earth, where I came from."

"That's impossible. So, the sooner you stop thinking about it, the better it'll be."

"There has to be a way." I shook my head.

"There isn't," he bit out. "Now, get in and stay there." He gave me a shove, pushing me through the door backwards.

"How did all of you get here?" I rushed out, holding onto the door frame. "How long have *you* been here?"

"All of my life." He closed the door in my face, leaving me alone.

Trapped.

"Wait!" I tried to slide the door open, pushing at it with my hands. It wouldn't budge.

I leaned my forehead against the cool material of the door. The horror of my situation descending on me.

"That's impossible."

Wyck's words echoed in my mind.

I had no reason to trust anything he said, but could I prove him wrong? Even if I managed to somehow fix the cut-out in the escape capsule door that Nocc had made, I had no idea what to do about the system malfunction.

"Not enough power to take off."

I distinctly remembered the warning message on the control panel, but I didn't know what had caused it or how to fix it.

Our team had been carefully selected. The distinct skill set of each individual was meant to add to the combined knowledge base we had as a group. My expertise, sadly, appeared to be the least useful for the current situation.

As a movie producer, my sole purpose on the team was to obtain appealing footage to create a documentary that would showcase the achievements of our expedition in the best light and make our sponsors look good. The cameras I had installed around the common areas of the ship would've recorded the carnage upon our arrival and the demise of my entire crew—nothing for the sponsors to brag about.

I had no idea how to fix any of the complicated space travel technology that had gotten me here. I'd spent nearly a year in training, learning how to *use* it. It would take years more of studying to learn how to *repair* any of it.

The people who could do something about it were now dead. My chest tightened as the image of the motionless bodies of my teammates rose in my mind's eye again. The horror of their murders churned painfully in my soul.

A little flicker of hope burnt through the darkness of my despair. Val wasn't among the corpses on the floor when Wyck had taken me off our ship. I hadn't witnessed her being killed. Could she have survived and made it out of there undetected? And if she had, how long would she be able to survive in this place?

According to Wyck, being anywhere on the Anomaly on your own meant risking being raped or eaten. After everything I'd experienced here in the short time since our landing, I was inclined to believe him on that one.

The horror of it all crept up my throat, making it hard to breathe and bringing tears to my eyes. I pressed my eyes shut quickly, refusing to let the tears flow. As long as I was still alive, I had to keep going.

First, I needed to talk to Wyck—or anyone who would speak to me—to find out more about this place and those who occupied it.

Letting go of the door, I finally turned around. My breath caught in my throat at the sight of the room Wyck had put me in.

It'd been made entirely out of transparent material. Attached to the pewter-colored wall with the entrance doors, the glass bubble extended out into the open space beyond. The bottom of it was flat, serving as the floor, the rest arched around me, surrounded by the rolling waves of multi-colored light. It ebbed and pulsed in an endless cosmic dance, impairing my sense of reality.

The space beyond the glass room was both beautiful and terrifying in its vastness. Staggering back, I pressed my hands into the door behind me, letting the sensation of cool solid metal ground me.

One didn't need to be an expert to realize this light show was not a normal occurrence. For all the wonders of space I'd witnessed on my journey here, I'd never seen anything like this before. The mesmerising beauty would've beguiled and excited me had Wyck not made it clear—this was now my prison.

Beautiful and terrifying.

Chapter 4

WYCK

He punched the code into the newly mounted panel to engage the lock, then leaned against the closed doors, grateful to have the female and her scent finally concealed behind them. The urgent throbbing in his cocks subdued somewhat, resuming the normal blood flow to his brain.

Now what?

"Take care of her. Feed her..." Vrateus had instructed.

She must be hungry. He needed to get her some food.

Since Vrateus's woman, Svetlana, had taken over meal preparation on the Dark Anomaly, the crew was no longer allowed to come and go in the kitchen whenever they pleased.

Three times a day, Krahkil served the crew the food Svetlana cooked. Outside of the meal hours, snacks were available in the mess hall.

Lunchtime had passed, and there was still some time before dinner. He should get something for the female—Nadia—from the mess hall, but first he needed to get Lesh.

He'd left the _mahdi_ chained in the humans' spaceship. Lesh could take care of himself, but Wyck didn't like leaving him alone for long anywhere but in his room.

Pushing away from the doors, he turned right, heading in the direction of the human's spaceship.

Three _errocks_—Nocc, Trox, and Gler—were working on stripping the ship of equipment.

Chained in the spot where he'd left him, Lesh lay on his belly. However, his posture was far from relaxed. His paws drawn under him, all six eyes trained on the *errocks*, the animal was ready to pounce on anyone who came too close.

"There you are," Gler growled as soon as he'd sighted Wyck. "Get your beast the hell out of here. He's in the way."

Lesh leaped to his feet the moment Wyck entered. He refrained from petting or even greeting the animal in the presence of the others, silently unwinding the chain from the bar on the wall, instead.

"Where is Vrateus?" he asked Gler.

"Took some boxes with weapons over to his storage."

Weapons.

He remembered about Nadia's knife in his pocket. It was resting right above the wound she'd made between his ribs.

Crazy female.

A warm thrill tickled inside his chest at the thought of her.

Vrateus didn't allow anyone but Svetlana to carry weapons. Although the laser knife was more of a utility tool, Wyck was certain his captain would classify it as a weapon and would demand Wyck surrender it to him. Any of the *errocks* present would love to get their hands on the blade, too.

He didn't always obey his captain, but he'd never concealed anything from his family before. Except for Lesh. His grip tightened on the chain connected to the *mahdi's* middle neck.

Wyck had found Lesh in one of the narrow passages that were plentiful around the Dark Anomaly, in which only the *mahdi* pup could fit. He'd been not much bigger than Wyck's forearm back then, whimpering in fear, his three heads pressed tight to each other.

The youngest on the Dark Anomaly, Wyck was only fourteen back then. Finding someone younger than himself had intrigued him. Having someone small and defenseless, who wouldn't order him around, had felt refreshing.

"Hey!" Nocc stomped out from a side compartment, hauling out an armload of spacesuits. He dropped them on the floor. "How is *my* female doing?"

Wyck's neck muscles stiffened, and his jaw tightened at the word "my."

"*Ours*," he corrected. "That's what the captain said."

"Fuck the captain." Nocc came closer and wrapped his arm around Wyck's shoulders.

Just a hand-width shorter than Wyck, Nocc was two decades older than Wyck's twenty-four years of age.

"The captain put you in charge of the female, didn't he?" Nocc said in a conspiratorial tone. "Whatever you do with her now is up to you, right?"

"That's not what he meant—"

"Since when do you care about what he means?" Nocc snapped. "All *errocks* are a family. Here, we're all brothers. And family comes first."

Wyck had been raised with this motto hammered into his brain—the *errocks* are one large family. His father had died in the crash. The remaining *errocks* raised him, with Crux taking the role of his father.

As one of the *errock* family, Wyck had even gone against the captain's authority before. Only a few weeks ago, Crux had poisoned Vrateus, intending to get rid of the captain. Wyck helped Crux and the others to bring the crew under their control. Had Vrateus and his woman not wrested back the power, things would've been very different right now. Nadia would've ended up in the *errocks'* possession. In which case, she might be dead already.

He'd heard *errocks* fucked in savage ways. Ever since Wyck grew big enough for his cocks to get hard, Crux showed him plenty of videos depicting sexual acts. Crux accompanied them with even more graphic comments, describing the gruesome details no video had.

"If you're that scared about upsetting your precious captain, there're many ways we could cover it up," Nocc kept talking while hugging Wyck's shoulders like a brother. "We can let the *kreers* eat her after you and I are finished with her—"

"Hey! How about me?" Gler had obviously been eavesdropping. "If you're sharing the female, I want some of her pussies too!"

"Human females only have one pussy, I've heard," Trox chimed in, shifting closer.

"Just one? What a waste of a warm body," Nocc spit through his teeth with disgust. "Anyway, we're a family, Wyck, remember? Whatever one of us has belongs to everyone."

"I don't *have* her." Unease crept up his back at the thought of any of his family coming near Nadia again.

"But you can *get* her. Let's do it tonight. We'll come in with you when you bring her dinner."

"She's in the glass room."

"What?" Nocc winced.

The mention of the glass room made Wyck cringe inside, too. The way the clear walls exposed the open space beyond made his head spin. Terror had filled him at a mere glance at that crazy room.

The sensation was typical for *errocks*. However, the glass room didn't seem to bother any of the other species on the Anomaly.

"Why did you take her there?" Nocc snarled, huffing a breath through his nostrils.

Wyck decided not to reply to that one. Telling Nocc that he'd obeyed the captain's orders would bring nothing but more scoffing and mocking.

"You can get her out, though." Nocc's voice filled with new hope and promise. "Tell her she needs to go to the mess hall for dinner, then bring her over to my room. I give you my word, she'll be yours after I'm done with her. I'll also let you watch what I'll do to her." He smirked, glancing over his shoulder at Trox and Gler. "It's about time, the boy got a real-life lesson on how to fuck."

Gler didn't seem amused. "To make the lesson worthwhile," he growled. "I'd have to go before the boy.

"Not a chance!" Trox shoved him aside. "I'll never go after Gler again. Remember what you passed on to me the last time? A piece of dead meat, unusable in any way."

Wyck had heard about "the last time" before. Before Svetlana's ship, the last time a spaceship with live females crashed here was over two decades prior.

He was too young to remember that night, but he'd heard plenty from the others. The *errocks* bragged often about the "great time" they'd had, though most of them admitted they'd been too drunk to remember much. Their accounts often contradicted themselves, leading Wyck to believe that a lot of what they said must be made up.

True or not, the idea of Nadia turning into a piece of "dead meat" sickened him. He hadn't asked to be tasked with the job of looking after her. In fact, he'd tried to decline "the honor." Now, that she was his responsibility, however, he refused to put her in harm's way.

"She is taking the place of Vrateus's woman in the mess hall." He shrugged Nocc's arm off his shoulder. "We'll all get to see her naked, more than once."

"That's not what I'm asking you to do, boy." Nocc stepped in closer. "Are you going against your family?"

Lesh released a warning hiss, and Wyck tightened the grip on his chain.

"That's not it, Nocc." He tried to recall some of the words Vrateus had used to convince them all before. "It's a chance to use the female in any way you like, but only in your imagination. As long as it's in your head only, she'll last longer."

"Are you protecting *her*?" Nocc scoffed, the expression of utter disgust distorting his face. "If so, your father must be rolling in his grave, laughing his head off, boy! Females are disposable. The Great Scodr changed his women more often than he did his clothes. He liked his females fresh every night. If they pleased him, he'd set them free on the next planet we'd come upon. Those who crossed him in any way were sent the fuck out the airlock."

Gler roared with laughter. "The human with her *one* fucking vagina would've been tossed out into the space, for sure! The good old Scodr wouldn't have put up with that."

Nocc and Trox guffawed at that, too.

Wyck didn't always find their jokes funny, and this one fell especially flat.

"Well, there you go." He shoved past them, tugging Lesh along. "Father wouldn't have approved of her, anyway. No need to bother."

"Hey!" Nocc yelled as Wyck exited the spaceship. "We'll make do with her. We don't have the fine choice of females that Scodr had—"

"Exactly," he snapped. Usually, he felt pride when hearing about his father, the Great Scodr, who once had a fleet of fine ships and led an army of free men, submissive to no law but his own. Now, irritation grew in his chest. "We can't be like my father. We only have *one* female. If I let you have her, we'd have none at all."

He didn't pause to listen to their objections, heading down the corridor and away from the humans' ship.

Vrateus was striding his way.

"How is she?" the captain asked quickly, passing him by.

"Good."

Vrateus nodded, disappearing into the opening of the humans' spaceship.

Wyck pressed his hand to the pocket with Nadia's knife. He was not surrendering the weapon. He sensed he needed it more than Vrateus did.

<u>*WYCK*</u>

He took Lesh with him to the mess hall. The *mahdi* needed some food, too, and with the female in his care, Wyck now had twice the responsibilities.

Once there, Wyck quickly grabbed a few of the hard, round disks Svetlana called *cookies*, and stuffed them in his vest pockets, promptly leaving the room right after. There was always someone mingling in the mess hall, and he had no desire to answer any question about the new female or to ward off any more mocking comments.

Out in the corridor, he fed three of the *cookies* to Lesh, and popped one in his mouth. The sweetness of the pollen sugar covered his tongue with every bite, reminding him of Nadia once again.

The wound in his side ached, bringing to mind the image of her fighting him in the corridor. He remembered her fear-filled eyes. The horror and desperation in them reminded him of the look Lesh had when he'd found him. The *mahdi* would've died had Wyck left him behind nine years ago.

Nadia wouldn't last long, either, if he allowed Nocc to have his way with her.

"Show the boy how to fuck."

Nocc's words followed him.

In all honesty, he would've *wanted* to see that. Even more so, he would've liked to *do* that to her himself. Nadia's sweet, tantalizing scent seemed to have soaked his lungs and permeated his clothes. Even with her no longer around, the mere memory of her scent teased his cocks like a stroke of a hand... Her hand.

He knew that Vrateus and Malahki added something to the soap on the Dark Anomaly that neutralized their scent, making them practically undetectable to *errocks'* acute sense of smell.

Before reaching Nadia's room, he made a sharp turn toward the closest storage, instead. He needed that soap for Nadia so she could wash off her tormenting scent.

The door to the storage room was open. He poked his head in to find Svetlana rummaging through one of the boxes on the shelf unit by the wall.

He cursed under his breath. He didn't expect to find her here, though it made sense that he would—they all used the same supplies stored in the same rooms.

Her shoulders jerked, and she stilled for a moment before turning to face him, laser gun raised in her hand.

"Oh, hi Wyck." Her voice was friendly enough, though she didn't put away the gun at seeing him. In fact, she adjusted her aim, pointing it straight at his head. "Looking for something?"

"Soap."

"Here." She stepped aside, gesturing at the box she'd just taken two soap bars from herself. "All yours."

She slid closer to the door, waiting for him to move so she could exit.

A whiff of her scent reached him. From this distance, even her daily showers didn't mask it completely. In addition, Wyck could clearly smell Vrateus's most recent kisses on the skin of her neck. The two scents mingled in an alluring, enigmatic combination, stirring tantalizing reactions inside him.

He hated having his cocks twitch in response to Svetlana. The fact that he had no control over it left him feeling powerless. He reached deep inside his emotions, searching under the thick layer of arousal for the resentment he had been breeding and cultivating toward Svetlana ever since she'd murdered Crux, the man who had been his father figure.

According to the customs of his family, the murder of one's father could only be avenged by the death of the killer. Crux might've been only his *adoptive* father, but he'd taught Wyck everything he knew.

Svetlana deserved to die, by his hand.

He wasn't sure why he hadn't done what the family honor demanded of him. Vrateus trusted him enough to have him guard Svetlana on occasion. Sure, Svetlana had always been careful and carried a gun on her at all times. However, there were ways for him to ambush her despite that. He'd had opportunities to kill her.

Of course, Vrateus would've ripped him limb by limb and fed him alive to the *vasai* centipedes if he so much as made a hair fall off Svetlana's head. But Crux would've been avenged.

"Well, um…" She edged closer to the door, keeping her distance, her gun trained on him. "I'd better go."

He stepped into the room and to the side, getting out of her way.

Her expression relaxed a little at having a clear escape route. Then her gaze slid to the wound on his side.

"You're hurt." Her dark eyebrows slid close together into a frown of concern.

Concern—the last emotion he wanted her to feel for him.

"It's nothing," he dismissed gruffly.

"It's from a fight," she stated, confidently. Plenty of injuries on the Dark Anomaly resulted from the nightly fights between the crew members. "I can treat it for you. If you let me—"

"No." He needed her touch even less than he needed her concern. "I'm fine."

"Okay, then. Well, there're some medical supplies right here, in this box." She pointed with the hand holding the soaps at a metal crate behind her. "I have more in our room if you need them. Come see me anytime if you change your mind."

She slipped out the door promptly. The sound of her light foot-falls moved away down the corridor.

He guessed Vrateus hadn't told her about Nadia, and Wyck had absolutely no reason to tell Svetlana about her either.

Grabbing as many soap bars as he could fit in his hand, he was about to leave the room, too. The wound on his side twitched with a sharp pain as he twisted his torso on his way out. A few drops of blood oozed out, trickling down the ridges of his abs.

Fucking Nadia and her blade.

He paused in irritation. The fact that the new female was of the same species as Svetlana added to his annoyance. Obviously, human females brought nothing but trouble.

The wound seemed clean and would probably heal on its own. Yet even with the slightest chance of an infection setting in, the fever would impair his abilities to take care of those in his charge.

Normally, he fussed little about his injuries. However, he'd never had as many responsibilities as he had now. He simply couldn't afford taking any time off to fight an infection.

With a grunt of displeasure, he reached for the crate. Finding some antiseptic and sterile gauze, he cleaned and bandaged his wound the best he could, then took the *cookies* and the soap to the human in his charge.

Chapter 5

I WAS PACING MY PRISON cell of glass when the doors swished open and the three-headed animal ran in, its chain rattling.

With a startled noise, I leaped back.

Covered in black shiny scales with red stripes on its side, the thing was terrifying, a true creature of nightmares. All three of its mouths hung open, saliva dripping from its sharp teeth, with three black tongues dangling out. Its long tail slithered behind it like a snake.

"Lesh, back," Wyck commanded in a quiet voice, and the beast obediently trotted back to its master.

"You trained it well," I said, with a genuine appreciation.

A corner of Wyck's mouth lifted in a half-smile.

"It took me a while to teach him who the boss was. Now that he knows it, he doesn't forget." With a flash of affection in his gaze, he placed a hand on one of the beast's heads.

The doors slid closed behind them. Wyck remained in the doorway, his feet firmly planted on the metal plate that covered the floor by the threshold.

"Here." He stretched his arm my way, holding a handful of flat, black disks. "*Cookies* for you."

"What did you just call them?" I couldn't believe my ears.

Shockingly, he'd used the English word for "cookies," carefully articulating each obviously foreign-to-his-ear syllable.

"Where did you hear that word?" I took the disks out of his hand and turned one between my fingers. It looked hard and glossy, like a flat hockey puck.

"From the woman who made them." He took one out of the pocket on his vest. "Eat." He shoved the whole cookie in his mouth. "See? Safe to eat."

My empty stomach tightened. With all the worry and adrenaline, I hadn't realized how hungry I was. I tentatively bit into one disk. Hard and crunchy, it tasted very much like the sugar cookies from back home.

"Who made them?"

"The captain's woman." He winced, as if mentioning her left a bad taste in his mouth.

"This woman is from Earth, isn't she?"

"How do you know?"

"She speaks one of the Earth languages I do." I lifted the half-eaten disk in my hand. "*Cookies*. That's English, one of the many languages from Earth, my planet."

To my knowledge, Svetlana Kostyk was the only Earth woman who'd come anywhere near the Dark Anomaly. She was of Ukrainian background but spoke fluent English. All of my spaceship's international crew had also spoken English to some degree, in addition to Universal. Though most were more fluent in the latter.

Back in Svetlana's time, however, Earthlings had just been introduced to the Universal language. Not many spoke it back then, and not on the same level as we did now.

It'd been assumed that Svetlana was long dead. Could she have been living on the Dark Anomaly, for the past fifty years? Baking cookies for these savages? Or was it someone else?

"Where is the woman who made the cookies? Can I meet her?"

"No." Wyck shook his head, evading my gaze. In fact, he'd been avoiding looking into the room ever since he got here. His body angled sideways, he persistently kept his gaze on the metal side of the doorway.

"Why not?"

His jaw muscles twitched. "It's not necessary."

"But I'd love to—"

"What you'd *love* is irrelevant," he snapped abruptly. "It's up to the captain to decide who meets her. She is *his* woman."

That was puzzling. The only Earth disappearance I knew of that had happened in this area was that of Svetlana Kostyk. It happened over fifty years ago, though. If Svetlana survived here somehow for that long, she'd be an elderly woman now.

"What exactly do you mean by her being *his?*"

"It doesn't matter." He shrugged, jerkily. "It's not *her* you should be worried about, anyway."

He wasn't wrong. I should be asking questions about my future. But this topic was too remarkable to give up. After all, I'd come here to find out what had happened to Svetlana. Now, there appeared to be another woman from Earth, which was a completely new mystery to me.

"Have you ever heard of a human woman named Svetlana Kostyk?" I asked. "She might have crashed here about fifty years ago. I know it was long before you were born..." Wyck appeared to be about my age, maybe even younger as *errocks'* massive size often made them look older and more mature than their age. "But maybe you've heard something from the others?"

Finally, he turned his head to me. His eyes narrowed to slits as he stared at me in some odd calculating way, not saying a word.

I took another bite of the cookie in my hand. "These taste similar to the ones we have back home."

"Don't all baked goods kind of taste the same?" he replied. "There's just so much one can do with eggs, bark flour, and some pollen sugar."

Clearly, he'd never been to an international bakery on Earth and hadn't been exposed to the vast variety of flavors different nations gave to the same ingredients.

"Could you at least tell me the name of the 'captain's woman?' How did she get here?" I insisted.

He shook his head resolutely. "What difference would that make to you?"

"I *need* to know. Is there anything at all that you could tell me about her? Who is she? How long has she been here? What else does she do, other than bake cookies?"

He made a face as if he'd bit into something bitter. Clearly, the "captain's woman" was not one of his favorite subjects.

"The only thing you really need to know," he said curtly, "is what *you'll* be doing here."

I vaguely remembered bits of what the captain had said back at the ship—something about entertainment.

"What is it?" I asked carefully.

He kept staring away from me, rubbing the back of his neck. The edge of his vest lifted up with the gesture, revealing the clean bandage on his side. Someone at least had taken care of his wound, I noted with relief. The sight of the blood-oozing hole I'd made in his flesh had been unnerving.

The medical capsule on our ship would treat a flesh wound within seconds and significantly speed up the healing. It might've gotten damaged during the crash, though, or the captain had ordered it taken apart, by now.

"Tomorrow night, I'll take you to the mess hall," Wyck said, bringing my attention back to him.

"Why? What is the mess hall here?"

"A room for large gatherings, among other things." He stared at the wall again.

"What am I to do there tomorrow night?"

"You'll have to take your clothes off. In front of everyone."

"What?" I nearly choked on the last bit of the cookie. "That's a joke, right?"

Please let this be a joke.

Alarmingly, after everything I'd seen of this place, what he'd just said seemed entirely possible. Dread gripped my heart with icy fingers.

"What are they going to do to me?" I asked, swallowing hard.

"They'll look at you." His casual tone sent a chill down my back. He obviously didn't think what he was saying was wrong.

"Why?"

Wyck had saved me before. Every time someone had tried to assault me, he'd put a stop to it. Was it because he'd been saving me for *this*?

"Because seeing you naked would excite them. And excitement feels good."

"Why should I care about them feeling good?" I raised my voice. Fear made it sound squeaky. "And who are *they*, anyway?"

"The crew of the Dark Anomaly." He pressed his hands into the wide metal stripe of the threshold, leaning into it as if for support.

Something was bothering Wyck. Sadly, it didn't seem to be the subject matter of our conversation.

"They'll want to see you naked, and they'll want to watch you come."

"Co... What?" Horror and shame rolled over me in a suffocating swell. "You've got to be kidding me. That's just—"

"You can do it yourself," he said without a shred of humor in his tone. I couldn't fool myself; he wasn't joking. "Touching I mean. Or like the captain said, you can choose one of the males to touch you instead."

"In front of everyone?"

"Yes."

It was simply ridiculous, except that he spoke of it earnestly.

"Do you even realize how absurd you sound?"

He glanced my way but quickly diverted his eyes again, staring back at the metal in front of him. I couldn't see his expression clearly, and it unnerved me.

"It can't happen." I breathed faster, as the room suddenly appeared to be short on oxygen. "You know it's wrong—you can't even look me in the eye when you say it."

What was up with that? What was so fascinating about that wall that he wouldn't take his eyes off it?

"I'll bring your dinner soon." He shoved away from the wall. "Tonight, you'll rest. Tomorrow, you'll do what you're supposed to do if you want to stay alive."

"Is that a threat?" Fear shook through me. "Is it a live-or-die thing? Are you going to kill me if I don't disrobe and let one of you touch me? Is that it?"

He finally leveled a stare at me. Heavy and cold, it made my skin crawl.

"I won't have to kill you," he said gravely, his every word falling into the room like a stone. "There're plenty of others who will if you don't give them what they want."

"And you'll do nothing to stop them?" I asked, my voice low and thin. I could have guessed the answer already—he didn't care.

"I hope it won't come to that," he said evasively.

"You *hope*? Why do you even think I'll go ahead with your plan?"

"If you have any brains in that head of yours, you will."

"Brains are the last thing required for what you want me to do," I muttered, glaring at him. "I'm not going to do it."

"You will. If you want to live."

He held my gaze with his, his yellow irises especially bright and unnerving.

"Or you'll starve." He suddenly snatched a cookie from my hand.

"Hey!" I leaped back, hiding the remaining two cookies behind my back.

Turning to fully face the room, he kept his gaze on me. His gloomy expression had smoothened out, giving way to calculation and...interest.

"You'll get to eat only *after* you cooperate." He suddenly looked annoyingly pleased with himself.

"Are you serious? You're going to starve me until I comply?"

He shrugged. "Whatever worked for a *madhi*, should work for a human, too, I imagine."

"Did you starve your pet, too?"

"Starve? No. I used food as motivation to train him. Lesh proved to be smart enough to learn quickly what's best for him—to do as I say. He never starved."

"So, you're hoping to force me into obedience, too?"

He shrugged.

"I can only hope you're as smart as a *mahdi*?"

I seethed with resentment at the indignity of it. He stared straight at me now, but I remembered the signs of his unease ever since he'd entered this room. I stepped aside, and his gaze followed me, as if glued to my face.

"How about these two?" I waved my hand with the two remaining cookies in front of me. "Aren't you going to take these away to increase your bargaining power?"

His gaze shifted, and his focus seemed to slip along with his composure. His self-indulgent smile disappeared. Confusion, mixed with genuine fear momentarily distorted his strong features. He grabbed on to the metal panel, turning sideways again.

The warm umber of his skin paled on his cheeks. His chest moved rapidly with shallow breaths.

Understanding dawned on me.

"You're afraid of this room, aren't you?"

"Afraid? Don't be ridiculous," he scoffed.

Afraid might not be the most accurate word, but something about staring straight into the glass room or the lights beyond it made Wyck uncomfortable, and judging by his reaction, severely so.

"Yeah? Then prove it." I took another step back, holding a cookie out to him. "Come and get it, big guy."

He wouldn't look at me.

"Come on," I taunted, dangling the cookie in my hand. "You want to starve me. Start now. Take this away from me."

He didn't move. His huge hands balled into fists at his sides, his jaw muscles tensed. The rest of his body stilled, as if packed with compressed power that threatened to explode.

Suddenly grabbing the metal corner strip, he roared, the deafening sound rolling under the glass ceiling. Muscles bulged like boulders in his arms. He yanked off the metal rail that protected the corner of the wall in the entryway and bent it in his hands.

His deep roar rocked the room and reverberated through my chest. The cookie dropped from my fingers, weakened by the terror of witnessing the crushing power of his temper and the graphic demonstration of his strength.

Now, I hoped whatever it was that prevented him from entering the glass room was strong enough to keep him from lunging after me in retaliation for taunting this beast of a man.

He yanked on Lesh's chain, threading it through the loop he had bent the metal strip into, then tied it to it.

"Lesh is staying here." He tossed a glare at me over his shoulder. "No more food for you from now on." He shoved the door open, tipping his chin at the last cookie in my hand. "Make that one last."

The door slid closed behind him.

Lesh's left head quickly swiped the cookie I'd dropped off the floor.

"You're in it with him, aren't you?" I narrowed my eyes at Lesh as his left head gleefully chomped on my cookie. The central head licked the crumbs off the muzzle of the left head.

"A bunch of thieves," I mumbled under my breath, moving away from the beast just in case, though he didn't look that threatening at the moment. My cookie, settling in their joined belly, must've felt nice, mellowing the fierce expression of all three heads. "You're no better than your master," I told him.

My stomach still rumbled hungrily, and exhaustion weighed me down, along with a depressing feeling of utter hopelessness. I wandered off to the far end of the room.

"I'm not looking after your dog!" I yelled toward the door. Not that Wyck would hear me, but yelling seemed to release some of the frustration pressing heavily on my chest. "I'm not giving him any water either!" I turned to Lesh again. "I bet that cookie made you thirsty, didn't it? Too bad your owner doesn't care about you."

Wyck obviously didn't care about anything or anyone.

I glanced at the very last cookie in my hand.

"Make it last."

What for? With the future that awaited me, it might be better to starve than ration this last pathetic little bit of sustenance.

Taking a big bite of the cookie, I examined the contents of the room.

A clothing rack with ridiculously bright, embellished long gowns and a small table on gilded rollers were the only furnishings. Behind the rack, I found a roll of blankets. They seemed clean enough, though I was so tired by now, I wouldn't have cared much even if they weren't. I took them as far away from the door and Lesh as I could and set up a bed for the night.

Wyck's beast sat down on his haunches, bringing to mind Cerberus with his three heads. All three moved in sync, following my every move. The three pairs of black beady eyes watched me intently.

The fact that the animal made no sound creeped me out. Completely silent, he appeared even more like an eerie creature from the underworld.

"You want water?" I asked. The middle head growled at the sound of my voice while the other two hissed. "You know, you three should be in an agreement whether you're thirsty or not—you look like you share a stomach after all."

I walked to the bathroom, getting a drink for myself. The cookie had made me thirsty, too. Thankfully, there didn't seem to be a water shortage in this place. It ran freely from the faucet in a wide continuous stream. I filled a large, empty soap dish then brought it over to Wyck's pet.

He got to his feet as I approached. All heads lowered to the ground with a joint hissy growl as the eyes glowered up at me menacingly.

"Great, *now* you're in agreement," I mumbled, setting the dish down. "All three of you unanimously hate me."

The chain clanked as Lesh strained to reach the dish, but it turned out to be just a little too far. All that growling from him had scared me from placing it any closer.

He glanced up at me.

"Hey, don't look at me like that. It's not my fault your master dumped you here."

He sat back on his haunches once again, and I shoved the dish a little closer with my foot. There was no way I'd come any closer to this beast than that, especially while he was watching me with his sharp, translucent teeth bared in warning.

Only once I'd stepped back to my sleeping pallet did Lesh lower his left head to take a sniff at the water. The other two kept watching me, unblinking.

"Are you picky or just mistrusting?" I threw him a glare of my own. "Well suit yourself, I'm going to bed." I climbed under the blankets.

The slurping sound of Lesh drinking reached me as I closed my eyes.

"If you need to go to the bathroom," I mumbled through the warm, heavy haze of the approaching sleep, "hold it until your master is back. There's no way I'm going to clean up after you."

Chapter 6

I WOKE UP TO A VOMIT-inducing stench.

"For the love of all that's holy, Lesh!" I groaned, burying my face in the blankets. "What the fuck did you do?"

What had Wyck been feeding him?

The cookie couldn't have caused that smell, could it?

"No, no, no," I moaned into the blankets. "No way. I'm not cleaning that. Wyeeeeck!" I yelled in desperation. It was unlikely that the broody *errock* would hear me or rush to my rescue.

I had no idea what time it was. The lights outside the glass moved in the same chaotic pattern as they did when I went to bed. I still felt tired, needing more sleep. But not in this stench.

Cursing and groaning, I rolled out of the sleeping pallet and climbed to my feet.

Lesh's chain clanked, but he remained lying by the door. All of his heads were wide awake, six glimmering eyes watching me intently.

On the glass floor between me and the hound from hell, a huge steaming pile lay.

"I can't believe this." I speared my fingers through my hair then shook my hands out. "I told you to wait for your master, didn't I? What am I supposed to do with this?"

There was so much of it, too.

Lesh tilted all of his heads to the same side. They moved simultaneously like a synchronized swimming team.

"Don't you stare at me like that," I snapped at him. "Like you're proud of what you've done."

I paced the floor in front of the offensive pile, pressing both hands to my nose and mouth and trying not to gag. It smelled like something huge had died in here, then had been baking in the sun for months while its decomposing corpse had been used as a place to go to the bathroom by every space creature imaginable.

"Wyck is insane!" He must be crazy. Only a man with an intense, unhealthy attachment to the animal would keep it around and clean after it regularly.

I had no idea how long the stinky Cerberus was supposed to stay with me. However, there was a good chance I wouldn't survive this stench long enough for Wyck to starve me.

"I hate him! I don't have anything to clean up this shit with." I stomped my foot. "Nothing!"

No automatic cleaning machines like we had on the ship. No soap, no rags, no hot water.

I stomped over to the rack that held the shimmering evening wear. The clothes were less useful to me than the bedding. If I had to rip something for rags, it had to be one of the dresses.

It hurt to ruin the gorgeous outfits, but they were out of place here, and I needed to do something about the gallon of alien poop on the floor.

Using my hands and teeth, I managed to rip off two long, voluminous sleeves of a velvet dress, then to tear one of them in half. I tied one long strip over my nose and mouth, using it as a face mask.

"Gaaawd, this is so, so gross." I crouched by the pile of Lesh's waste as he kept staring at me, not moving a muscle. Despite his lying position, he appeared tense, like he was ready to pounce on me if I made a wrong movement. I knew his chain was long enough for him to reach me. After all, it'd been long enough for him to take a dump in this very location.

At this point, however, the risk of a vicious animal attack seemed irrelevant when faced with the dire need to breathe some fresh air.

Holding my breath, I quickly scooped the mess with the pieces of fabric then tossed it into the toilet. I had to do several trips, scooping and tossing, before most of it was gone. Then, I filled the empty soap dish with the water from the bathroom faucet and scrubbed the floor the best I could.

I rinsed out and dumped the dirty pieces of fabric into the waste basket in the bathroom, then washed my hands thoroughly and shut the door.

The place still smelled awful, but at least the sharp edge of the stench was now gone.

"I'm going to kill your master with my bare hands," I vowed to Lesh afterwards. "Even if it'll be the last thing I ever do."

"DID YOU HAVE A GOOD night?" Wyck's voice woke me up. There was an uncharacteristically warm note in his tone.

I lifted my head off the pallet and opened my eyes. Wyck wasn't talking to me, which explained the affection in his voice.

Lesh's front paws planted onto Wyck's chest, the heads of the scaly monster fought over the patting that Wyck was generously shelling out to them. Having not enough hands to pat all three at the same time, Wyck did his best to give an equal amount of attention to the flat heads of his pet.

"How did it go, my friend?" he cooed, scratching the side of the right head's neck. The animal literally smiled in response, baring his teeth, his three tongues dangling out. His heads leaned toward Wyck's hand, the snake-like tail wound around one of Wyck's short boots. "Did she give you any trouble?"

I huffed, dropping my head back to the sleeping pallet.

"*I* gave him trouble?" I asked curtly, my voice hoarse from the lack of sleep. "He took a huge dump in here! What on earth do you feed him, it reeked like decomposing flesh."

"It still does." He wrinkled his nose.

Whatever air filtration system they had in this room had done its job, in my opinion. I couldn't smell anything anymore. I'd heard that *errocks'* sense of smell was superior to that of humans, though. Also, I might've gotten used to the smell and no longer noticed it even if it lingered.

Whatever the case, the disgusted expression on Wyck's face irritated me. It wasn't my fault the air in the room was not entirely to his satisfaction.

"You know what..." I got up and stomped to the bathroom.

A nauseating wave of stench assaulted my nostrils the moment I opened the door. The soiled rags in the waste basket had done a great job at overpowering any efforts of the air filtration system.

Pressing my nose into my shoulder, I grabbed the basket then went back to Wyck.

"Here" I shoved it into his chest as he stumbled back, astonishment mixed with deep repulsion on his face. "Get rid of this, will you? Make yourself useful instead of just complaining."

He stared at the offensive basket, his full, shapely lips curved in disgust.

"Take it!" I urged.

He shoved at the door behind him, sliding it open, then tossed the basket out into the corridor and closed the door quickly.

"Now, get out." I heaved a long breath. "And take your pet monster with you. I need to get some sleep if I still can."

Wyck glanced down at Lesh who stood at his side, keeping an eye on me. I was well inside the reach of his chain, I realized. He didn't attack me, and I felt too tired to care if he still could.

"Lesh stays here." From the hip pocket of his pants, Wyck produced a long meaty bone wrapped in a piece of plastic.

"No, he is not," I protested.

Wyck calmly unwrapped the plastic and tossed the bone on the glass floor. Lesh lunged after it, his three mouths soon gnawing at the meat with gusto.

"I'm not cleaning after him again." I glared at Wyck from under my brow.

"He's trained to use the bathroom."

"How much good does it do if he can't *reach* the bathroom? He's chained."

"Lesh," Wyck called, quiet enough. The animal heard him. Immediately letting go of the bone, he trotted back to his master. "Here you go." Wyck unclipped the chain off the black leather collar around the middle head's neck.

"What are you doing?" I gasped, instinctively stepping closer to him as Lesh ran back to his bone.

"Releasing him, so he *can* use the bathroom next time."

"What next time?" I fought the panic rising inside me at the prospect of sharing the room with Lesh *unleashed*. "I don't want him here. He'll chew my head off in my sleep."

"Do you want me to stay and watch him while you sleep?" Even with my eyes to the three-headed monster, I could tell by the smile in Wyck's voice that he was teasing me.

"I want you here even less than I want him," I snapped. "Both of you need to get out."

"Someone else may come in, then."

"Who?"

"Anyone."

"You lock the doors, don't you?"

"Yes. But the palm-reader panel was broken a few weeks back. It's been replaced with a numeric code one. Who is to say it won't be broken again by someone. Or hacked." He gave me a suspicious glance. "How good are you with technology?"

"Me?" As far as technology went, I had the expertise of a user. Any kind of hacking or tampering was way out of my skill base. "Rest assured, I won't be able to get out of here when the doors are locked. There is absolutely no need for you to leave your guard dog here."

"*Dog?*" He gave me an incredulous look. "Lesh is a *mahdi*."

"Whatever." I waved him off, stumbling back to my pallet. "I've had a rough night. I need some sleep. And you need to get out and leave me alone."

"Lesh will stay here," Wyck reiterated in a firm tone. "For your protection."

"No. Please." Dread washed away my sleepiness. "Don't leave me with him. He's unchained."

The creature appeared calm enough, occupied with his bone. However, the scraping sound of his teeth against it was unnerving enough to drive me mad with fear.

"He won't touch you if I tell him not to," Wyck assured me casually. "He's had some time to get used to your presence by now and will be calm, unless you irritate him in some way."

"*Me* irritate *him?*" I screeched.

"Yes." He turned to leave. "That shrieking voice you just used, for example, may set him off."

"What? Wait!" I rushed after him.

"I'll be back at lunchtime," he tossed over his shoulder as the doors closed, shutting me in the room alone with the three-headed beast gnawing on a bone.

Chapter 7

LYING ON MY PALLET, I could no longer sleep, despite being tired. I couldn't relax enough to fall asleep while Lesh freely roamed the room.

He took his bone to the door. Lying across the entranceway, he kept chewing on it, even as there no longer seemed to be a shred of tissue left.

The smell of cooked meat had replaced the earlier stench of his excrement in the air. This one was at least pleasant and increasingly more appetizing to me.

My stomach growled. The sound rivaled that of the scraping of Lesh's teeth.

He lifted his heads in alarm, staring at me.

"Yeah, well, if you wanted complete peace and quiet, you should've shared that bone with me, you know, back when it still had some meat on it."

The sound of my voice, snarky as it was, oddly appeared to pacify the beast. He turned his attention back to the bone.

After what felt like an eternity, the doors finally slid open again.

Lesh leaped to his feet at the first sound of them moving and pivoted to face the entrance. The bone completely forgotten, he lowered his heads to the ground and made a loud hissing noise.

For what it was, I had to admit he did make a good guard.

The beast relaxed as Wyck entered. The tip of Lesh's tail brushed by Wyck's ankle, as if in greeting.

"Hungry?" Wyck murmured, lowering himself to the floor.

The large plate in his hands irresistibly attracted my attention. It was huge, the size of a tray, piled high with weird looking but probably delicious things.

Wyck sat by the door, his back propped against one side, his long legs stretched across the entire entranceway. Lesh made himself comfortable alongside him, resting his heads on his master's knee.

"How has it been?" Wyck's gaze remained on his pet, but I knew he was talking to me this time. The tone of his voice had changed, lacking the note of affection it held when he spoke to Lesh.

"Splendid." I pursed my lips, trying and failing to tear my gaze away from the food.

He lifted a piece of what appeared to be a stew meat and tossed it to Lesh. The center head snatched it from the air, its teeth snapping loudly.

Swallowing the saliva that had gathered in my mouth at the appetizing smell of cooked meat, I schooled my features into what I hoped was a casual expression before meeting Wyck's gaze. He'd been watching me, with a knowing look in his eyes.

I shifted on my pallet, annoyance muffling my hunger.

"It's tonight," he said calmly.

"All right."

"'All right' means you'll do it?"

"'All right' means 'I know' and 'fuck off.'"

"*All right*, then," he said pointedly, rising to his feet.

My eyes moved back to the food, completely against my will.

"Wait!" I yelled as he bent over to place the plate down for Lesh.

"Yes?" He straightened, the plate still in his hands.

"I'll think about it, okay." I couldn't even remember the last time I'd eaten. It must've been a ration bar, back on the spaceship right before our failed landing.

"You had enough time to think." He lifted another juicy chunk of meat off the plate and tossed it to Lesh's left head. I couldn't help but follow it with my eyes. "I need your promise, now."

"Why do you think I won't break the promise once I've eaten?"

"I suspect that's possible." He paused for a moment, eyeing the food on the plate. "I'm gambling on the belief that you're a person of honor. And if you're not..." He shrugged. "I can always resort to dragging you to the mess hall by force."

"Why don't you just do that?" I scoffed. "Why pressure me for a promise?"

"I'd love to have some cooperation from you." He shifted his weight to his other foot. "I want you to have whatever choice I can give you. Because *I am* a person of honor."

"I don't believe there is any *honorable* way to deal with this fucked-up situation." I sighed. "Whose idea was this anyway?"

"The captain's. If you have one female and over six hundred males who want her—"

"Six hundred!" I gasped.

He nodded.

"There used to be over seven hundreds of us just over a month ago."

"What happened to the rest then?" I asked mechanically.

He shrugged his wide shoulders before replying evasively, "Power struggle." Gazing at me with curiosity, he asked, "Does the size of the crowd bother you? Is there a smaller number that you would prefer?"

"Yes!" I exhaled sharply. "How about zero?"

"That's not going to happen. They want you."

"But why?"

"Isn't it clear? They all want to fuck you. Only if they do, you will die, and they'll be left with nothing. Vrateus gave them the next best thing—they'll *watch* you and pleasure themselves. They'll get their fun, and you'll live."

From the captain's perspective that might be a win-win situation. Except that no one took my personal feelings into consideration.

"And if I refuse?"

"You'll die." He huffed a breath, his thick brow ridges twitched in annoyance. "Listen, I don't have much patience, and long explanations bore me. So, you either go out there and do it on your own or I'll drag you to the mess hall myself and—"

"You'll molest me?"

He stared from under his heavy brow.

"It doesn't have to be me. In fact, I'd prefer if you choose someone else but me."

"Oh, it'd better be *anyone* else but you," I said quickly.

His jaw muscles flexed again, the way they tended to do when he was irritated or angry. I'd learned some of his tells already.

"I'm sure Nocc would love to give it a go," he gritted through his teeth. "Or Kex and Tezul, the two males who tried to climb on top of you yesterday."

The recent memories of that made my stomach churn with nausea, which must be what Wyck had been hoping for when he'd brought it up.

"You're not helping by scaring me." My voice came out gravely hollow.

"I need your promise," he insisted, stubbornly.

The promise to allow someone to assault me in front of hundreds of over-sexed aliens. Or to die.

There had to be another way.

"So... They need entertainment?" I asked, slowly. "Of...a sexual nature?"

"Right."

I bit my lip, mulling over an idea in my head.

"What if I gave them that—something like that. But without, you know, the whole touching and coming part."

"What are you talking about?" He shook his head.

I raised my hand, as if about to make a vow.

"I'll give you my promise that I'll provide entertainment for your buddies." I waved my hand in the air. "But on *my* terms."

"I'm asking again." He frowned. "What's that supposed to mean?"

"I'll be needing a few things..." I glanced back at the clothing rack. It held enough dresses for me to make a costume. "Do you have something that plays music?"

"Why music?" He stared at me, clearly dumbfounded.

"I'll dance, okay?" I explained. I'd taken dance lessons for years in school and then in art college. I'd even won a few competitions, back in the day. Not that any of that mattered much to a group of males searching for stimulation to get themselves off. "I'll take my clothes off too," I added, reluctantly. "Some of them."

I stifled a sigh. Sadly, I wouldn't be the first woman in history pressured into stripping by necessity.

"Dance?" Wyck scrubbed his hand over his face, not looking convinced at all. "How is a dance supposed to be exciting?"

Clearly, he'd never seen a striptease before. That could work to my advantage: they'd have nothing to compare me with. I'd have the sense of novelty on my side.

I really hoped that would be enough.

The idea could be tested right here, I realized.

"Oh, Wyck. Dance can be so many things," I said in a deliberately low, raspy voice, moving toward him. Swaying my hips, I gave him a sultry look. "It can also be very, very sexually stimulating."

I hoped *errocks*—as well as the rest of the aliens here—responded to body language similarly to human men. Because that plate with steaming stew looked and smelled more amazing the closer I got.

Wyck's nostrils flared as I approached.

"Hungry?" he asked, his voice came out rougher than normal.

"Very." I held his gaze, licking my lips.

His thick eyebrow ridges shifted together, his bright eyes glaring with menace and heat. At this distance, I spotted grass-green spots floating in the yellow-gold of his irises—a touch of calm amongst the wild light.

"Come and get it, then." He took a piece of meat off the plate, holding it out between his fingers. The same way he'd done when he'd tossed food to Lesh.

I was sure he intended to insult me, but I was too hungry to care. Stepping closer, I rose on my tiptoes, tilted my head back, and opened my mouth.

"That's a good girl." His voice rumbled with approval. He sounded almost delusional, as if caught in a surreal dream with me.

This place certainly felt like a dream—teetering on the edge between a nightmare and a hallucination.

He dropped the meat between my lips, quickly withdrawing his hand, not giving me a chance bite his fingers. This might not be the best meal I'd ever had, but it certainly felt like it. I quickly chewed and swallowed the piece of meat right there.

"More." I reached for the plate in his hand, but he lifted it up higher.

"Not so fast."

"I've given you my promise." I stepped on the toes of his boots, to get higher. I'd never thought of myself as short, but Wyck would dwarf any human with his height and bulk. Next to him, I felt petite, and the plate remained out of my reach.

"Not exactly the promise I'd asked you for." He moved the plate even higher.

Hooking one arm around his massive neck, I pulled myself up, straining to get to the food. "Who cares? As long as you get the same results?"

His other arm wound around my waist, holding me in place.

My attempts to get to the plate suddenly halted, the awareness of our position rushed in.

I was hugging his neck, my face at his eye level, my body pressed flush to his so tight I could feel the firm beat of his heart against my chest. Every breath I took was filled with his scent—strong and masculine like him.

"That hungry, are you?" The velvet rumble in his voice gave his phrase a whole new meaning.

He dipped his face to the place where my neck met my shoulder, and his wide chest rose with a breath so deep, it lifted me up.

"I want you to *listen* to me," he growled against the skin above the collar of my suit. "And *obey*."

"Keep dreaming, buddy." My voice came out breathy. For whatever reason, I kept clinging to his neck and shoulders instead of letting go and retreating into the safety of the room where I knew he wouldn't follow. Despite my upbeat words, the closeness of his massive body appeared to subdue if not paralyze me completely. "It's not going to happen."

He yanked his head back up. His yellow eyes glistened bright like two flashes of lightning.

"You *will* listen to me," he said with force. "You'll do *what* I say, exactly *when* I say it. Or you'll end up as a piece of 'dead meat.'"

His nostrils flared as he drew in the air around me again. The look in his eyes turned from wild to outright feral, and he shoved me away from him.

Startled by his words and his actions, I still managed to snatch the plate from his hand the moment he lowered it. I then scurried backwards into the middle of the room.

Whatever kept him at the door restrained him more effectively than Lesh's chain. He didn't follow me. He didn't even appear to notice the plate was gone. Closing his eyes, he kept breathing deeply, a pained expression on his face. It was as if he were eager to fill his lungs with the drug he knew would hurt him.

"Take a shower before I come back," he finally growled, tossing a small rectangular package on the floor next to me. "Make sure to use the soap."

Then, he was gone.

Chapter 8

FIGHTING WAS NOT IN my nature. The confrontation with Wyck had drained me. It had done something else, too. For whatever reason, I could no longer think about him without an odd feeling fluttering in my stomach.

The sensation of the hard as rock muscles in his neck and shoulders stayed with me. The brutal power I sensed in this man could be frightening if directed against me. Yet there would certainly be some comfort and reassurance in his strength, were he on my side.

The feeling of his presence lingered in the room, even after he was gone. I couldn't forget his scent—warm and heady, with a hint of some exotic spice. I found it pleasant and...invigorating.

He obviously thought that I stank, though.

Resisting the urge to sniff my armpit, I threw a resentful look at the bar of soap he'd tossed to me.

My suit was made from an experimental self-cleaning material. It kept a pre-determined shape, requiring no undergarments. It also absorbed impurities, leaving only a thin layer of body oil to maintain healthy skin but eliminating dirt and offensive odors.

While wearing the suit, I could go without taking a shower for weeks. It helped reduce water consumption in space. None of my crew had ever complained about my smell. Neither had I ever noticed any of them stinking.

But then again, *errocks* did have a superior sense of smell. And something about my body odor must have offended Wyck.

Not that I should care about offending the man who had intended to starve me into obedience. Chasing the thoughts of Wyck away for now, I focused entirely on my bounty—the plate full of food.

As hungry as I was, it filled me up quickly. With still more than a half of the meat, grains, and bread left on the ginormous plate, I offered the rest to Lesh.

The beast eyed me suspiciously when I placed the plate on the floor in front of him. I stepped back to give him space to eat in peace. Slowly, he crept toward the plate. His central head keeping its eyes on me, while the other two salivated over the leftovers.

"You have more control than they do over that stomach of yours, don't you?" I asked the central head, which somehow seemed to be in charge of the other two. Although Lesh was one animal, there were subtle differences in the behaviour of his heads.

The left one, the most impatient of the three, lunged for the food first, snatching the dark dinner roll. The right one gave me a once-over then calmly started eating as well. The middle head watched me intently for a few moments as the other two ate.

"I'm not planning to attack you or to snatch the food from you," I assured it.

My presence obviously unnerved the creature. I decided to follow Wyck's advice—more of an order, really—and take a shower. Not because I worried about offending Wyck's sensibilities with my body odor, of course, but because the chance to have a soothing shower felt enticing.

Picking up the bar of soap off the floor, I headed to the bathroom.

There was nothing soothing about the brief, cold shower I ended up having. The water was barely room temperature, and it stopped running before I even managed to properly rinse all the soap out of my long hair. I ended up using the sink for that. Even as there wasn't a shortage of drinking water in this place, the water consumption must still be regulated.

The cold shower, however, felt invigorating. It woke me up and brought me into action. Since I had no plan beyond surviving tonight, I put all my energy into that.

Selecting a few dresses off the rack, I lay them out on the floor. I wished I had a pair of scissors or at least my utility knife. Since I had neither, I used my teeth and hands to rip sleeves off some of them, separate bodices from the skirts and shorten their length the best I could.

It wasn't easy. My fingers hurt after a while.

"I could use your teeth here," I said to Lesh, who had finished the food, licked the plate clean, and now was resting in his usual place by the door. His two heads were taking a nap while the middle one continued to watch my every move suspiciously.

I wasn't quite finished with my work when Wyck returned with an armload of flat, opaque tiles that glowed in different colors.

Lesh greeted him as enthusiastically as ever.

"Here, here." Wyck patted his pet.

Taking a cookie from his pocket, he tossed it to Lesh. The animal paid little attention to it. His left head licked the cookie once or twice before Lesh settled down on the glass floor by the wall. All three heads sleepily dropped to the floor, one by one.

Wyck's gaze landed on the empty plate on the floor.

"We shared," I explained before he had a chance to ask. "He seemed hungry."

"You're not to feed my beast." He glowered at me.

"Well, you've never told me that before. And it's too late, now."

At the sound of Wyck's grumpy voice, "the beast" gave us a sleepy glance with only half of his eyes open. He then went back to his nap, the long, scaly tail forming a circle around his body.

"What are those?" I pointed at the stack of tiles under Wyck's arm, diverting his attention.

His brow still furrowed in displeasure, his lips pressed tight, Wyck followed my gesture with his gaze.

"Data slates," he bit out curtly. "You've asked for some music."

"Oh, yes!" I jumped to my feet. "Let's see what you've got."

He shuffled back a little as I approached, then tentatively drew in some air through his nose, his chest rising.

"What?" I winced. "Do I still stink?"

From the impression I got of this place, the air around here wasn't pristine or completely odorless. His excellent sense of smell aside, I couldn't possibly smell worse than anyone else in here.

"Stink?" He frowned. "Who said you do?"

"You keep making faces whenever I'm near, as if my smell offends you." I snatched a few slates from him. "How do these work?"

He shuffled through the remaining stack of slates, producing a black frame.

"Slide a slate in here, it'll light up for you to use." He handed the frame to me, then added in a softer voice, "And you don't stink, never did, even before you took the shower."

Something in his tone made me look up at him. His eyes on me, he appeared absolutely serious, genuine.

"How do you know I took a shower?" I brought a hand up to my slightly damp hair. "Can you smell it?"

"Yes. And it's...nice, either way." He shifted foot to foot, tipping his chin at the slates in my hand. "Tell me which color has what you need, I can bring more."

Color?

I turned the slates. Two of their spines glowed yellow. Two were gray. The remaining few that Wyck was still holding were green.

"What do the colors mean?"

"The data slates are organized by color in the library."

"You have a library here?"

He nodded.

"The captain put it together."

I quickly ran my gaze over the words etched into the glowing spines. These were in Universal, with a line of text under it in a language I didn't recognize—*themul* most likely, since that was the species of the captain.

According to the titles, the yellow slates contained documentaries on the lives of indigenous tribes of some distant planet. These wouldn't be the obvious choice in search of some fast, catchy music to strip to, but I'd have to see the videos on them first.

The gray ones had words "The Dark Anomaly" imprinted on them. There were even less likely to contain the music I needed, but the words piqued my interest.

"Let's see this one first." I slid one of the gray slates into the frame, and it came to life, its surface turning into a touch screen. "I've heard about this technology in my Interplanetary History of Film class in college. I can't believe you're still using it."

Holding the frame in my hands, I sat down on the floor right where I stood. Wyck sat in his usual spot in the entrance way, and I scooted closer to him, so he could watch with me.

"Tell me about this place."

Humans had learned about the Anomaly having a solid core inside, but we weren't sure whether it was a planet or something else. Finding life existing in its core was a complete shock.

"The Dark Anomaly is a disk, made of crushed ships it has been sucking in," Wyck started, somewhat hesitantly. "They used to crash here more often in the past, but we still get a few a year. Most of them unmanned."

"So, there is no solid planet here at all? No atmosphere?"

"No."

"You don't go outside?"

"Only for maintenance purposes. While wearing a suit with an oxygen supply."

That would be like spending an entire life inside a spaceship. A sickening feeling of claustrophobia tightened my chest.

I pulled up a chart, or possibly a map, on the screen.

"What's this?"

He leaned closer, peeking over my shoulder at the device.

"That's the habitable sector of the Dark Anomaly, by the look of it. We're here." He pointed at a spot on the map with a thick finger, tipped with a smooth nail. His skin, the warm color of reddish clay, darkened to charcoal-gray on the protruding ridges over his knuckles. "This is the main corridor," he continued sliding the tip of his finger along an arched line. "It runs from the place where your ship crashed, all the way here, past the *vasai* farm and the airlock on the other end."

I read the labels, following the movement of his finger. The gardens, the library, the captain's room, numerous storage and utility rooms along the way. The mess hall.

I had yet to see most of that with my own eyes, but from the map, this looked like a fairly large area, equipped not just for survival but for a lifestyle allowing for some recreation. This place had been built to live in long term.

Wyck had mentioned that he'd spent his entire life here.

"How did all of you get here, Wyck?"

"Crashed, the way you did."

Except that I didn't crash. We had deliberately come here. Our landing, as rough as it was, was not an accident.

"Why have you never left?"

"You can't leave the Dark Anomaly," he stated simply.

"Why?"

"It won't let you."

Despite his casual tone, his words sounded ominous, like a line from a horror movie. What he had said made the Anomaly appear alive, like a being with a mind of its own—a dangerous mind.

"But has anyone tried?" I asked, refusing to accept it.

"Many times."

"And they ended up staying?"

"They ended up dead."

The dreadful feeling grew stronger, prickling cold down my spine. Instinctively, I leaned even closer into the warmth of Wyck's large body at my side.

"Why?" I ventured another question, already wary of the answer. "What happens?"

"Every ship that has tried to take off ended up crashing back, killing everyone."

"So, you're all stuck here for life?"

"As are you." He gave me a side glance.

I wondered if I should tell him about the true purpose of our expedition. Could I trust him to help me get off the Dark Anomaly? Or would he try to stop me?

"You see. Ours wasn't exactly a crash," I started carefully. "We came here on purpose."

He shrank away from me, catching my gaze, his expression shocked.

"How? Why?"

"This was a planned mission."

"Why?" He stared at me in bewilderment, obviously unable to comprehend why anyone would voluntarily travel to this place.

His expression gave me hope that he might not be entirely opposed to the idea of getting out of here.

"Ever since the solid mass inside the Anomaly was discovered, there have been talks about sending a ship here."

"But what for?"

"To see what it's like. It's a mystery, you know? Kind of like a modern-day Bermuda Triangle—" I cut myself off, realizing the analogy would be lost on him, since he most likely had no idea what the Bermuda Triangle was. "Anyway, there was a lot of interest from the public. All our unmanned probes have disappeared without a trace, so the Earth governments were reluctant to send a live crew. Especially, since Svetlana Kostyk had gone missing…"

A muscle in his face twitched when I mentioned Svetlana's name again.

"Do you know what happened to her?" I asked him.

He sat quietly for a moment, assessing me the way I had assessed him minutes earlier. Slowly, he reached into a pocket on his vest and pulled out one of the black, glossy cookies.

"Did she end up crashing here, after all?" I prompted since he kept quiet.

"She is the one who makes these," he finally said, staring at the cookie in his hand.

"It is her!" I stared at it, too, as if it were an object from another dimension, or at least from another time. "Is she here, then? Alive?"

"She is very much alive." He heaved a sigh then bit into the cookie with a vengeful expression. "She's Vrateus's woman."

"The captain's?"

Hearing that the human scientist, whose disappearance hadn't left the news for decades, ended up as someone's "woman" felt so wrong. Was she his property? Had she been forced to submit? By the same means Wyck had been coercing me into stripping—do it or die?

Of course, I didn't know Svetlana Kostyk personally, but I believed this would not be the life she would've chosen for herself.

"I can't believe she survived here all this time," I muttered to myself.

Svetlana would be about eighty years old, now. The captain appeared to be around thirty.

"In what way is she *his* woman?" I asked.

Wyck shrugged. "In every way there is."

"Do you mean like...sex, too?"

"Sure. I smell them on each other all the time."

"Oh God," I looked away. "All the time? Are you sure it's consensual on her part?"

The thought of the captain molesting the helpless elderly woman made me sick to my stomach. What would be unimaginable on my world, seemed to be plausible around here.

Wyck's mouth twisted in a sarcastic smile.

"Not that Svetlana would ever confide in me about her sex life, but she seems content with the captain."

"How long has it been going on?"

"Pretty much since she got here. Why is it of any interest to you?"

I wondered if that was the way to avoid the sex sessions in the mess hall—being claimed by one of the males here as his own. Not that I personally wanted to be claimed in any way.

"Did Svetlana ever have to do what you want me to do tonight?"

"A few times." He nodded. "At the beginning."

"Fifty years ago?"

"Why fifty? Svetlana got here just about two months ago."

"What? Where has she been for the fifty years that she's been missing, then?"

He shook his head.

"She couldn't be missing for that long. She isn't much older than you or me. Vrateus's age, maybe."

I sat up straighter.

"It can't be the same Svetlana, then. The one we've been searching for disappeared over fifty years ago. She'd be at least eighty, now."

He gave me an incredulous look. "How many Svetlanas have your people lost around here?"

One, that I knew of. The things didn't add up.

"Are you sure this Svetlana is a human?" I asked. "Does she look like me?"

He gave me a long assessing stare then said with something oddly like regret, "She does. Well, her hair is darker than yours and her eyes are brown not green, but she is most definitely a human."

"I need to talk to her. Wyck, please. Does she even know I'm here?"

"I don't think the captain told her."

"Well, can *you* tell her?"

He grimaced again, as if the very idea of him talking to Svetlana repulsed him.

"I'll ask the captain," he promised reluctantly. "Is that why you came here? To take Svetlana back?"

I shook my head, still reeling from his revelations.

"We never thought we'd find her alive. The most we hoped for was to learn what happened to her. Her age doesn't make any sense, though. Unless there is some kind of a time warp—"

"Probably."

"Do you know anything about it?"

"Not much." He shifted into a more comfortable position. "When Malahki got here about five years ago, it said it'd been thousands of years since my father's fleet traveled space. There is a difference between a year on the Dark Anomaly and a year out there." He waved a hand in the direction of the lights outside the glass, without looking up from the tablet in my hands.

"Who is Malahki?"

"The last sentient being who crashed here before Svetlana. You won't see it much. It works in the gardens and keeps to itself."

"It?"

"It's a *damirian*, without a gender. It probably won't even be in the mess hall tonight."

"Thousands of years..." I thought about Malahki's words. "How old is your father?"

"*Was*," he corrected. "My father died during our crash here, twenty-three years ago. I was still a baby."

Two decades on the Dark Anomaly equaled thousands of years out there in the galaxy. Yesterday, I'd had a thought about landing in pre-historic times. It turned out I hadn't been that far off.

"What kind of fleet did your father have?"

"A fleet of fine ships led by the crew of free men," he said somewhat mechanically, like the words had been repeated so often, their meaning had lost its luster to him. "The men who answered to no law."

"Pirates, you mean?" I exhaled slowly. I'd heard about the cosmic pirates of the past. Brutal, unruly, and bloodthirsty, they used to terrorize this part of the Galaxy millennia ago.

"Pirates, mercenaries, free traders..." Wyck ran his fingers over one of the raised ridges on his head. "They had many names."

"How about your mother?" I asked carefully. It couldn't have been easy to be a woman back then.

His expression hardened.

"She wasn't on the ship when it crashed," he replied evasively.

From his tone, I understood he wasn't willing to elaborate, and I decided to leave it at that for now.

"So, the other *errocks* raised you?"

"Yes. Crux, Nocc, and the others. We are a *family*," he said with emphasis.

Nocc would be the last person in the Universe whom I'd want in my family, but the obvious pride in Wyck's voice stopped me from saying anything out loud.

"Would you mind if I kept these?" I pointed at the gray data slates, changing the subject. "I'd like to read some more later, after..." The thought of what was supposed to happen in the mess hall tonight sent anxiety vibrating through me. "I need to get ready."

I quickly searched through the remaining slates. Neither of them had any even remotely suitable music I could use. The green slates contained detailed information on *damirian* best practices for cultivating some crops. Which made me wonder why would Wyck bring them here at all.

"None of them will work," I exhaled in disappointment.

"I'll get you some more, then." Wyck climbed to his feet, and I followed, getting up, too. "What color do you prefer? Green or yellow? Or should I grab different colors? There are some in blue, pink, and purple, too."

I stared at him in some confusion.

"It's not about the color. I need music—human or of any other race—a track I can dance to. These have some music, but not what I need." I pointed at the documentaries on tribal life. "And these have no music at all." I gestured at the rest.

"Okay." He brushed the cookie crumbs off his pants. "I'll get more yellow ones, then."

"But what do the pink and the blue ones have on them?"

"I don't know." He shrugged, not meeting my eye.

"Well, make sure you read the titles first. Something with words like 'music,' 'dance,' or 'concert' could be it."

He just stood there, shifting foot to foot.

"Is there a problem?" I asked, confused by his hesitating.

Suddenly, understanding dawned on me as if someone dumped a bucketful of ice-cold water over my head.

"You can't read, Wyck, can you?"

Chapter 9

I COULDN'T BELIEVE it. Did Wyck really not know how to read? There wasn't a civilized person—human or alien—out there in the Universe who didn't know how to read and write. Even the most isolated tribes on remote planets, who actively refused technology, had advanced written languages, and some read and wrote in Universal. The use of translator implants by the general public had been declining because so many spoke the same language now.

I knew for a fact that most *errocks* on Hexol, their home world, spoke Universal just as well as their native language.

Maybe things used to be different back when the *errocks* of the Dark Anomaly had been on their home planet last?

"Can you read Hexolian?" I asked. "The *errocks'* native language?"

With a furtive glance at me, Wyck reached for the slates in my hands. "I'll take these back."

"No one has ever taught you how to read?" I had to clarify, shocked and shaken by this discovery. "In any language?"

He didn't reply, refusing to meet my gaze, which was an answer of its own.

Wyck was a grown man, raised by his own kind, and he couldn't so much as read the few words of the title on a data slate.

Something inside me twitched—compassion with a hint of pity. Not being able to read could be considered a form of handicap in the modern world. It greatly impaired one's quality of life and independence.

"I'll get you some more slates." He turned to leave.

"No. Wait a second." I stopped him by placing my hand on his forearm.

There was no point in sending him to fetch something he wouldn't be able to find.

"Is there someone..." I intended to ask if he could bring along one of the crew to help him, then realized that if no one had bothered to teach him how to read all his life, there probably wouldn't be anyone who'd want to help him with reading labels now, either. "Is there a way for me to come with you?" I asked instead.

"No," he said resolutely before the last word even left my mouth. "Not safe."

I realized that, I hadn't forgotten the attacks by the crew on me.

"Is there a way to sneak in undetected? You'll be with me. We'll make it quick."

"No." He sounded just as resolute, but it took him a little longer to say the word "no" this time. I hoped it meant he might be considering taking me along.

"Are there lots of people around here this time of the day?"

This time, he took a considerable pause, definitely thinking about something.

"What time is it?" he asked.

"How am I supposed to know that?"

He silently pointed at the tablet in my hand.

"Oh, is it connected to a network?" I turned it on again.

"No. There is no network on the Dark Anomaly. But the clocks of all devices have been synchronized. Makes it easier to keep a common schedule."

"Okay. So..."

He glanced at the tablet screen. "Lunchtime."

"Which means?"

"Most of the crew will be in the kitchen where Krakhil is serving food."

"So, we can go, then?" Despite, the potential danger, I was looking forward to getting out of this crazy room with its restless dancing lights. Having Wyck with me made me feel safer.

Wyck took the tablet out of my hands and placed it on the floor. "We'll leave all the slates here for now. I'll pick them up later, when I'm on my own."

I guessed that meant I was coming with him.

"I'm ready." I clasped my hands in front of me.

He gave me a long measuring look, as though assessing my worth in battle. It wasn't much, I had to admit. At five feet five, I had less than average muscle tone. My self-defence strategy would be kicking my opponent between the legs and running as fast as my legs would carry me. That obviously hadn't worked during the previous attacks.

Wyck had already gotten a preview of my limitations—he'd thrown enough males off me yesterday.

"Stay close," he said grimly, probably thinking about the same thing right now. "Keep your hands free. If something happens, don't get in my way."

"Got it." I chose not to clarify what exactly he meant by "something."

He slid my knife handle out of his pocket and clutched it in his right hand, then opened the door. Making sure no one was out in the corridor, he grabbed my arm and dragged me out of the room with him.

"Lesh," he called back into the room.

The animal leaped out of the door before Wyck closed it. All three of us were going, then.

"Watch our back," Wyck said to me, not letting go of my arm.

I glanced over my shoulder as we promptly moved down the corridor in the direction of the crash site of my ship. Fear rose the fine hairs on the back of my neck. I half-expected someone to leap at me any minute.

Wyck kept me a little ahead of himself, shielding me with his shoulder from the back, and I shifted even closer to him. The enormous size of his body felt comforting, it was like having a fortress wall move along with me.

Lesh followed us closely, his warm breath reassuring against my calves. I knew the animal didn't have any particular loyalty or attachment to me personally, but I hoped the mere presence of the fierce-looking beast would make anyone think twice before attacking us.

A little while later, Wyck stopped in front of an opaque-glass double door. Tossing a glance up and down the corridor, he punched in the code in the panel by the door and poked his head through when the doors slid open.

"Come." He ushered me inside then promptly closed the doors behind us.

Once we were in the room, his shoulders relaxed a little.

"That's the library?" I took in the large area filled with floor-to-ceiling shelves with glowing data slates neatly arranged on them. "Impressive."

"Is it?" Wyck cast a glance around the room as if seeing it for the first time or from a new perspective.

I walked over to the closest shelf unit by the door and slid my finger along the red-glowing spines.

"The captain did all of this? On his own?" It must have been a long tedious task.

"Yes." Wyck cleared his throat, standing close behind me. "The red ones have sex videos, not much music there, other than in the background in some."

"Oh." I jerked my hand away. "How about the rest of the colors?"

The collection was clearly color-coded. From what Wyck had brought to me earlier, I assumed the gray-marked slates contained data on the Dark Anomaly itself. The yellow ones must have something to do with history or studies of various alien ethnicities, and the green ones were on agriculture. There were more colors here, though.

"I'm not sure," Wyck confessed.

He'd sounded rather confident about the red section earlier.

"So, you're only familiar with that part of the library?" I waved back at the shelves glowing red.

"I'd watched most of those by the time I was fifteen years old." He didn't appear embarrassed or uncomfortable admitting that. "Crux brought me here."

"Crux is one of those who raised you?" I skimmed over the titles of the slates in the blue section then moved on to the pink one.

"Was. Crux *was* the man who raised me after my father's death."

"Has he passed away, too?"

"Yes." His features shifted into a stern expression.

"I'm so sorry to hear that."

"Why?" He narrowed his eyes at me.

"Why am I sorry?" I blinked, staring at him for a moment. How easily did people say these words when a tragedy happened? What exactly did they mean when they said they were sorry? "Because I believe you're hurting, Wyck. The loss of a loved one is always painful, no matter how long ago it happened. If you loved the person, it hurts when they're gone."

"Avenging their death is supposed to ease the pain," he said grimly, not meeting my eyes.

"Was Crux murdered?"

He nodded.

"And you believe that killing his murderer would make you feel better?"

"Vengeance is an honorable thing," he replied mechanically, as if reciting something he'd learned by heart.

"Vengeance doesn't always give you closure. Justice does. Have those who killed him been brought to justice? Was their punishment equal to their crime?"

His brow furrowed, he appeared to be deep in thought, then his expression turned troubled, confused. Something bothered him, deeply. Without knowing his entire situation, I couldn't tell what exactly it was.

"What do *you* know about vengeance and justice?" he asked.

"Personally, not much," I admitted. "But I do know loss. My parents died when I was a teenager."

My dad passed away from a heart condition when I was sixteen. Mom died from cancer two years later. Both were in their eighties when it happened.

They'd spent most of their lives building their careers. I was conceived from a frozen egg when they were in their late sixties. By then, they'd decided their lives were comfortable enough to start a family. They knew they might not live long enough to see me graduate college or even high school and had made sure I had the means to complete my education when they were gone. Financially, I had been okay without them. Emotionally, however...

"I miss them every day." Our happy family time had been cut short by my parents' weakened health in their later years and then by their deaths, yet I'd always treasure every minute spent with them.

It was comforting to know that they had accomplished a lot and had done everything they ever wanted to do. They'd shared a long, happy life together. I just wished I'd been there for a much bigger part of it.

That was the main reason why I'd decided to start my own family early. I wanted to spend as much of my life as possible with my child. With my parents taken from me so early, I couldn't wait to start my own family. The fact that I hadn't found a man I'd consider a suitable life partner wouldn't stop me.

I'd had a sperm donor selected and a clinic appointment booked for the scheduled end of the mission. The financial reward promised to me upon the completion of this mission was supposed to supplement the money left to me by my parents. It would ensure a more than comfortable future for me and my baby. If I ever got back, I'd be a wealthy woman who no longer needed to work and could dedicate her entire life to raising her child.

I had so much waiting for me back on Earth.

Aware of Wyck's large figure looming over me, I thought back to the conversation we were having.

Loss and grief were the things I knew way too well.

"What has been helping me deal with the pain is all the good memories we'd made when we were together," I said softly. "Before I fall asleep, I often think about a trip we took together or our family celebrations. All moments are precious, even the smallest ones—like the many times my dad made me laugh or when my mom held me close while I cried over a scraped knee. Keeping my parents alive in my memories helps me deal with them no longer being here."

Wyck held still, and I looked up to see his reaction. He stood over me, watching me like some kind of a novelty, as if the concept of honoring the loved ones through memories was entirely new to him.

"Tell me about a good moment with Crux," I asked, hoping that talking about the one he had lost would help ease his grief, too. "Something you two did or shared that made you feel happy."

The furrows on his heavy brow grew deeper. His features hardened in concentration, then he winced, not saying a word.

Were there no good memories of the person who had been like a father to him?

The most recent thing Wyck had said about Crux was that he'd introduced him to all the sex videos in the library. Yet Crux didn't seem to show him any of the other ones in this large collection.

What kind of a parent was Crux if he hadn't even bothered to teach Wyck how to read in all those years?

The silence that stretched between us threatened to remain infinite.

"Well," I spoke first since it didn't appear Wyck would say anything any time soon. "I think some of these slates might work." I crouched by a shelf at the wall farthest from the entrance. It contained purple glowing slates with titles suggesting the subject of arts and entertainment.

I accidentally pushed a slate with the side of my hand while taking a few others out. Instead of stopping at the wall, the slate disappeared somewhere behind it, landing in the darkness beyond with a thud.

"What's there?" I asked Wyck.

"Where?"

"There's no wall behind this shelf."

"Really?" Pressing his shoulder into the corner of the unit, Wyck easily shifted the whole thing aside, revealing a dark cut-out in the wall.

"What is it?" I moved to poke my head in, but Wyck stopped me quickly with a hand on my shoulder.

"A sure way to lose your head on the Dark Anomaly is to stick it into unknown places."

He got a flashlight out of his pocket and flicked it on.

The beam of light fell inside a windowless room beyond the wall.

"Is it someone's hiding place?" I ventured a little closer since the place seemed completely deserted. "Why is it here?"

"There are a lot of hidden places all around. When ships crash into each other, pockets of space end up being created. We don't know about all of them. Many aren't easily accessible."

"Well, the access to this one has been created by someone." I slid my finger along the edge of the cut-out. The paneling had melted around it, as if it'd been cut through with a tool that produced heat.

Lesh released a hissing sound, and Wyck stilled suddenly. A moment later, the sound of footfalls out in the main corridor reached me.

"Someone's coming."

"Maybe they just need some slates?" I suggested.

"Maybe, but they may want something else if they see you. Here." He shoved me into the space behind the wall.

Wyck then quickly got in with me, too, and called Lesh to follow us as well. He then yanked the shelf unit back in place from the inside.

The footfalls stopped at the entrance to the library as the person entered a code in the panel.

Lesh hissed in warning again.

"Quiet." Wyck placed his hand on the animal's middle head.

Crouching by the opening, I peeked out through the gap between the slates on the shelf.

The tall boots of Vrateus, the captain, came into my view as he entered. He headed to a unit that held gray glowing slates and added the two he'd brought with him to the shelf.

I felt air stir as Wyck lowered into a crouch at my side. His thigh brushed by my knee—the contact cost me my concentration. I kept staring at Vrateus, watching him browse the shelves. My mind, however, was momentarily overtaken by the awareness of Wyck next to me. I had to shift away from him a little, to regain my composure and focus on what was going on in the library.

After selecting a few slates of various colors, the captain headed for the door. He paused just before the exit. Bending down quickly, he pulled out a slate from the red-glowing section then left.

"Did the captain just take a sex video?" Wyck's eyebrow ridges rose in shock.

"Looks like he wants to have some fun tonight," I let out a short giggle. "To spice up a date, maybe?"

He gave me a questioning look.

"What's a date?"

I gazed back at him. "You really don't know what it means?"

"I suspect it has something to do with sex." It wasn't exactly a question, however his voice sounded uncertain.

"A date is when two people who are interested in each other romantically get together to spend some time. Back on Earth, that would often be a dinner or a trip to a movie or a show. And yes, if they like each other enough, there may be sex, too."

"Why would he need a video if he has Svetlana?" Wyck appeared genuinely puzzled. "They share a room."

"Maybe they'll watch the video together?" I was just speculating here since I didn't know either the captain or Svetlana that well.

"People do that?" he squinted at me, curiosity and disbelief evident on his face.

"Well, some couples do, I guess. It makes sense when you think about it," I tried to explain. Not that I had that much experience in that department myself. A high school boyfriend and a few casual dates in college were all I had in terms of romance in my past. "If you're watching a sexually stimulating video, it's nice to have someone nearby to turn the fantasy into reality, don't you think?"

He tilted his head to the side. "Have you had a date?"

"A few."

"With a sex video?"

"Um, I don't recall watching porn with a guy," I admitted. "But I'm sure my ex and I have watched movies with love scenes in them, at some point."

"Does 'ex' mean he is no longer your man?"

"That is exactly what it means."

"Did he die?"

"What? No. We both went to different colleges, and the long-distance thing didn't work out after a while. Why would you think he'd died?"

He shrugged. "That would be the only way I'd ever give up something that's mine."

"Something? You mean a woman?"

He gave me a long look.

"*Especially*, a woman."

He kept his eyes on me for a moment longer. "*Errocks* don't keep women for long, but—"

"That's not true," I objected. "*Errocks* form long-term family units very similar to humans. They get together for procreation, but many remain as couples for life. If you like each other's company why separate, right?"

Wyck shook his head. "That is not the *errocks'* way."

"Here on the Anomaly, maybe," I argued. "But the world is so much bigger than this place."

He seemed to ponder my words, then shoved the shelf aside, clearing the exit for us.

"We should go back." He took my hand in his, leading me out and back into the library.

Only when we were already walking down the corridor had I realized that he kept holding my hand, instead of dragging me by my arm the way he'd done on our way to the library.

My thoughts went to what lay ahead for me tonight, and I felt betrayed by the comfortable feeling I got in Wyck's presence. At the end of the day, he was still the man who was forcing me to strip for the entertainment of strangers.

I carefully worked my hand out of his. With a glance my way, he took a hold of my arm once again then led me down the corridor like the prisoner that I was.

Chapter 10

On his way to Nadia's room that night, he fought a feeling he'd never had before—he was extremely worried...about a woman.

He'd allowed Nadia to go ahead with her plan to dance instead of being touched.

Frankly, he had no idea what to do if he were to touch her in front of everyone. That might be the main reason why he'd agreed with her plan in the first place. The thought that he might do something so wrong it would upset her, make her dislike him, or laugh at him filled him with anxiety.

The closest he'd ever come to that level of intimacy was when he watched Vrateus and Svetlana in the mess hall during those few sessions.

Unlike the rest of the crew, Wyck hadn't touched himself, then. He'd been fascinated by what had been happening in front of him. Svetlana, always distant and on guard with everyone, had melted into Vrateus's touch, becoming soft and pliable in his hands. Their calm and collected captain had nearly come undone when he held her in his arms.

After that, Wyck became intrigued, watching the connection grow between the two, week after week. All of it was so new to him—a woman willingly committing to a man, not just in body but in spirit and soul. He saw the way Svetlana looked at Vrateus, as if she were ready to cuddle him or to die for him or both.

She'd ended up fighting for Vrateus and even killing for him—both things that, according to Wyck's upbringing, only a family would do for each other. For as long as Wyck knew him, Vrateus had always been alone. Until Svetlana became his family.

The *errocks* on the Dark Anomaly abhorred and ridiculed this kind of connection between a male and a female. Yet Wyck found it...enviable.

Why didn't he feel the way the rest of his kind did? There must be something wrong with him. He wished he could talk to Nocc or any of his brothers about it. He'd venture speaking with Crux had he been alive. Except that Wyck was absolutely certain he'd only be laughed at, provided he could even find the right words to express what he felt.

The best way he knew to touch a woman would be to copy Vrateus's hands on Svetlana's body. As much as the idea of feeling Nadia's bare skin excited him, he wouldn't like having to recall Svetlana when touching her.

At the same time, the idea of letting someone else touch Nadia filled him with a rage so strong, it burnt through his insides like acid, urging him to punch something.

He drew in a long breath, fighting the feeling of worry and unease about Nadia's performance tonight. He'd never seen a woman dance before and was actually looking forward to experiencing something new. He just hoped the rest of the crew would find the dance an acceptable substitute for the entertainment they were expecting.

He punched the code into the door panel, bracing himself for the onslaught of panic that always hit him the moment he faced the glass walls of the room and the open space beyond.

Lesh slinked around his legs in greeting the moment he'd entered.

"Ready?" He asked...and froze, speechless.

It wasn't the lights that shocked him this time but the sight of the smiling Nadia, standing in front of the clothing rack. She was wearing something so beautiful it could've only come out of a dream.

Her outfit consisted of several layers made of the dresses she'd cut to various lengths. The top one was trimmed with yellow feathers along the edge of the long skirt. The material of different colors was light and transparent, each layer slightly visible through the rest, giving the entire outfit the iridescent effect of a rainbow. With the most layers being over her breasts and hips, he couldn't see all of her body through the fabric—just a teasing whisper of her curves underneath it.

Her scent was only a slight tendril at this distance. Combined with the sight of her in this outfit, however, her scent had the effect of a punch to his chest, leaving him breathless.

"Do I look okay?" She smoothed a hand over her straight, light-brown hair she'd let down for the night.

The dancing lights of the Anomaly cast streaks of gold on her long tresses. The fear in her green eyes was softened by the smile on her lips.

"Yes, um... You look...okay," he mumbled as soon as he'd found his voice.

His insides twisted at the thought of taking her out there to be gawked at by hundreds of males. Everything in him urged him to hold her tight, to keep her to himself. He closed his eyes and clenched his hands into fists, fighting the unexplained wave of possessiveness.

"We should go," he croaked.

Before I change my mind, take you for myself, and get us both killed.

"Okay," she said softly. "Let's do it."

He opened his eyes, finding his worry and anxiety reflected in hers.

"I'll keep you safe," he vowed, fully intending to keep his promise, no matter the cost.

She picked up the frame with a purple slate inserted in it. He took her arm and opened the door.

They headed down the corridor, with Lesh walking slightly behind them. The *mahdi* remained unchained. Wyck needed his hands free and Lesh ready to leap to their defence if needed.

Nadia hugged the frame with the slate to her. Her chest rose rapidly with shallow, uneven breaths.

"I'll keep you safe," he reiterated.

Even if it's the last thing I do.

He could almost sense her fear. The soft, layered outfit made her look exceptionally vulnerable. He had the urge to grab her and hide her away from everyone.

Would she fit in the small room near the *vasai* farm where he had kept Lesh for years before Vrateus took over and Wyck thought it was safe for the one surviving *mahdi* to join the crew? But no one had known about Lesh's existence back then, no one had searched for him. If Nadia went missing, every male out there would be tracking her, hunting her.

"She belongs to all of us." Vrateus's words came to mind.

Irritation at his captain rose in his chest. Vrateus had cleverly avoided sharing Svetlana with anyone. Nadia had been thrown to the crew in place of her. And she was scared.

As they approached the mess hall, some members of the Dark Anomaly crew came into view. They lingered by the entrance to the room, glancing down the corridor impatiently.

Nadia tensed at the sight of them. She slowed her steps and moved so close to him, he nearly tripped over her feet.

From the corner of his eye, he noticed someone reaching for her. He threw his elbow out, shoving them out of the way.

"Stand back," he gritted the warning through his teeth, leading Nadia into the room.

It appeared that the entire population of the Dark Anomaly had gathered here, except for Vrateus and Svetlana. Even Malahki had shown up and now lingered casually at the back of the crowd. Curiosity must have brought the genderless *damirian* out tonight.

The tables in the room remained the way he had them arranged about an hour ago. Pushed close to each other, they formed a long line in the middle of the mess hall, just as Nadia had told him she needed them arranged.

"Where to?" he asked her.

Her face had paled, the green eyes open wide, as she stared at the half-naked males who filled the space.

The crowd was agitated, charged with anticipation and energy.

He slid his hand from her arm up to her shoulder, "Where do you want to start?"

"Oh." She snapped from her fear-induced stupor and gestured at the line of tables. "Either end is fine."

With shaking fingers, she fumbled to turn on the frame in her hands. The sound of an upbeat, sultry song filled the room.

"Could you hold this, please?" She handed him the frame, approaching the first table in the long line.

He placed the frame on a corner of the table. "Do you need help getting up?"

She nodded quickly.

His hands under her arms, he lifted her up onto the table. In his arms, she felt light like one of the feathers from the top layer of her clothing. In her multi-colored outfit, she truly reminded him of the rainbow-colored bird he'd once seen on a poster in one of the ships.

Now, she was positioned above the crew.

A few *ognuts* and most of the *kreers* were clinging to the walls, some of them hanging off the lighting cables dangling from the ceiling. However, most of the males sat in the haphazardly arranged chairs all over the room. The first crooked row of chairs was a few paces away from the line of tables—and from Nadia.

"Are you ready, boys?" Her upbeat voice startled him.

Forgetting all about the room and the expectant males, he snapped his gaze to Nadia.

Her fear was still there, he sensed it. Her fingers never stopped trembling. Her eyes remained open so wide, the entire room could drown in them.

Yet her back was straight, her head held high. She had a smile on her lips—a wide, inviting smile.

"What the fuck is she doing?" he muttered under his breath.

An excited roar rolled through the room. The rest of the crew appeared to be just as surprised as he was, though they seemed to recover quickly, shouting, clapping, and stomping their feet.

Nadia tilted her head playfully.

"Let's start then." She stomped her foot as the music picked up with the next beat.

Pinching the side of her skirt between two fingers, she lifted its top layer up and cocked her hip. Before he had the chance to fully appreciate her sassy stance, Nadia waved her skirt with a flourish and lunged along the line of the tables, moving in rhythm to the music. Her feet fluttered deftly along the hard surface of the tables. Her skirts billowed like the clouds of shimmering colors as she twisted, twirled, and turned.

He stared, mesmerized by the vivid show of the young woman jumping, swaying, and spinning, within the iridescent swirls of fabric. As the pace of the music increased, so did the speed of her dance—her feet but a blur beneath her skirts.

Suddenly, the clasp of the wide gold-tone belt around her waist clicked open and the upper, pale-yellow layer of her outfit slid loose—the one with the longest skirt trimmed with feathers.

She shrugged it off her shoulders in a slow, seductive gesture, then tossed it off into the crowd. The crew roared, growled, and hissed, fighting over the garment.

He watched in horror as the fabric was ripped to pieces in seconds. For one terrifying moment, he imagined it being Nadia herself.

She did not belong here—delicate, beautiful, and vulnerable—like a bright flower tossed into a dirty fighting pit. He had to get her out of this room and lock her up again—safe.

He balled his hands into fists so tight, his fingernails dug into the skin of his palms, but he ignored the pain.

"Nadia." He moved along the tables, keeping himself between her and the males who were devouring her with their eyes.

She didn't skip a beat in her dance. Her movements light and easy, she leaped into the air as if taking off to fly through it. He had never seen anything more spectacular in his life. Nadia was now his definition of beauty and magic.

Deliberately slow, she unwrapped the next layer of fabric from around her. Crimson red, it fluttered through the air like a wisp of the Anomaly light, landing among another group of males who immediately shredded it, too. Nadia followed it by yet another layer, without stopping her dance.

As she revealed more of her body, the movements of her limbs had become more apparent and even more fascinating to him. Her legs propelled her through the air. Her arms undulated smoothly, like wings, as if the music gave Nadia the power to conquer gravity and levitate.

He couldn't take his eyes off her, enthralled by her dance. Reality ceased to exist. She no longer appeared as a person but a magical being from another world.

Eventually, the music slowed down then faded away. With a graceful sweep of a leg to the side, Nadia lowered herself into a deep bow.

Her chest heaved. Her eyes shone with life and excitement when she rose and glanced around the room. The wide smile on her lips was genuine.

His consciousness slowly floated back from the blissful feeling of awe her dancing had plunged him into. A new kind of pleasure rolled through his body, warming his chest. He wanted more of this, so much more. At the same time, he was afraid his heart would burst from emotions he couldn't name.

Raising his hands, he clapped—the only way he could remotely express his deep delight and appreciation for her performance. The noise of his clapping seemed to grow and multiply, as others joined in his applause.

Whistles, stomping, and roaring took over.

Nadia looked around nervously. Her gaze landed on him. Then, she smiled again, just for him this time. He nearly staggered from the charge of pleasure rushing through him at the sight of recognition in her eyes.

He had to get her back to her room, the sooner the better.

"Hey!" Nocc's voice cut through the noise of the crowd like a rusty knife. "How come she's still wearing clothes?"

A short purple skirt and a narrow matching scarf tied around her breasts were all that remained from Nadia's outfit. Yet it proved too much for Nocc and some others who started joining him with growls of disapproval.

Nadia raised her hands in front of her as if trying to stop an approaching disaster.

"Step back, everyone!" Her voice rang high with fear, though she visibly made an effort to remain calm and to calm down the crowd. "Stay were you are if you want to see more."

She moved a hand up to the knot of the scarf around her breasts.

Judging by the musty smell of semen saturating the air in the room, most of the males had already come during her performance. Wyck guessed that seeing her naked might satisfy them further, but it wouldn't stop their demands. The more she gave, the more they'd want.

Tossing a glance back to the door, he estimated the number of steps it would take him to reach the exit with the weight of Nadia in his arms—too many—especially with the agitated crew between him and the door.

Someone crashed into his back as a scuffle broke out behind him. Lust came hand in hand with aggression here. A massive fight was brewing. He flicked the laser blade on, stabbing without looking. Enkail, the *dimo* rushed him, the hard-plated skull painfully ramming into his shoulder. He shoved Enkail aside.

"Nadia." Wyck twisted in her direction just in time to see Nocc leap onto the table next to her. He ripped the end of the scarf from her fingers and yanked at it forcefully. Nadia spun around as the scarf unwound from around her, freeing her breasts.

At the sight of her naked flesh, wild roars ripped from hundreds of throats. The lust-crazed males rushed to Nadia, shoving the chairs and tables aside and trampling each other.

"Nadia!" Wyck yelled at the top of his lungs.

She swung her head toward his voice, her arms pressed to her breasts, her expression terrified.

"Come here!" He punched a *kreer* out of the way, crashing through the crowd to her.

Lesh launched himself at someone's throat. He left him to it.

There were at least as many tables as fingers on his hand between Nadia and him. The males filled the space separating him from her quickly, punching each other to get closer to her as she stood on a table, hugging herself, terrified.

He couldn't get to her fast enough. She needed to be moving, too.

He opened his arms for her, and she ran.

Those light feet of hers leaped from table to table even as the pieces of furniture were moved and shoved aside by the thickening crowd. Her strong legs propelled her forward as she evaded the greedy hands reaching for her from all sides. Jumping in the air from the last table, she briefly landed on the back of Enkail who had fallen to the ground in a scuffle.

The *dimo* grunted then tried to turn around to catch her, but she had already jumped up and into Wyck's arms before anyone else could get to her.

"I've got you," he exhaled. As soon as she was in his arms, something loosened inside him, allowing him to breathe freely once again.

"Lesh!" he called the *mahdi*. The animal had been gnawing on some tentacles that were still attached to a *yourlu* who was writhing and screaming in pain. "Lead," he ordered.

The *mahdi* dropped the whimpering *yourlu* and plowed through the crowd separating them from the entrance. His three heads snapped, bit, and ripped to pieces the flesh of those who stood in their way.

Wyck held Nadia to him with one arm. Her limbs wound tightly around him, she buried her face in his shoulder, surrendering all control to him. With the knife in his other hand, he slashed through the air, deterring any attempts to attack them from the side.

Once in the corridor where the crowd had thinned, he ran. Lesh fell behind slightly, snapping at anyone who tried to pursue them.

When all three of them made it back to her room, he allowed himself to release a long breath, feeling the tension drain from his muscles and letting the worry finally ease in his chest.

His back to the closed doors, he slid to the floor, settling Nadia in his lap.

"Nadia?" he called softly, stroking her long, mussed hair.

She wouldn't move.

Chapter 11

IF I KEPT MY EYES CLOSED—THE wild faces distorted by madness, the fangs dripping with saliva, and the hands grabbing for me wouldn't come back. There would only be the warmth of Wyck's large, hard body and the safety of his strong arms around me.

Forever.

Among the sea of scowling faces and hulking figures, Wyck had stood out as the biggest and the most intimidating. Yet as soon as he had yelled my name, I'd run to him. I'd run so fast, I practically threw myself into his arms.

"Nadia." His voice filtered through the dark fog of terror, like a ray of sunshine breaking through the storm clouds. "Are you okay?"

His wide, callused hands rubbed my back—my *naked* back. My front was bare, too. The scarf had been ripped off my chest. My naked breasts pressed directly into Wyck's chest as the sides of his vest had fallen apart.

I shifted in his lap, realizing that my body was practically plastered to his, head to toe, while the short, flimsy excuse for a skirt was the only piece of clothing I was wearing.

He must've become aware of that, too, as his erection started to harden and grow against my core.

I peeled myself from him.

"I'm fine. Thank you. For getting me out of there..." I leaned further back, wrapping my arms around my chest. "I'll need to get changed."

"Stay," he rasped, flexing his arms around me. Trapping me.

His erection kept growing. How huge *was* this guy?

His green-speckled golden eyes pinned me in place, the expression in them increasingly more unhinged, wild, so similar to what I'd just seen in the eyes of the others.

Alarm lanced though me.

"Wyck..." Covering myself with one arm the best I could, I pressed my other hand into his chest. "I—I should go."

He yanked me to him. My heart sped up. I desperately tried to hold back fear.

"Please," I begged. "Let me go."

A pained groan rose from his throat. He buried his face in my neck.

"Just give me a moment," he growled against my skin, the short dark stubble on his jawline prickling lightly.

This very instant, he appeared more tortured than dangerous.

"What for?" I asked, tentatively placing my arm around his shoulder.

He inhaled deeply, then again, and again.

"If I smell you long enough," he said, without lifting his head, "if I let your scent fill me inside and out, without holding back for once, then maybe there is a point when I can say I've had enough of you for a while."

His hold on me was as firm as ever, but he didn't let his hands wander. He simply held me close.

I managed to relax a little against him. Placing my hand on the back of his neck, I soothingly trailed my fingers along the three gray ridges. They ran all the way along his head. The one in the middle went down his spine, disappearing under his vest. The two on the sides split at the base of his neck, running along each of his shoulders then down his arms to the knuckles on his hands.

"I thought this might make it easier letting go of you," he said, uncharacteristically softly. "I was wrong, it doesn't." He unwrapped his arms from around me, setting me free. "But go on, get changed."

I wasn't sure what all of that meant exactly, but he did appear calmer after our hug. The wild expression in his eyes didn't entirely disappear, but it had softened somewhat, turning wistful.

Climbing out of his lap, I found my suit then took it to the bathroom to change.

Tonight's events wouldn't leave my mind. My hands still shook and the anxiety about next week had already started to build.

"Why are they like that?" I asked Wyck upon my return from the bathroom. He remained sitting sideways in the doorway, his eyes focused on the metal panel ahead of him. "So...brutally feral?"

"The crew?" He shifted, making some space for me in the entranceway. "That's what they are, what all of us are by nature."

"That's not true." I sat opposite him, my back pressed against the panel he'd been staring at. He had no choice but to look at me, now. "Violence and disrespect are not inherent characteristics of any nation in the modern world. They might've been prevalent in some places, at some point in history, but that's not how things are anymore."

I studied his features for a while, really *seeing* him for the first time.

The three gray ridges on his head met in a peak over the bridge of his nose. The typical for *errocks* heavy brow gave him a fierce expression. The bright yellow eyes glistening underneath appeared almost glowing in the shadows. His proud, angular nose and high sharp cheekbones with dark stubble clashed with the sensual shape of his mouth. The shapely upper lip had a defined curve of the cupid's bow, and the full lower one seemed to be made for kissing.

Wyck was a handsome man, I realized. I had no way of knowing whether an *errock* woman would find him good-looking, but I was positive that many human women would.

He flinched under my scrutiny, and I promptly shifted my stare away from his face.

"Sorry," I mumbled. "I've never spent so much time in the company of a non-human before. I've never even been this close to one of your species. It's all still new."

"*Errocks* and humans don't get along out there?"

"Oh no, we do. There are many joint projects between Hexol and Earth, your planet and mine. Most of them are done remotely, though. Earth is just so far away from the rest of the planets in the Federation. We're also still the newest member."

"You're saying *errocks* out there—people in general—are not the same like they are here?"

"Absolutely not." I shook my head. "Believe it or not, I could be completely naked in a room full of men and no one would dare to touch me without my explicit permission."

He lifted a brow ridge.

"Have you done that?"

"Um, no," I blinked, then gave him a smile. "That is not a common practice. It was just an example."

"Then how can you be so sure no one would touch you?" He gazed at me inquisitively. "You said you haven't been this close to an *errock* before—clothed or not."

"Because I know a lot about the larger nations of the Federation, including the *errocks*. I studied their art and culture. I know the *errocks* nation has been an active member of the Federation, instrumental in making the organization what it is—a safe, peaceful place where all nations live and work together in harmony. Their laws protect personal freedom of all individuals, and they strictly enforce them."

His brow furrowed, Wyck stared at me with suspicion.

"One of the most esteemed politicians in the Federation government is an *errock*," I continued. "His name is Krix Kussur. He came to Earth as part of a delegation, about a year ago. I was sick that day, but my friend went to the welcoming rally and got to meet him in person. He shook her hand and gave her a hug." I crossed my stare with Wyck's. "He did not attack her. Trust me, Nocc's way is *not* an acceptable way of treating women."

"It's not..." he sounded as if thinking out loud.

It blew my mind that personal freedom and respect—something that I'd taken for granted—were a complete novelty to Wyck.

Did he really think that what was happening on the Dark Anomaly could be the norm anywhere else in the Universe?

But then again, had he ever had a chance to learn the truth, before now?

"You only know what the others told you," I said, realizing just how isolated Wyck's life had been in here. Their library was the only window into the world, and he couldn't even use it fully because he didn't know how to read.

Most of his life knowledge came from men like Nocc. I'd never met Crux, but I had a feeling he couldn't have been much better than Nocc. This group of *errocks* had last seen the world outside of the Anomaly thousands of years ago. A lot had changed in the Universe since then.

What had happened out there since *my* arrival here? I'd been on the Dark Anomaly for over a day now, which must be close to a year out there. A dreadful feeling slithered down my spine. Aside from a few close friends, I had no one left on Earth to mourn my disappearance. However, I knew that the rest of my team had families who must be frantic to learn about their fate.

Since I might be the only one who'd survived, I owed it to everyone and to myself to find a way to get out of here.

Once again, my thoughts went to the ship and the damaged capsule. I needed to get out of here, and I might have the means to do that, but I needed help.

I moved my gaze back to Wyck.

"Would you like to see what the world is like out there?" I asked tentatively.

He shot me a glance, and I glimpsed a spark of curiosity in his expression. As grim and unaffected as Wyck tried to behave, I believed he was thirsty for new experiences. It couldn't be easy for him to be cooped up in one place all his life. He had been soaking up every word I'd said about the world beyond the Dark Anomaly.

"No," he said quickly, the light in his gaze dimming. "There is no leaving this place. Dreaming about what's out there only leads to disappointment or death."

Obviously, I wouldn't try to get off the Dark Anomaly without making sure it was safe to do so. Yet Wyck didn't believe it was possible to escape, at all.

I had to find another way to approach this.

"Can I get more slates from the library?"

"It's not safe for you out there, even less so after what happened tonight." He tipped his head in the direction of the mess hall.

"Would you bring me some, then?"

"You need more music?"

"Actually, I'd like to read more about the Dark Anomaly, please. Here..." I grabbed one of the slates lying around. We'd left the frame behind while escaping the mess hall, and without the frame, the slate wouldn't work. I blew a breath on the smooth surface then drew two words in the condensation with my finger. "This is how Dark Anomaly is spelled in the Universal language."

He threw a sideway glance at the words.

"What is it that you need to know about this place? Knowledge won't affect your life in any way."

In some ways, he was right. My life here was not much different than that of a caged animal, let out only for the entertainment of others. However, knowledge was power that could potentially enable me to change things.

There could be a way for me to make Wyck more interested in those changes, too.

I wiped the slate off with my sleeve, then blew on it again.

"Have you ever seen your name in writing?" I asked, tracing the letters in the fog on the slate. "Here, this is how it looks in Universal."

This time, he studied the slate a little longer.

"That's my name?" He took the slate from my hands to take a closer look at the word.

"Yes." I nodded. "These are letters—the written record of each sound in your name. By rearranging the letters, we write words."

"What does *your* name look like?" He handed the slate back to me.

"Here is mine." I wrote it quickly. "See? We have the same sound in yours and mine, which in the Universal language corresponds to the same letter. There it is." I pointed at the letter that in Universal stood for both sounds that the letters *y* and *i* made in his and my names, respectively.

"We share a letter?" He seemed especially pleased by that fact.

"Right." I smiled.

"Is it the same in *my* language?"

"I don't know." I rubbed my forehead. "I don't speak Hexolian. There might not be. There are no common letters in our names in either English or Russian—the two Earth languages that I speak. Both have more complicated structures. But that's the point of Universal—it simplifies things. It was created to unite people of many planets by making communication easier. That's why it's one of the easiest languages to learn, if not *the easiest* one of all."

He kept staring at the slate until the condensation evaporated and the letters disappeared.

"I can teach you how to read," I offered quietly and held my breath in anticipation of his answer.

"Why?" he said after a short pause.

To me, his inability to read was an impairment that could be easily fixed. There was no downside to it. Wyck didn't need to continue going through life in ignorance. I sensed a keen interest about the world in him. He wanted to learn more about it, but he couldn't do so independently.

"Because we have some time to kill," I replied casually. "And being able to read is handy, even around here."

He slid his gaze aside, biting down on that plump lower lip of his.

"I don't think I can learn. Crux used to say I was too dumb for that," he said it simply, without bitterness, as if stating a fact.

Suddenly, I wished Crux was still alive, so I could slap him.

"Crux obviously had no desire to bother teaching you."

Knowing what I did about the men responsible for Wyck's upbringing, there might be more to it. Having Wyck grow up unable to learn things for himself must've made it easier for them to control him. The only truth he'd ever known was whatever they'd told him.

"Knowledge is a kind of power, Wyck."

He rolled his shoulders back, flexing the bulging muscles in his arms.

"I've got enough power as it is." He gave me a crooked grin.

"Physical strength is only part of it. Your captain is not as big or as strong as an *errock*, yet he holds the authority over all of you."

"Because he is smart," he replied slowly.

"See? Knowledge *is* power," I said with conviction. "It'd give you the ability to think for yourself and to make your own decisions based on the information you'd be able to access on your own if you could read."

He kept quiet for a little while. I could almost *see* the thoughts running through his mind.

"You may think you're one of them," I continued. "But you are your own person, first and foremost. And you're not like them."

He stirred, ready to protest, but I wouldn't let him.

"When they all lunged at me back there, ready to rip me to pieces, you got me to safety. You've held me, almost completely naked, in your arms and you let me go without causing me any harm. Would any one of those over six hundred males have done the same?"

Maybe I was wrong. Maybe I had too much faith in him and not enough in the others, but he no longer tried to argue.

"You're not like them, Wyck. You don't have to be."

Chapter 12

"SO, THIS GUY HERE..." Wyck shifted into a more comfortable position on the floor, in his usual place in the doorway. The tablet frame with an orange slate was in his lap. "He invented the medicine that cured a large portion of the population of a *themul* country on Nofoi."

Leaning against his side, I nodded. "Hundreds of thousands of lives were saved. More than that, though, the process the *errock* Professor Lercur created has been used to make life-saving medicine for other species, too, not just the *themul*."

"And that's why he is celebrated as a hero everywhere."

"Right."

It had been three days since I started teaching Wyck how to read Universal. His nearly photographic memory allowed him to memorise entire words, which proved a hindrance sometimes. I had to force him to break the words into letters, so he could then learn to read words yet unknown to him, too. Despite some slight setbacks, once he had grasped the concept, he was moving forward with astounding speed.

Wyck had been spending most of the days here with me, leaving only to get us food and to exchange slates from the library. I'd noticed he was especially eager to read biographies of famous men. I believed he loved learning about the many ways in which a person could distinguish themselves in the modern world. At first, he listened with fascination and admiration when I read the stories to him. Now, he had slowly started reading them himself.

"Has Professor Lercur ever visited Earth?" he asked.

"No. I don't believe he has."

"Do you know anyone who has been to Hexol?"

"Not personally. No." I shook my head.

"Would you like to go there one day?"

I snapped my gaze up to his face. It was impossible to tell whether his question was purely hypothetical. I hoped he might be considering the possibility of traveling beyond this place one day.

Other than this mission, I hadn't travelled much. Until now, my life plan had focused on settling down, then creating and raising my family. Now, when I imagined myself taking a trip to Hexol, in Wyck's company, it seemed extremely appealing.

"I'd love to see Hexol," I replied sincerely then added, "If it were possible, that is."

We sat in silence for a while, each lost in our own thoughts.

"Did you have to learn how to dance?" Wyck spoke first, changing the subject, for which I was grateful. "Or are humans born knowing how to do that?"

"No, that's not a born ability. I took dance classes for many years. Though, I did love dancing probably from the day I was born."

"Why?"

I blinked at him in confusion. Why did people like dancing? Or art in general? How could I best explain it to him? And was an explanation even possible?

I often had to adjust my way of thinking around Wyck. He questioned many things I took for granted, forcing me to look at the world from a different perspective. For him, so many things I grew up with were new as he learned about them for the first time.

Dancing seemed to be one of them.

"I always loved it." I shrugged. "While in school, I considered becoming a professional dancer, but when I got a little older, film production attracted me more as a career. Dance just stayed a hobby for me."

"Do you dance at home, when you're alone?"

"Sometimes," I confessed. "But I also go out with friends. I've done a few dance competitions, too. It's been fun. You see, dancing is both my way to relax and revitalize."

It didn't escape me that we both were talking about my life in the present tense, as though I still *had* that life.

"How so?" he asked. "I'm sure it's a strenuous exercise, though you do make it look easy."

I smiled wider.

"True, after a performance I feel tired, but also energized. There is a sense of accomplishment—satisfying and fulfilling. Don't you wish you could express yourself through something bigger than words, sometimes? Don't you ever feel so full with emotions that no words would do? None seem good enough. That's when dancing becomes a necessity for me."

"When I'm *full of emotion*?" He arched an eyebrow ridge, a corner of his mouth lifting in a half-smile. There was a genuine desire to understand behind his amused expression, though.

So, I continued.

"Yeah, like..." I searched for words to describe that mix of longing and energy that grew and bubbled, threatening to explode if I didn't move—the *need* to dance. "I believe it's in everyone, the desire for another form of self-expression. Everyone has something that brings them happiness while they're doing it. It doesn't need to be dancing, of course. It could be any form of art—music, painting, singing—or crafts, creating something with your hands—carving, sewing, knitting."

"You think everyone has that?"

"Sure. Sports could be that, too, for some. Any physical activity."

"Like fighting?"

I bit my lip. The type of fighting that took place on the Dark Anomaly, I suspected, was not what one would call "relaxing and revitalizing."

"Do you feel satisfied after a fight?" I asked.

"If I win. Which I always do." He gave me a cocky grin.

I thought back to the fighting he'd done in the mess hall the night of my performance. He threw punches and maimed people with a sole purpose of allowing us to get away, not because he enjoyed it.

He couldn't be talking about that.

"Do you have some kind of sparring here?" I clarified. "When you fight without the intent of seriously hurting your opponent?"

"There are one-on-one fights organized, nightly. There is always plenty of intent to hurt, but seriously harming each other is not allowed during those fights. Vrateus has strict rules against intentionally inflicting serious injuries." His face lit up with a wide smile. "It's still fun, though."

"Well, I guess fighting without injury could be seen as a form of couple dancing," I mused. "One person attacks, another parries. One leads, another follows."

He tilted his head, as if considering something.

"Sex then could be viewed as a dance, too," he said, unexpectedly.

"Um..."

How exactly did it come to talking about sex?

"One partner attacks," he explained, "the other submits."

I felt I owed it to every woman who might have sex with him one day to correct him on that one. Then, I winced at the thought of Wyck with another woman. It was not a pleasant one, and I chased it away like an annoying fly.

"The goal of having sex, other than for procreation, is the pleasure of both partners," I said to him, "which means it shouldn't be approached like a fight, where there could only be one winner."

"Why not?" He slid his gaze to my lips as I spoke, and I found myself staring at his mouth, too. "Doesn't one person lead and another follow in both cases? Isn't there also some power involved?"

I forced myself to look up from his sensual lips and into his eyes. "Power? Are you talking about something like the power of passion?" I muttered.

His eyes lit up, making me warm inside.

"You see," I cleared my throat, dropping my gaze into my lap, "unlike a fight, there are no losers in good sex. If it's done right, both partners end up winning. That's what so great about it."

"Women also experience pleasure." It wasn't a question. His statement sounded as though female pleasure was not an entirely new concept to him.

"Yes." I glanced up again. "Women do experience pleasure, Wyck. With the right partner, the sex is like a most wonderful dance, with a beautiful finale for both the man and the woman."

He licked his lips, his eyes on me, and I followed his tongue with my gaze.

If I kissed that full bottom lip of his, would his taste have the same flavor as his scent?

The thought was sudden and wrong.

I'd been spending so much time with Wyck, hoping to eventually convince him to assist me in getting off the Anomaly, not to be seduced into daydreaming about the taste of his kiss. The way he was looking at me right now—the glowing gold of his eyes making my insides melt like warm butter—didn't help, either.

"So many wonderful things have happened since your arrival," he said softly.

Had anything *wonderful* ever happened on the Dark Anomaly? For me, it had been nothing but fighting off various aliens and a constant struggle for survival.

That would be Wyck's regular life, I imagined—both rough and monotonous. For him, my arrival here *had* brought some changes to that life, and probably some new excitement along with them.

Turning at the waist to face me, he lifted his hand to my face, and I halted my breath in anticipation of his touch, unsure where it would lead but not willing to stop him.

With a soft whimpering sound, Lesh scooted closer to us from his spot by the wall. He placed all three of his heads across my legs and onto Wyck's lap.

I froze in alarm as the animal's long scaly necks stretched across my thighs, his black curved claws resting on my shin. His right head, the more outgoing one, nuzzled my hand.

"He wants you to pet him." Wyck huffed a laugh, dropping his hand down without touching me after all.

"This one wants it, maybe." I tentatively stroked the red stripe of scales on the side of Lesh's right head. "I'm not so sure about the middle one, though."

In the past three days, as I'd worked on taming his master, Lesh and I had also grown closer. The animal had been staying in my room all this time. Wyck had brought us both food, and all three of us had eaten every meal together.

Unchained, Lesh was free to roam my room, but he appeared to respect my space, sticking mostly to the area along the wall and near the door. He was guarding me when Wyck was not around. And for that, I was beginning to feel a real appreciation for him.

Wyck wasn't lying when he'd said that Lesh had been toilet trained. Ever since he'd unchained him, Lesh had been using the bathroom without fail, which had gained him a new level of respect from me. There hadn't been any more stinky incidents.

Yet until today, Lesh hadn't allowed any physical contact between us.

"The middle head looks like it wants to move away from me as soon as possible." I continued gliding my fingers over the hard, smooth scales on the side of the left head. Lesh's left head also appeared relaxed, but the central one kept watching me with its shiny, black eyes. "It has a rather suspicious personality, doesn't it?"

"What are you talking about?" Wyck petted the middle head then scratched under its jaw. Lesh closed all his eyes, releasing a soft hiss of pleasure. "They're all one animal."

"They are," I agreed quietly. "But if you look closely, each head has its own personality. The middle one is obviously in charge, I'm going to call him Lesher. This one is Leshic." I scratched under the right head's chin, the way Wyck had done to Lesher. Leshic let me do it, its thin lips stretching into a blissful smile.

This was the most amazing ability of Lesh's, in my opinion—he could smile. With his razor-sharp teeth now on display, the smile wasn't far from a scowl, but I could tell the difference.

"You're a mellow fellow, aren't you?" I murmured, petting the smooth flat top of the right head. "That one, on the left, is cuddlier than the rest. That's how he gets away with much more, too. You are a troublemaker. Right, Leshy?" The left head opened an eye at my question, as if responding to the nickname. I'd seen him demanding and getting more attention than the rest from Wyck.

Wyck watched me intently as I spoke. I wondered if it annoyed him that I'd gotten to know his pet this well and even was taking the liberty to name his heads.

"I call them Boss, Calm, and Cuddly," he finally confessed, his expression a little sheepish. "You're the first one to notice the difference in their behaviours. Normally, I keep Lesh away from everyone."

"Why? He can be friendly once he gets to know you."

He exhaled sharply, shaking his head.

"There is no need for others to know that. Being friendly and approachable may get him killed."

"That's horrible." I hugged Leshic with both hands. "Why kill a friendly animal?"

Wyck shrugged his shoulders, with a somber expression.

"For fun."

I could point out that there was no fun in murdering anyone, let alone an animal. Sadly, I'd gotten to know the dwellers of the Dark Anomaly well enough by now to agree that most of them would possibly derive a perverted kind of pleasure in murder.

"Lesh arrived with the ship that was transporting a large group of *mahdis*," Wyck explained. "All of them were killed within days. He must've escaped the cage somehow because I found him hiding in a short, narrow passage near the *vasai* farm. I was fourteen at the time, and he was only a pup. I hid him away from everyone and kept him alive until both of us grew big enough to protect each other. When Vrateus became the captain, I told him about Lesh. He made Lesh part of the crew, which gave him the same rights as everyone else. Under the captain's rules, Lesh can't be killed without punishment for the murderer. That doesn't mean some still wouldn't try to end him if they got a chance."

He rested his hand on top of the middle head of the animal.

"Lesh needs to be vicious and scary in order to survive and to protect you and me. Deep inside, however, he is still the cuddly playful pup he's always been. We'll just keep your happy side a secret from everyone, right Lesh?" He patted his pet.

Being the only one who was let in on their secret made me feel even closer to both of them, as if I was now officially included into their tiny group.

Stroking Lesh's smooth scales, I snuggled into Wyck's warm side. These few square feet of space by the door might be the only place in the entire Dark Anomaly where both of us felt the most comfortable.

"I'll tell you what," I said. "You'll finish reading this chapter, then we'll take a break from learning. This afternoon I'd say let's watch a movie together. There are a couple you got from the library last time. One even looks like it may have some dancing in it."

He wrapped his arm around my shoulders and settled the tablet between us, re-opening the biography he'd been reading.

I listened as he read out loud, still haltingly and tripping over some long or unknown words. His perseverance was admirable, though, and the speed with which he soaked up everything new simply astonishing.

Sitting like that, cuddling next to Wyck under the blanket, I could almost forget where I was and what lay ahead of me.

Almost.

Chapter 13

"Hey, boy," Nocc stopped him outside of Nadia's room. Trox and Gler were with him, as they often kept together. What surprised Wyck was that Krakhil, a *dimo*, was also standing nearby, looking as if he were a part of their group, too.

"How is the female doing?" Krakhil asked, a smirk stretching the lipless mouth on his hard-plated face.

"Fine." Wyck started walking towards the mess hall.

It'd been eight days since Nadia landed on the Dark Anomaly. Another session in the mess hall was scheduled for tonight. He had left Nadia in her room because he needed to set up the tables for her dance. He also had to get some lunch for her and Lesh.

The four males who'd accosted him in the corridor were too close to Nadia's room, which troubled him. He walked faster, eager to get them as far away from her as possible.

Thankfully, all four followed him.

"You've been selfish, Wyck." Trox elbowed his way closer to him. "One of the only two females available is in your reach, and you've been keeping her all to yourself for the entire week."

"I'm keeping her safe, for all of us." The statement sounded wrong even to his own ears.

Vrateus had said that Nadia belonged to them all. By now, however, she was more Wyck's than anyone else's.

Only his.

Mine.

The powerful urge to proclaim that out loud vibrated through him. His muscles ached to be put to a good use. He balled his hands into fists, ready to strike.

"If she is ours how come *you're* the only one who smells like her?" Trox growled.

Did he?

Nadia had been taking showers with the soap regularly, making her scent barely discernible. There hadn't been any sex or even kisses between them, of course. The scent Trox was talking about must be coming simply from him being in her proximity daily.

She'd sit next to him in the entryway, the only portion of that room he could tolerate because it had a solid floor instead of glass. He loved the feeling of her body pressed to his—one of the reasons why he'd been spending so much time in the room he hated. He'd often wrap his arm around her shoulders, to get her even closer.

It wasn't much, but they would spend hours siting side by side—enough time apparently for her scent to transfer to his clothes and skin.

Knowing he had her scent on him pleased him, even as Trox continued to harp at him, "We're a family, Wyck. What yours is ours."

"How about *him*, then?" Wyck tipped his chin at Krakhil. "Is *he* a part of the family, too, now?"

"Hey!" the *dimo* roared, the fingers on all four of his hands twitching. "Why do *you* get to fuck her all the time while the rest of us only see her once a week? And even then, she wouldn't spread her legs for us to see or do anything!"

Wyck's temper flared.

"Listen you!" He pivoted into the *dimo's* direction. "No one is fucking her. Definitely, not *you*." He raised his fist, searching for the least armored place on the *dimo's* face to land a blow.

"There, there, now." Nocc stepped closer, draping his arm around Wyck's shoulders. "Krakhil is a friend. A family friend. Okay?"

"He is *not* family." Wyck glared at the *dimo*, keeping his fist aimed at the male's face.

"No, of course not." Nocc patted Wyck's arm in a gesture that felt more patronizing than calming. "But *you* are." He led Wyck down the corridor again, with the rest of the group catching up. "We're a family, Wyck, don't forget that. We live together. We fight together. And we die together. Our loyalty to each other is what has kept us alive all these years—here on the Dark Anomaly and out there before that."

Nocc slowed down, making the two of them fall behind the rest of the group.

"Women are whores to be fucked and tossed out," he continued casually.

Wyck had heard these words often. Never before, however, had they made his skin crawl with revulsion as they did now. His mind and his heart rejected the notion.

"That's what your father did to the female who gave birth to you," Nocc kept going. "He left her in the filthy brothel he'd found her in. It's your luck you were born a boy, so he brought you on his ship. One day, you would've taken over his entire fleet. You're the true leader of this family, Wyck. And the leader is always just and generous to his people. The human girl is our bounty. And as such, she should be shared fairly among all of us. That's what the Great Scodr would've done. It's your legacy, Wyck."

"If I am the 'true leader' of the family," Wyck had chosen a portion of Nocc's speech to focus on, "then I want you to help me carry out this task."

He stopped outside the mess hall, gesturing to the rest of their group to carry on walking.

Krakhil folded his arms across his chest, taking a stance that said he was not moving anywhere. Trox and Gler also paused, glancing at Nocc for directions.

So much for Wyck being their leader. After the death of Crux, Nocc had been the one who held the true power in their group.

Nocc waved his hand, making them all move away, then turned to face Wyck again.

"You don't need to be afraid of Vrateus, boy," he said in a conspiratorial tone. "His days are numbered. He and his woman are as good as dead. I promise I'll let you have the final round with Svetlana, so you can fuck her to death and have your vengeance."

Wyck knew it was his obligation to avenge the death of Crux, but *that* wasn't how he'd do it. When he finally killed Svetlana, he'd do it the way she killed Crux, by shooting her in the belly. That was the reason he kept taking his time, Wyck told himself, he needed to get hold of a gun first.

"Nocc." He diverted the male's attention to what he felt was more important than vengeance at the moment. "I don't want any harm to come to Nadia."

"Who is Nadia?" Nocc made a face, as if the sound of any female name was offensive purely because it was female.

"The woman in my charge."

"You know her name?" Nocc slid him a suspicious glance, his expression sour.

"I have to call her something, don't I?" Wyck snapped.

Nocc shrugged instead of an answer, and Wyck made an effort to rein in his temper.

"We are a family," he used Nocc's own words. "I have a task to complete, and I'm asking for your help."

"Which is?" Nocc narrowed his eyes at him.

"To keep the female safe. I can't do it alone," he added as Nocc curled his lip in disgust. "You saw what happened the last time."

Nocc tilted his head. "Did you hear anything of what I've just told you, boy?"

"I heard every word, Nocc." Keeping his rising anger and frustration at bay was proving harder by the minute. "And I'll tell you the same thing I've told you before—no one harms Nadia. She's here to entertain six hundred males, and the only way for her to do that is if I— if *we*—keep her well and alive. I need to know you're with me on that. Can I count on my family to support me?"

Nocc gave him a long, penetrating look.

For the first time in his life, Wyck felt that the *errocks'* loyalty to each other was not a given. Nocc had spoken the truth when he'd said that the *errocks* on the Dark Anomaly had stood up for each other. Until now, Wyck had always felt the support of their entire group behind him. His strength stemmed from their collective power. The feeling of being on his own lately had been destroying him from the inside. He needed the loyalty of his people, he wanted them on his side. Yet, he also felt that it was *he* who had been drifting away, going against the group.

"You want all of us to help you keep her alive?" Nocc's expression turned calculating.

"Yes. I want you to protect her with me."

"Did Vrateus say something about this?"

"No," Wyck replied firmly. His task had grown way past Vrateus's orders. Keeping Nadia safe had become Wyck's personal mission. "It's because *I* want her safe. And I need you—all of you—on my side."

Nocc shifted his weight to the other foot, his expression finally relaxing. "What exactly do you want us to do?"

Wyck released a short breath. It was too soon to breathe with relief, but Nocc's words gave him hope.

"I want you to keep the crew at bay tonight, away from her. Let her do her dance and let me get her out of there without anyone laying their hands on her."

"Her dance?" Nocc folded his arms across his chest. "She'll need to do more than that tonight."

Wyck's heart hollowed with dread.

"You didn't like her dancing?" he asked flatly.

"It was...*lovely*," Nocc spat the word out as if it burnt his mouth. "But I barely caught a glimpse of her tits before you hauled her away. That was hardly fair, boy."

His thoughts drifted back to that night. The moment Nadia had run to him something had snapped in his heart. Since then, she'd been becoming his main reason to wake up every morning. By now, he felt he would die to protect her. Except that his death would leave her completely on her own. And he might need help to stay alive.

"If you want to see her naked," he said to Nocc, slowly, "you'll have to make it safe for her to do so. No one touches her, no one even comes close enough to breathe on her. Do you understand?"

Nocc chewed on the inside of his cheek, taking a pause that was too long for Wyck's comfort.

"It's a deal," he finally said, and Wyck was able to inhale deeply.

"Promise she won't be harmed," he demanded, needing to hear it said out loud.

"Promise." Nocc nodded.

Getting Nocc's word on it was as good as securing a promise from their entire group. Having his family fully behind him again took a load off Wyck's shoulders.

Errocks were the largest group on the Dark Anomaly, both in size and in number. Vrateus recognized their power, giving them the honor of being his personal guard. Even after Crux had taken over the Dark Anomaly, naming himself the captain, and Vrateus had fought him to get his title back, he'd kept the *errocks* as his guards. The captain needed their power.

No one dared to mess with *errocks*, and Wyck loved that. He enjoyed being a part of something bigger than he could ever be on his own.

Feeling somewhat lighter at heart, he got some food for Nadia, Lesh, and himself. Then the three of them had lunch together. It was easy to forget about the world outside of their glass bubble when he was talking with Nadia.

She smiled, telling him another story about the outside world that was beginning to truly fascinate him. Lesh lay at his side, gnawing on a bone. And Wyck didn't want to think about anything beyond the present moment.

Once he finally forced himself to leave her side, he turned right from her room, not left. Then, he headed toward Vrateus's room instead of his own.

"Captain!" He slammed his fist into the set of double doors, identical to those of Nadia's.

Vrateus had occupied this room ever since he'd become the captain of the Dark Anomaly. Wyck was sure that the reason the captain had selected this space out of the many available on the carcases of the crashed ships that made up the solid body of the Anomaly was its glass walls the *errocks* found unnerving.

Wyck harbored no illusions. The captain used and tolerated the *errocks*—that didn't mean he liked them or trusted them in any way.

Yet he had to make the captain trust him this one time.

"Captain!" He slammed his fist into the door once again. "It's me, Wyck. I need to talk to you."

The door slid aside a little, the gap not big enough for Wyck even to slid his hand through. He wasn't planning to get in anyway, even if he'd been invited.

"I need a gun," he blurted out as soon as Vrateus's face came into view through the gap.

"No."

Wyck wedged the toe of his boot into the gap, afraid the captain might shut the door in his face.

"You told me to protect Nadia, the human female," he rushed out. "I need a real weapon to do it effectively."

"Who is it, honey?" Svetlana's voice cooed from somewhere deep in the room.

Her tone was warm and soft, the words swaddling Wyck's heart like a fuzzy blanket. He knew she wasn't talking to *him*, but that didn't lessen the wonderful effect of the love in her voice.

"It's Wyck, my treasure," Vrateus replied softly over his shoulder. "Just give us a minute." He slid the door open a little wider and slipped out into the corridor.

Suddenly, Wyck knew *why* he'd never honored the ancient tradition of his family and hadn't killed Svetlana. This feeling between her and the captain that he'd sensed weeks ago had captured his curiosity. He'd never witnessed anything like that between a man and a woman. It was like a puzzle, an enticing mystery to him.

He'd let her live, while he'd watched them together, day after day, trying to decipher whatever this relationship was that they shared.

What he'd seen and heard had bred a new feeling inside him.

Envy?

He wondered how it would feel if *he* had someone to speak to him the way Svetlana did to Vrateus. He wished to have someone he could *treasure*, too.

Well, he did have someone he needed to protect like the dearest treasure there was.

"I'm not leaving here without a gun," he said stubbornly, giving the captain a glare.

Vrateus folded his arms across his chest, leaning back against the closed doors.

"Whom are you going to use it against?"

"Against anyone who tries to hurt her," he replied earnestly.

Vrateus gave him a long stare, and he firmly held it with his own.

Resentment rose inside his chest, heating up the anger he'd carried since the day of Nadia's nearly tragic performance. Under the captain's scrutiny, his temper rose higher with each passing second—Vrateus was the one who'd put her in the situation that had nearly led to a disaster last week.

"How do I know you won't turn the weapon against me?" Vrateus asked calmly. "Like you did a few weeks ago, with Crux."

That was a valid question. Vrateus had every right to be cautious. However, Wyck didn't care about his precautions right now. The thin film of his composure broke, and the anger boiled over.

"You did this!" He grabbed handfuls of Vrateus's pristine white shirt at the captain's chest and shoved him against the wall near the door. "You threw Nadia to the crew to protect your own woman, didn't you?"

Vrateus's facial muscles barely twitched. With a sharp click, one of the guns he always carried on him slid out of his wide sleeve. The cold metal of the tip pressed against Wyck's temple. "Cool your temper, Guard Leader," the captain said slowly.

Wyck's temper had caught on fire, though, even the cool metal of death at his head failed to stop him.

"You know that human women find it disgraceful and terrifying to undress in front of the hundreds of males here," he gritted through his teeth, scowling into the *themul's* face.

"I do." The focus sharpened in the captain's bright orange eyes, the vertical slits of his pupils narrowed. "But how did *you* learn about that?"

"I saw it last week," Wyck seethed. "She was scared. She is outright panicking right now."

"And you care?"

"Yes!" He gave the captain another shove, ready for a fight. Blood coursed hot in his veins, pumping his muscles with energy to punch and crush.

Shockingly, Vrateus lowered his gun in response.

"Good. That means I didn't make a mistake by assigning you to her."

The captain's calm reaction left Wyck with no opponent. Confused, he relaxed his grip on Vrateus's shirt.

"If you really care for her," the captain said. "Then you should understand better now what I did back then. If you had to choose between protecting your woman or Svetlana, which one would you have sent to the mess hall?"

Wyck dropped his hands, releasing the captain, and took a step back. The realization rushed him—were he in Vrateus's place, he would've done exactly the same. He'd sacrifice others to keep Nadia well and happy.

"I didn't simply replace Svetlana with Nadia," Vrateus continued. "By the time the human ship arrived here, I'd already found a way to keep my woman away from the crew. If you care about yours, find a way to keep her out of their reach, too. Your chances are even better than mine because you're not alone. As one of their own, you have the *errocks'* loyalty. No one would dare go against you while you have your brothers by your side."

That should be true. Why did the unwelcome doubt scratch inside him when he was reminded about his family's loyalty to him?

Vrateus must have caught something in his expression.

"How is Nocc?" he asked.

"Fine."

He would never admit to Vrateus that he had to talk Nocc into helping him. Vrateus didn't need to know about the inner dealings of the *errock* family, definitely not about any rifts between them. Wyck had gotten Nocc's word, that should be as good as gold.

"Whatever you decide to do to protect her," the captain continued, "you'll have my support. I can order the end of the sessions in the mess hall any time, but my orders are only as good as their enforcement. Can you and your brothers contain the rest of the crew when they learn you'll be keeping the female away from them? Are you confident you can stop them from rushing her room or ambushing you on your way to her or attacking all of you in your sleep?"

Listening to the captain, Wyck realized how much worry this man must be living with every day. Protecting a woman was not a battle but a constant war on the Dark Anomaly.

Vrateus briefly placed his hand on Wyck's shoulder. "Think about it, then let me know."

"For now, I just need a gun," he said. "Nadia was attacked last week, I won't let it happen again. You've put me in charge of her, give me the means to do my job well."

After another long, assessing stare, the captain finally nodded. "Just one?"

"I only have two hands, and I prefer to keep one free and ready to punch." Besides, more guns potentially meant more chances for them to be stolen.

"Wait here." Vrateus went back into his room and when he returned, he had a black leather holster with a laser gun in it.

Wyck grabbed it, but Vrateus held on tight.

"Promise me you will only use it for her defense."

"I promise," he said sincerely. "I need it for tonight only. You can have it back first thing tomorrow morning."

"Find a way to keep her out of their reach," the captain had said, and that was exactly what he intended to do. He needed some time to figure out how, but he vowed right then and there that tonight would be Nadia's last dance for the crew.

"Keep it." The captain released his hold of the holster belt. "I hope you won't have to use it."

Vrateus might be right. With his family at his side, managing the mob should be much easier.

"Captain?" he said as Vrateus turned to go back into the room.

The *themul* glanced his way, his long furry tail whipping across the tops of his tall boots.

"Is there something else?"

"Yes." Wyck rubbed the back of his neck, unsure how to word his other request. "Nadia has been asking about Svetlana."

"What?" the captain growled. His tail lashed wildly and the orange in his eyes darkened. "Why?"

Wyck shrugged.

"She wants to talk with her. The two of them are the only humans here."

For him, Nadia's desire to see someone of her own species made perfect sense. However, he had no idea if as a *themul*, the captain shared the same sense of family.

"The only surviving women, too," he added.

Vrateus heaved a long breath, leaning back against the door again.

"You haven't told Svetlana about Nadia, have you?" Wyck asked, already knowing the answer. He wanted to find out the reasons for the captain's silence.

"No."

"Why? Are you afraid they'd plot another escape plan?"

Vrateus glanced up at Wyck from under his dark eyebrows. "You know there is no way to *escape* here." He raked his claws through the wide stripe of long, thick fur on his head. "I'm not afraid that Svetlana would leave. Fuck, I'd go with her if that were possible. What scares me is that she would try again."

"She *has* tried," Wyck reminded. "She knows she'd die if she tries again."

"She does." Vrateus heaved another sigh. "However, the risk of death wouldn't stop her, I'm afraid. Svetlana is a scholar, with an unquenchable thirst for knowledge. She is willing to risk her life in the quest for more knowledge, in the name of research."

Still a week ago, the meaning of this would've been lost on Wyck. Now, he realized he understood it well. Moreover, he could *relate* to Svetlana. He, too, had developed a thirst for knowledge, looking forward to every new chapter and each new book. He asked questions and searched for answers. Except that so far, he'd been able to find answers to most of his questions. How far would he go to get answers to the yet unanswered ones?

Vrateus shifted his weight to his other foot. "If Svetlana learns about a human ship crashing here, with significantly more advanced technology—"

"They didn't crash," he blurted out.

"What do you mean?"

"It was a controlled landing," he explained, there was no point in holding this information back now. "They planned to eventually take off and leave."

"Leave? They thought they could do that?"

"That's what Nadia says. Yes."

The captain huffed a sad laugh.

"They might have *planned* it. Doesn't mean they would've succeeded." Vrateus furrowed his brow. "More reasons not to tell Svetlana about it. I'm worried she would be tempted to test their theories."

"So, how long are you planning to keep the new ship a secret from her?"

The human vessel had landed at the very edge of the habitable sector, at the end of the corridor past the gardens. There might never be a reason for Svetlana to wander that way. The crew rarely spoke to her—the possibility of someone telling her about it was low. Unless she somehow accidentally discovered the cut-out, she could remain ignorant about its presence for a very long time.

"Will you ever tell her?" Wyck asked.

"I don't know. Maybe. One day." The captain flashed him a warning look. "Don't you dare tell her yourself."

"I won't," he promised. He hardly ever spoke to Svetlana himself. Keeping her informed was not on the list of his duties. "Thanks for this." He swung the holster on the belt the captain's way.

"Take good care of it," Vrateus said, on his way back to his room and to his woman. "And take good care of your female."

Your female. Wyck loved the sound of it, and he no longer needed the captain's orders to care for Nadia.

Chapter 14

"READY?" WYCK WALKED into my room.

I knew it was time for my next performance. But I was *not* ready.

I had changed into a new outfit with a floor-length, purple gown for the top layer. I'd put on a pair of golden sandals I'd found in the trunk under the clothing rack. I had been standing in front of the door for a few minutes now, waiting for Wyck to take me to the mess hall.

But I was not ready to go through with it after what had happened the last time.

"Yes," I said, pressing the tablet with my music to my chest. "Let's get it over with."

Because it would be over soon. Tomorrow morning, we'd be having breakfast together. And I wouldn't have to dread taking my clothes off in front of a wild crowd for another week.

"Nadia." He placed his large hands on my shoulders, peering into my eyes.

I nodded quickly. "I know. They'll want me completely naked this time."

They'd made their preferences very clear last week. My artful half-disrobing hadn't been enough for them.

His fingers flexed on my shoulders, digging in to the point of pain.

"This is the last time, I swear," he gritted through his teeth.

I winced, and he eased his hold on me.

"I've made sure you'll be safe."

"I know." I nodded again, my voice clipped from nerves. "I trust you."

I did. I trusted Wyck. Last week as I'd been surrounded by the crowd of lust-crazy males, he stood out as the largest and the most intimidating of them. Yet I had run to him for safety. Instinctively, I'd known then that he would rescue me from them. I believed he would protect me tonight, too, if it came down to it.

"We'll be fine." I patted his hand on my shoulder, trailing my fingers over the hard ridges on his knuckles.

His expression was grim and focused, but concern warmed the gold of his eyes. With the last encouraging squeeze, he let go of my shoulders, then produced a device from the holster under his arm. It took me a few moments to realize that he was holding a weapon.

I only had some theoretical knowledge of guns. To me, they were mostly costume props we used when filming historical movies. I knew just enough to distinguish between the projectile shooting handguns that the captain had used to threaten his crew the day of my arrival on the Dark Anomaly, and the slightly more modern laser gun that Wyck was now holding in his hand.

Both kinds of weapons had been long eliminated from use by civilians back on Earth. I'd never had a chance to see a real gun until I got to the Dark Anomaly.

"Are you planning to use it against your own crew mates?" I asked. My hands started to tremble from the anxiety caused by that thought.

"Let's hope I won't have to," he replied with an ominous note in his voice.

Clutching the tablet so hard my fingers hurt, I nodded silently, following him to the door.

Wyck clipped the end of Lesh's chain to his belt, holding the gun in one hand while he took my arm with the other.

As we walked down the corridor, his hand gradually slid down my arm. By the time we stopped in front of the entrance to the mess hall, his fingers were laced through mine.

I gripped his hand tightly. It was large and rough, warm and strong and most importantly, unlike mine, it did not tremble. That alone was more comforting to me than anything.

The air in the room was rich with sweat and charged with lust. I tried to avert my eyes from the half-naked male bodies. It was challenging to find a safe place to rest my gaze, however. Every chair in the room was occupied. Some of the crew were reclining on the floor, leaning against the walls. Others clung to the walls or the pipes and cables under the ceiling.

The mass rippled and stirred with excitement as Wyck and I entered. I felt the weight of their attention on me, their gazes sliding down my body, their nostrils flaring to suck in my scent.

"Show us what you've got, sweet thing!" someone yelled.

"Yeah but give us more to see this time!" another one warned.

I stopped myself from raising my eyes to search for them. The less I saw, the less I'd remember and the fewer nightmares I might have later.

Letting go of Wyck's hand regretfully, I turned on the tablet. The upbeat music of my selected song filled the space, drowning out the noise of the crowd.

"I'm ready," I said to Wyck quietly.

Hands on my waist, he lifted me up onto one of the tables that had been pushed next to each other to form a makeshift catwalk-style stage. I glanced back at him, getting some comfort from having him here.

His yellow eyes focused on me with wonder and anticipation.

Was Wyck just as excited as the rest of them to see me strip?

What would it matter if he were? He was one of them after all.

I drew in a deep breath, letting the music take over my senses. The dancing part was easy. I hadn't practiced the choreography beforehand, it just came to me as I went. Letting my heart guide me freed my mind. After having spent a week locked in a room, I found any movement liberating. I twirled, leaped, and glided, wishing I could simply keep dancing like this, lost to the world.

Except that *they* were waiting—the world of the Dark Anomaly.

Blindly, I found the tie of the top layer of my outfit and tore at it. The long, wrap-style dress fell away. Someone snatched it out of the air before it had a chance to flutter to the ground. I was left in another long, flowing skirt and a cropped, sleeveless top.

A roar rolled through the room.

"Too many clothes!"

They didn't want to be teased. They demanded *everything*, and they wanted it *now*.

I glanced Wyck's way. His expression momentarily made me forget about the restless crowd. Wonder and appreciation shone on his face—the expression that every artist longed to see on the faces of their audiences.

Out of the hundreds of individuals here, Wyck was the one who truly appreciated my dancing. He appeared happy to watch it even as I remained fully clothed.

I gave him a smile, just before someone's arm or tail lashed against me, knocking me off balance.

Fear slammed at me full force as I fell, my knees painfully hitting the hard surface of the table. Hands, tentacles, and other appendages reached for me. They tore at my clothes, slithered under them, groping for my body underneath.

"Nadia!" Wyck's voice was like a lifeline in the ocean of chaos. I crawled toward it, making my way through the mass of male bodies fighting on top of me. They shoved and punched each other out of the way in their strife to get to me first.

Thin, crackling sounds of laser shots pierced the noise of the crowd, followed by the stench of burnt flesh.

"Wyck!" I yelled, frantically kicking at someone's hand gripping my ankle.

Another rough hand grabbed my arm, and I was yanked out of the pile of gyrating bodies on top of me.

"And there she is," an *errock* said with a smirk, my arm painfully clammed in his massive hand. "Our bounty, at last."

"Trox, let her go." Wyck's voice sounded strangled.

He lay on the ground. A *dimo*—Enkail, I remembered his name from the day of my landing—had his hard-plated knee planted between Wyck's shoulder blades. Another huge *dimo* sat on Wyck's back, behind Enkail. A whole swarm of *kreers* held down Wyck's legs and arms. His knuckles were bloody. One side of Enkail's face had been smashed in despite the plated armor that *dimos* were born with.

A *yourlu* lay on the ground with his head twisted aside, motionless. Quite a few other males littered the floor. Bearing laser wounds, some of them remained unmoving, others writhed in pain.

Wyck had fought hard before they'd all swarmed him and wrestled him down.

"Let's see what she's got." Nocc stepped from the crowd, making my skin crawl at the memories of his hands on me.

Enkail handed Nocc the laser gun they had taken away from Wyck. Nocc already had my knife in his other hand.

A growling hiss from the middle of the room made me glance that way. Poor Lesh was tied to a cable dangling from the ceiling. A bunch of *yourlu* taunted him with their tentacles. They slapped him from all sides then leaped out of his reach before he could bite any of them.

Nocc pressed the gun into my belly, snapping my attention to him again. Lust burned bright in his yellow eyes—lust for both my flesh and my life.

I halted my breath, even my heart seemed to stop as terror spread in cold tendrils through my chest.

"Nocc!" Wyck growled. "You promised!"

Nocc narrowed his eyes, his jaw muscles twitched in annoyance.

"I know," he barked over his shoulder. "I'm not going to *harm* her." He slid the gun higher up my belly, between my breasts, then stuck the end of it into my neckline. He smirked, keeping his eyes on me. "She'll live." His words sounded more like a threat than reassurance.

I shrunk away from him, but Trox yanked me back in place.

"Nocc. Fuck!" Wyck roared and bucked, shaking the hulking *dimos* off his back as if they were bowling pins. "Get off me!" He rose to his feet.

His massive figure towered over the scattered males—imposing and intimidating. Hands fisted at his sides, eyes glowing with rage, nostrils flaring, the sight of him was sure to send fear into the hearts of anyone.

"You promised!" he bellowed, moving on Nocc.

A foolish *kreer* stumbled in his way, and Wyck swiped him aside with his fist. The *kreer* screeched, flying through the air, then wedged under one of the tables behind me.

Nocc promptly pointed the gun at Wyck. Faced with the approaching menace, Nocc's expression changed from smug to worried.

"Stand back!" he yelled. "Or I'll shoot!"

"Go ahead. Shoot." Wyck slammed a fist into his own chest, taunting. "Or would you rather do it when I turn my back to you? You backstabbing puddle of slime."

Nocc leaped to me, jamming the gun under my chin.

"Or maybe, I'll shoot her first." Some confidence returned to his voice. "Kill your pretty little toy, then no one gets to play with her."

Wyck halted abruptly, as if he'd hit a brick wall.

"Don't."

Nocc smirked, no doubt feeling the power over Wyck.

"That's better." He tipped his chin at the youngest *errock*. "You stay where you are, and I'll let you both live. I'll keep my promise, it's the *errocks'* way after all. I know we're a family, it's you who keeps forgetting it, boy."

He took a pause, for emphasis, then continued, "You're the one who's been acting like a slimy softy around this one." He shoved the gun harder against my throat, making me cough. "Your father would've been long done with her. He was just and always shared his women with his crew, too. If there was anything left to share, that is."

Moving his stare away from Wyck, Nocc slid it down my body in an assessing way.

"I'll tell you what." He licked his lips. "I'll show you just how kind and generous I am. I'll let *her* choose her first fuck."

"No one is fucking her!" Wyck lunged my way. Two *errocks* grabbed his arms, aided by two *dimos*, straining to hold him back.

"Stay where you are, boy." Nocc grabbed a handful of my hair, tipping my head back. The cold metal of the gun trailed a chilling path along my throat. "Or I'll change my mind on being kind and generous tonight."

"We had a deal." Wyck glared at him.

"The deal was for her to entertain us. And none of us find her fancy moves entertaining enough."

"I'll touch her, no one else." Wyck shrugged his shoulders, making those holding him stagger. "Like Vrateus touched Svetlana."

"Too late, boy. I don't care about touching. I want to see some real fucking."

"No!" His teeth clenched, Wyck yanked his right arm free then punched the *errock* on his left in the jaw.

Nocc jerked the gun Wyck's way again. Two more *errocks* leaped from the crowd and onto Wyck. Someone kicked the back of his legs, sending him to his knees.

"Don't hurt him." A sob ripped from my throat, warm tears rolled down my cheeks as my entire body shook from shock and terror.

How did it all go so wrong so fast?

"I said stand back!" Nocc pressed the gun to Wyck's head, between two bony ridges. "I swear on the memory of the Great Scodr, I'll burn a hole in your brains, my promise be fucked."

Nocc's threat charged the air with a new level of brutality. The room stilled, everyone watching the *errocks* going against each other. The tension grew so thick, I could hear it ring in my ears. It seemed a drop of a pin could set the fire off, resulting in the murder of an unarmed man.

"I'll do it!" I said, barely realizing myself what I was doing. My voice sounded high but strong enough to carry through to the far walls of the room. "I'll do what you want me to do. Put the gun down."

If Nocc shot Wyck, I'd be on my own. I didn't dare imagine what would happen to me then, but it wasn't the reason why I'd stopped Nocc. At that very moment, I didn't think far enough ahead to worry about myself. I simply couldn't let Wyck die.

The two men broke their stares from each other to gaze at me—Nocc with an obvious triumph, Wyck with utter shock.

"Nadia." There was so much in Wyck's voice—warning, regret, sadness...

"Unlike you, the girl has some brains." Nocc beamed with satisfaction that quickly turned to eager anticipation.

"Or maybe she's horny, too!" Trox snorted, shifting closer to me.

I'd come here tonight fully expecting to be degraded. What they wanted from me, however, added an entirely new level to it.

"You said I can choose," I hurriedly reminded Nocc. Panic pulsed inside me as I'd seen how little weight Nocc placed on his promises.

"Do you have someone in mind already?" He gave me another one of his leering stares.

I bit my lip, holding back a curse and a slap to wipe that repulsive smirk off his face. Unfortunately, he was the one with the gun at Wyck's head, and therefore the one with the power over both of us.

"I want Wyck," I said firmly.

Nocc's brow ridge rose.

"Him?" He released a roar of laughter. "You want the boy?"

Trox growled low at my side, his grip on my arm tightened from bruising to agonizing.

"Did you hear that, Wyck? Your newest pet wants you to fuck her." Nocc kept guffawing. "The hassle of looking after her might be paying off for you."

I dropped my gaze to the floor, dreading to look at Wyck. Whatever camaraderie we had shared before, whatever fragile friendship might've developed between the two of us, I felt it would now be crushed by the brutality of this situation.

Wyck was the last one I wanted to see me as nothing more than a sex object. His was the only opinion that mattered to me here. I didn't want any intimacy between us to happen this way.

Yet there was no other choice. The thought of being touched by anyone else in here made my stomach churn with revulsion.

"Well, what do you know," Nocc mused, stepping aside. "The boy will get to fuck for real, after all."

"About time!" Trox scoffed, finally letting go of my arm.

I rubbed the soreness out of it, keeping my gaze down.

"Go get her!" Nocc slapped Wyck's back as he rose to his feet. "Then, we'll all show you how the real men do it." He howled with laughter again, the rest of *errocks* joining him. "Here." Nocc shoved the laser knife into a tentacle of a *yourlu*. "Make sure she doesn't do anything funny."

I stepped back, away from all of them, until my backside hit the table behind me.

How much could a woman go through?

How much could *I* take?

Since I'd landed in the Dark Anomaly, I'd seen my colleagues brutally murdered, I'd been assaulted and humiliated. Every time I thought I'd reached the limit of what I could take, more had been thrown at me. Every time, I went through it, my limits grew. And here I was now, about to have public sex in order to survive for just a little bit longer.

Was this life even worth living? Any struggle to prolong this existence suddenly seemed useless. I closed my eyes—the fight, the light, and the energy draining from me.

I recognized his warm, spicy scent and knew he'd come closer.

His chest touched my forehead, and he put his hands on my waist.

I didn't want this to happen this way.

I wanted to tell him. My throat tightened too much for me to speak. The words weren't strong enough to convey the anguish I felt, anyway.

He lifted me up onto the table behind me then stepped closer between my legs.

Everything inside me tensed. I no longer felt the relaxing comfort I'd grown accustomed to in his presence. Right now, even Wyck's touch felt foreign and invasive.

He lowered his head to my ear and whispered, "I have no idea what I'm doing."

My heart leaped with a loud thud in my chest, and I blinked in shock. I'd been expecting to be ravaged publicly, hoping that with Wyck, it would be more bearable somehow.

I did not expect this confession.

Slowly, I lifted my gaze to his. His warm, golden eyes were on me, a light smile curved his full lips.

Relief flooded me. There was no resentment, no cold hostility I'd dreaded to see, not a trace of any violent lust in his expression. Though, the burning desire was prominently there, but it was softened by kindness and affection that melted my heart.

I wasn't alone, the Wyck that I knew was still with me.

"Come here," I said softly, cupping his face.

The music was still blasting out of the tablet, the same upbeat song playing on a loop. It helped with drowning out the noise of everyone else in the room.

"Keep your eye on the gun and the knife," I whispered into his ear before planting a kiss on the side of his neck. "I'll do the rest."

"I—I'll try..." he breathed out, wrapping his arms tighter around me.

Nocc sat in a chair nearby, the gun in his hand still trained at Wyck's head. The *yourlu,* with my laser knife clutched in one of his tentacles, took a place on the table right behind me. The blue-flame blade was hovering just above my shoulder.

I focused on the music for a moment, thinking only about Wyck. Sliding my hands up the hard planes of his chest, I savored the sensation of his warm skin under my palms. I hooked one arm around his neck, to bring his head lower. Using the moment, I finally did what I'd wanted to do for so long now—I kissed him.

I gently took that plump lower lip of his between mine, and he released a soft gasp into my mouth. The spice of his scent was in his taste, pleasant and familiar. I slid the tip of my tongue between his lips, and he yielded, parting them for me.

He splayed his large, warm palms on my bare back between my top and the skirt. The sensation tingled with warmth along my arms and thighs.

This could be so good.

Being with Wyck could be amazing, it dawned on me—had this been for real.

But it wasn't, this was all for show.

"What the fuck is she doing?" Nocc's rough voice yanked me out of the soft, blissful haze of kissing Wyck. "Spread your legs and take his cocks in. Now!"

The blade of the knife in the *yourlu's* tentacle jerked closer to my neck, searing a lock of my hair off.

I whimpered in terror, dropping my hands away from Wyck.

"Ssh." He cradled my head to his shoulder. His other hand went for the clasp on his pants. "I won't hurt you, promise."

I knew I could trust *his* promises. This did not ease my anxiety, though. It spiked even higher when his erection came into view. The same reddish brown as most of his skin, it had a slight greenish undertone where the thick veins protruded all along his length. Incredibly, it appeared longer and thicker than my forearm.

Errock males had two penises, I remembered something I'd heard back in college and recently from Nocc. Their females had two vaginas, too. I didn't. I couldn't even begin to think what to do with one of those, let alone two.

I stared at it in horror.

"This will never work," I mumbled, cold with dread.

"Why?" Wyck asked innocently.

"Too big..." was all I could manage, swallowing hard.

He took my hand in his and placed it on his massive shaft, wrapping my fingers around it.

"Make it smaller, then."

"How?"

He felt hot and hard in my hand. The smooth, silky skin stretched thin around his massive girth. The thick veins bulged and pulsed under my palm as he slid my hand along his length.

Wyck pressed my fingers tighter, and miraculously, the hard flesh in my hand squeezed smaller.

He hissed, his expression pained.

"Does it hurt?" I asked quickly, trying to yank my hand away.

"Somewhat." He wouldn't let me remove my hand, pumping it along his length with me. "But in a most wonderful way."

As I squeezed and moved my hand, a thin layer of slippery moisture seeped between my fingers. "What's this?"

He shrugged. "Makes the rubbing easier."

"I see." I smiled at his words. I could actually smile in this situation. How? I had no idea, only that with Wyck's wide back shielding me from most of the room, breathing had become easier.

"Does it feel...right to you?" he asked.

Right? Nothing about this felt right.

But that wasn't what Wyck was asking about, I understood. He wondered how I felt. He cared about my feelings. And that was the one thing that actually *was* right.

He asked because he had no frame of reference whatsoever. He'd told me that after Svetlana, I was the only woman he'd ever seen in his life. I realized I must be the first woman he'd ever touched.

More than that, his earlier confession could also mean that he'd never even seen two people making love. He'd seen people fucking in the videos that the men who raised him had made him watch. Consciously or not, however, he didn't want to repeat what he'd seen in the videos with me. Right now, Wyck was trying to do something entirely new to him with me—he wanted to be gentle. Something he had never been taught to be.

"We'll make it right, Wyck," I whispered, kissing the ridge of his cheekbone. "We'll make it right for *us*."

Shifting back on the table a little, I lifted my legs, planting the heels of my feet on the edge. The long, mint-green skirt I was wearing draped between my raised knees, concealing me from the lewd stares of the others.

"Come closer." I tugged him to me.

His erection in my hand had shrunk to a much more manageable and far less intimidating size by now. Holding him in my fist, I slid my hand under my skirt and positioned him at my opening.

"Closer..." I whispered.

He bucked his hips, his well-lubricated length sliding inside me effortlessly.

I buried my face in the base of his neck and closed my eyes. This moment was for Wyck and me only, even as hundreds of others were witnessing it.

He inhaled a shuddered breath. "Fuck...Nadia..." His arms clamped tight around me. No one would be able to pry me away from him now.

"I need to move," he groaned.

"Mhm." I nodded as he began to pump his hips.

With each smooth slide, he grew inside me, filling me entirely. A slight flicker of pleasure low in my belly grew brighter, spreading in hot tingles along my thighs.

"Is this right?" he asked.

"This is perfect..." I murmured, griping his vest below his shoulders and tugging him to me.

I did not expect this. I was not prepared to enjoy any of this. I'd braced myself to get over tonight and hoped to still be alive in the morning. Now, as Wyck moved inside me in smooth tantalizing thrusts, pleasure kept growing, spreading through me in waves.

My reply must have given him more confidence. Gradually, he had taken over. With one hand, he continued to cradle my head, the fingers of the other dug into my hip, holding me in place as the power of his thrusts increased.

A low growl vibrated in his chest, resonating through me. His arms slid around me once again, as he pressed me to him so tight I could barely breathe. His massive body convulsed with his release, pushing the table back with a loud screech against the floor.

I ventured a peek over his shoulder, quickly sweeping the place with my gaze.

Nocc remained in his chair, with Trox sitting on the floor next to him. Both held their enormous dicks in their hands.

Though Wyck was only using one of his, the rumors were true, *errocks* did have a pair each. With a dick in each hand, Nocc had no hands left to hold the gun. It lay on the corner of the table I was sitting on, a little too far for me to reach in one move. I believed I only had *one* move, one chance at it while Nocc was still coming, spurts of shimmering green goo shooting all over his hands.

Wyck leaned his head on my shoulder, spent after his orgasm. I slid my hand up, trailing my fingers along the bumpy line of ridges on the back of his neck.

"The gun," I whispered so softly only he could here. "Can you get it?"

Wyck's arms were longer than mine. While standing, he also had a wider range of motion.

His muscles tensed at once, all post-orgasmic softness completely gone from his body. Tucking himself in with one hand, he dashed sideways, going for the gun.

The knife over my shoulder dipped, slicing through my hair and scorching the skin at the base of my neck. I squeezed the tentacle that held the knife handle and leaped off the table. Twisting my wrist, I flipped the blade back, toward the tentacle.

"You filthy whore!" The *yourlu* scurried to the edge of the table after me, his other tentacles lashing at me as I cut through the one that held the knife.

"*Filthy?*" I snapped at him, yanking the knife from his loosened grip. "Do you consider yourself *clean?*" I wrinkled my nose at the soiled, greasy shirt he was wearing.

He scurried back, away from my knife. The cluster of tentacles he had for legs undulated under him, sliding and slipping along the surface of the table.

I saw Wyck point the gun at the two *errocks*, their limp dicks draped listlessly over their thighs. He was in control, now. Knife in my hand, I dashed to Lesh.

He hissed and growled as I made my way to him, dodging the males. Some of them still had their pants around their ankles.

His teeth snapping at everyone around us, Lesh didn't so much as nip at me. Grabbing his chain, I sliced with my knife through the cable it was attached to.

"Good boy." I patted Lesher. "Now, let's go get your master."

With the vicious *mahdi* clearing my way, moving through the crowd proved much easier. However, there were still too many of those who wanted a piece of both of us.

"Wyck!" I yelled over the crowd, hoping that he'd be able to meet us halfway.

He was easy to spot, towering over the rest. His head snapped in my direction, then he shoved aside at the aliens surrounding him, parting the crowd like the sea on his way to me.

He reached me in a few wide strides, firing at those who were too slow to move away in time.

"Come here." He hugged me to him with one arm. Without slowing down his pace, he swept me off my feet, half-carrying me out of the disgusting mess hall.

"She's dead meat, boy!" Nocc's voice shot from the room like a bullet at our backs.

Chapter 15

"NEVER AGAIN," WYCK hissed under his breath when we got back to my room.

A storm raged in his eyes, his chest heaved with heavy breathing, his expression dark—he was furious.

Never again?

God knew, I agreed with him. But what could we do to stop this? What could anyone do in this lawless place forsaken by the rest of the world?

His gaze fell on me.

"Nadia." He took a step closer.

He wanted to hug me, and I quickly stepped back into the safety of the glass room where I knew he wouldn't dare follow me. My body retained the memory of him being inside me, and my mind was still reeling at how it'd happened.

We'd been forced, both of us. They'd used us to violate each other. The last thing I wanted right now was to have anyone's hands on me, again. Not even Wyck's.

"This was not how it was supposed to happen," I said quietly in reply to his questioning stare, backing all the way to my sleeping pallet by the far wall.

"We'll make it right," he said resolutely, repeating what I'd said to him earlier.

He swept a glance around the room then winced and quickly averted his eyes.

"You'll need a better place than this." He made the doors open again. "I'll be right back."

Lesh hissed with a whimper as the doors closed behind Wyck. My legs gave in under me, and I sank onto the sleeping pallet.

The animal trotted to me. After restlessly pacing in a circle for a minute or two, he lay down on the floor next to me, his tail snaking in a circle around him. Lesh fixed all of his eyes on the door behind which Wyck had gone.

I found myself staring at it, too. I worried about how my thoughts and my heart trailed behind that man, refusing to leave him even as he was no longer with me. I didn't want him to touch me, yet I hated when he left. I *needed* him to be here. No place on the Dark Anomaly felt safe unless Wyck was there with me.

The future seemed grim. I knew I had to keep faith that things would get better if I wanted to hold on to my will to survive. Yet faith was so hard to come by.

WYCK

He slowed down his pace, walking along the corridor.

His lower cock, the one that hadn't known the bliss of being inside Nadia, remained painfully hard. Every step added to the agony. The only way to get rid of the pain was to make himself come, but his thoughts weren't on it.

As long as everyone knew where she was, Nadia was not safe. That thought was like a thorn in his chest. He needed to find a better place for her. He wished to hide her, lock her up, chain her in somewhere she wouldn't be able to escape from and where no one would ever find her.

The hurricane of feelings for her raged inside him—new and confusing. Ironically, the only person whom he could talk to about them was her. No one else would even begin to understand.

He'd gone against his family over her. When he thought back to the moment he'd held the gun pointed at Nocc, he felt he was ready to kill one of his own kind for her. How did she become so important to him that he would go against everything he'd been raised to believe in, against everything he'd been taught he was supposed to be?

His room was on an ancient ship behind the mess hall. He shared the space with the rest of the *errocks*, his bunk separated from theirs by just a curtain. There was barely enough space on the floor for Lesh's dish and sleeping mat.

Living in the tight quarters had never bothered him before. For the first time in his life, however, he didn't feel entirely safe spending the night here. The memory of Nocc's betrayal burnt through his heart. His own family turning against him made him look over his shoulder everywhere he went.

Thankfully, the ship was empty right now. He grabbed all the blankets off his bed and left promptly before anyone showed up.

Passing by the mess hall, he realized why the *errocks* weren't back in their sleeping quarters despite the late hour. A number of fights were taking place. The crew had decided to deal with their lingering lust by physically releasing aggression against each other.

"Hey, Wyck." Krakhil, a *dimo*, sauntered from the room, a tattered rag draped over his shoulder. "Wonna fight? Place a bet?" he asked casually, as if nothing had happened just a short while ago. As if Krakhil wasn't one of those who'd held Wyck down while the rest threatened to violate his woman.

Wyck gritted his teeth, reining in his rising anger. His muscles ached with strain and tension. He'd love to throw a punch or two or even let a few land on his body. A fight might bring a welcome distraction to the mess happening in his head.

He had other priorities, though.

"Busy." He snatched the rag from the *dimo's* shoulder and shoved it in the pocket of his pants.

"Hey!" Stretching his four arms, Krakhil reached for the corner of the rag sticking from the pocket. "I need that to wipe blood and stuff."

"Use your shirt." Wyck swatted his hands away.

"I'm not wearing one!"

Ignoring Krakhil and the curses he was throwing at his back, Wyck headed toward the *vasai* farm.

There, behind a row of centipede cages, was a wide crack in the wall. Making sure no one was around to see him, he squeezed his large body between the two ragged edges of paneling and into a room with a low ceiling behind the wall.

At the far end, there was a short passageway. It was narrow. Even at fourteen years of age, Wyck had had a hard time wiggling through and into another small room with a window behind it. Now, that he had doubled in size since, he could only get his arm through, up to his shoulder.

It was just as well. The room on the other end of the passage had a small window, and he'd seen enough of the dizzying lights of the Anomaly to last him a lifetime.

He shoved the blankets through the passage into the small space behind it. This was where he had kept Lesh as a puppy, many years ago. And this was where he now intended to bring Nadia.

The place was not ideal. There were no bathroom facilities. He'd have to take Nadia out to use the bathroom in the farm a few times a day. It would mean a higher risk of being discovered for her, but she needed to take daily showers to avoid being tracked by scent.

Unlike the hated glass room, however, he didn't experience any discomfort from being here. Since other species on the Dark Anomaly weren't bothered by the glass room, he'd always worried that someone might find their way in when he wasn't around.

The narrow passage to the room with the window was too small for any male to fit through. Nadia's slender dancer's figure should be able to fit, though. That put his mind at ease somewhat.

Sitting down on the floor next to the entrance to the passage, he opened his pants. Taking care of his throbbing erection had become a necessity. The agony of lust had been clouding his mind, making it difficult to focus on anything else.

His second cock had swollen by now, too. Both pulsed hot and hard when he took them in his hands.

His mind flashed to the moment when Nadia's small, delicate hands held one of them, kneading and reshaping it to her liking. The memory of the sensation shot through his core like lightning, bringing an intense pleasure.

Both cocks prickled and ached as he squeezed them in his hands and slid his fists up and down, spreading the sleek moisture that seeped through his skin.

Ecstasy raged through his body, the memories of Nadia fueling pleasure into an inferno.

She'd kissed him. Her lips had been as sweet as the pollen sugar collected from the *endoi* flowers in the gardens.

Her warm hands on him, so gentle and...loving. He'd never experienced anything like her touch in his life.

The unforgettable sensation of being inside her...

There'd been fog after that—the hot, sticky haze of desire and ecstasy mixed into an explosion of climax. The feeling of complete bliss he'd been plunged into was incomparable to any orgasm he'd brought himself to.

His climax hit him now, bringing physical release. The long spurts shot out of both cocks simultaneously, and the pain of the pressure had finally dissipated, draining the tension from his body.

He wiped off the mess, using the rag he'd snatched from Krakhil, then tugged his pants back up.

There was no energy to get up right away, and he allowed himself to rest for a moment. The thoughts of Nadia wouldn't leave him, even as the lust had subsided. Now, he wished to feel her relaxing against him, imagining holding her soft body in his arms.

An achy feeling seized his heart—the longing for having her at his side. He could no longer truly rest when he was away from her. A feeling of loss tormented him, as if something was missing and he needed to go search for it.

Restless, he crawled out into the *vasai* farm and got to his feet.

A sudden tremor ran through the walls and floor, making him sway on his feet. He got a hold of the nearest cage to steady himself, feeling the receding vibration through his palms.

Shakes and tremors happened on the Dark Anomaly. Sometimes a spacious cavity deep in its bowels compressed, causing the aftershock to rumble through. Every now and then, it reached as far as the outer edge of the habitable sector.

Other times, it happened when a large, heavy ship crashed on the surface nearby.

It wasn't unusual. He knew it from the lifetime spent here and from what he'd learned while reading with Nadia. Held together by the incredible gravity, the structure of the Dark Anomaly was fairly stable.

An inexplicable worry, however, nagged at him to hurry to Nadia.

The last of the crew were clearing the mess hall as he passed. It should be all empty by the time he brought Nadia here on the way to their new hiding place.

The corridor seemed endless. The feeling that something was wrong gripped his heart. He kept increasing his pace, finding himself practically running the last few paces.

Lesh lay in the threshold inside the glass room. He didn't move when the doors opened.

"Lesh?" Wyck dropped to his knees, lifting the animal's middle head...*Lesher*, Nadia had named it. "Are you okay? What happened to you, buddy? Where is Nadia?"

Lesh didn't respond. His eyes remained closed.

Alarm spiked higher. *Mahdis* lived as long as *errocks* did. Lesh had always been healthy.

"Lesh!" He shook the animal, in desperation. Lesh released a soft hiss, it sounded like it came from all three of his heads at once. "You're alive."

"Nadia." Wyck darted a glance around the room. His head swam with dizziness at the sight of the lights behind the glass. Even while he was sitting on the solid floor in the entranceway, the unsettling feeling of floating churned his stomach.

There was a reason why the *errocks* of the Dark Anomaly never went on spacewalks to repair the battery panels outside. None of them could stand the sight of open space. Solid walls grounded him and brought the comforting sense of normalcy.

An unknown massive dark shape outside obscured the lights on the right. This must be the newest ship that had just crashed, causing the tremors he'd felt earlier. The side of it touched the glass of Nadia's room.

"Nadia!" he called into the room.

Squinting against the lights, he made out her shape on the sleeping pallet by the far wall.

"Nadia!" he roared as loud as he could.

She didn't move, and his heart dropped into the hollow of his stomach. Dread chilled his insides, making it hard to breathe.

"Nadia, wake up!" he kept yelling, but she didn't seem to hear him and wouldn't come to him.

What the fuck had happened here?

Fighting the dizziness, he examined the dark shape leaning against the glass on the right—the newly crashed ship. Even judging by the small part he could see, it must be massive. A fine web of cracks spread through the glass from the point of its contact with the side of Nadia's room. The clear material from which the room had been constructed was infinitely stronger than any regular glass. Yet it obviously wasn't indestructible.

Wyck realized that his difficulty breathing didn't come merely from his worry and stress. The air inside the room was thin—the oxygen must be steadily escaping through the cracks.

From Nadia's safe haven, the room could quickly turn into her grave.

Lesh sucked in a long breath, releasing a choked coughing noise.

At least he was most definitely alive, which Wyck couldn't say for sure about Nadia.

Chilling anxiety buzzed through him with urgency. He needed to go to Nadia to get her out of the death trap this room had become. With the oxygen seeping out, this place was slowly killing her if it hadn't already.

There was no time to get help, provided there even was anyone in the entire Dark Anomaly who would help him without asking for something in return.

He needed to get her out as quickly as possible, only he couldn't fathom the thought of entering this place. The idea of stepping off the metal floor panel and onto the clear glass felt like diving headfirst into the abyss from which there'd be no return.

His breathing turned shallow, his lungs straining to draw in enough of the receding oxygen. Fear suffocated him even more effectively than the lack of air.

He ripped his vest off and tossed it on the glass. With a bracing breath, he took his first step onto the vest.

The room seemed to sway around him. He spread his arms wide for balance, as if he were treading a tight rope suspended in nothing.

The lights swirled, assaulting him with a new bout of nausea. His stomach churned, and his vision narrowed to a peep hole.

The small figure of Nadia curled under the blanket on her sleeping pallet became his only focus. He stared at her as he reached for the clothing rack on the right and ripped from it the first garment his fingers touched.

The voluminous skirt of the dark green dress puffed out, spreading on the floor when he tossed it in front of him. The material covered the clear glass, giving him a point of stability—small and unreliable, but stable enough for him to continue.

Quickly, he leaped onto the dress, then crouched down to move his vest from behind to ahead him. All while keeping his eyes glued to Nadia.

One more flip of the clothes on the floor, and he made it to her.

"Nadia." He dropped to his knees by her pallet.

She appeared to be sleeping peacefully but didn't wake up when he shook her shoulder.

"Please, don't leave me, now." It was a half-plea, half-threat as anger and desperation both took over.

He picked her up, blankets and all.

A screeching noise came from the right as the crashed ship leaned heavier against the glass capsule. The Dark Anomaly tightly gripped its newest acquisition, pulling it firmly into place.

There was no time to lose. He had to get out of here before the glass gave in completely.

Step after step, he moved back toward the exit, along the vest and the dress he had spread on the floor. The clothes only reached into the middle of the room, though. With Nadia in his arms, shifting them farther up the floor would take some extra time he might not have.

Drawing the thin air in through his nostrils, he closed his eyes and ran.

The sound of his boots hitting the uncovered glass filled him with panic. The sickening feeling made his blood pound in his ears. His chest tightened. His throat felt sore, each particle of oxygen seemed to scratch it from the inside on its way to his air-starved lungs.

Dashing through the exit and into the corridor, he placed Nadia on the floor then punched in the code to seal the doors behind him.

That was all he'd managed to do before a violent bout of nausea sent him crashing to his knees. His stomach twisted in agonizing knots then emptied itself onto the floor tiles between his knees.

Lesh whimpered, crawling to him.

He placed a hand on top of one of his heads, leaning back to catch his breath. His heart thundered in his chest, wildly beating against his ribs. He panted loudly, greedily sucking in lungfuls of air, again and again, until some clarity of thought returned.

Nadia.

He darted a worried look her way.

He'd been ready to kill for her. Now, he'd nearly died for her. There was no way back for him—this woman owned him. And he wouldn't have it any other way.

"Nadia..."

He crawled on all fours to her, afraid he'd get sick again if he tried to get up.

Her eyes remained closed.

He stroked the side of her face tenderly, just like she had touched him before.

Dying was one sure way to leave the Dark Anomaly.

"Stay with me, my sweet human woman." He leaned his forehead to hers, breathing in the tendril of her irresistible scent he now loved more than feared.

A faint breath puffed against his lips—Nadia's exhale.

"Breathe," he pleaded in a whisper, afraid to hope. "I'll get you out of here."

Gathering whatever strength he could muster in his shaking legs, he rose to his feet, holding her in his arms.

With a sad whistle, Lesh crawled after him, too weak to get up yet.

"Stay here," he ordered. "I'll come back for you."

Instead of going left, to the new place where he was planning to hide Nadia, he turned right in the direction of the captain's room. Just like Nadia's, it was a glass capsule. There might still be the danger of it being crushed next.

With his hands occupied, he slammed his boot into the captain's door.

"Captain! Get up!"

The alarm must be apparent in his voice, as the door opened within seconds.

Sleepy and completely naked, Vrateus looked ready to jump into action, nevertheless.

"What is it, Wyck?" he asked, his voice clipped, his eyebrows pinched together in a frown.

"A ship crashed. Broke the glass in Nadia's room. You may want to get the doors to it permanently sealed shut, now."

Svetlana's worried face appeared behind Vrateus's bicep. She darted a confused gaze at Nadia in his arms.

"What...*Who* is this?" she moved around the captain while clutching the blanket she had wrapped around herself to her chest. "What have you done?" She raised an accusing glare at Wyck.

She saw him holding a motionless woman and assumed it was his fault she wasn't moving. Of course, Svetlana would think that. She must have heard about what the *errocks* of the Dark Anomaly did to women. After the way Crux and the others had treated her, it was no surprise she'd assume the worst about him.

He had no time and no desire to explain himself, though.

"The new ship hasn't settled yet," he said to Vrateus, turning to leave. "Your room may not be safe either."

"Hey, where are you taking her?" Svetlana yelled at his back.

Where hopefully no one would find her.

"Vrateus, who is that woman?" Svetlana wouldn't give up.

"Wyck!" Vrateus's commanding tone made him pause for a moment. "Is she okay?"

"She will be," he said over his shoulder, heading down the corridor in wide strides.

She'd better be.

He let Vrateus explain to Svetlana the things that the captain should've probably explained long ago.

Wyck had something else to worry about. Someone else.

Nadia *had* to be okay.

As he passed her old room, Lesh rose to his legs, all four shaking. Unfortunately, the animal still wouldn't be able to keep up with him, and he had no time to wait.

"I'll come back for you Lesh." He kept going.

As he'd hoped, the mess hall was almost empty by now. The few crew that still lingered around were too far away to notice his precious cargo or to even pay attention to him as he quickly sneaked by the entrance on his way to the *vasai* farm.

Once safely in the room behind the cages, he carefully laid Nadia down on the floor. A faint light filtered from the farm, barely enough for him to inspect her face. She was breathing. It took him a few moments to detect her pulse, but it was there.

"Nadia," he said softly, touching her cheek. Her skin felt cool and soft under his calloused hand. "Please, wake up." He gently slid his thumb along one of her eyebrows, the short hair rather coarse but silky. She parted her lips, and the hope in his heart grew. He never forgot the taste of her mouth when she kissed him—sweet and intoxicating. "Open your eyes, my sweet pollen sugar," he cooed in a voice softer and more tender than he'd ever thought he was capable of.

Her features crinkled into a frown. She rolled to her side.

"How are you feeling?" he asked, shifting closer. "Anything hurt?"

"My head..." she groaned.

He sympathized, despite feeling almost hysterically happy at finally hearing her voice.

"And my throat... Thirsty."

"I'll get you some water." He moved to leave.

She caught a hold of his wrist.

"Wait... What happened?" She blinked her eyes open. "Where are we?"

"In a safe—" He winced and corrected himself, "well, *safer* place. Your room got destroyed by a ship crashing into it."

"Why don't I remember it?"

"You went to bed. There was a crack in the wall. A small one, but it sucked out enough oxygen to make you pass out."

"How did I get out, then?"

"I got you."

She blinked again, taking a moment before replying.

"You got me? From my bed? I thought *errocks* couldn't enter that room."

"It wasn't fun," he admitted, cringing inside at the memory of that nauseating place. "But I had to enter, to get you out."

She studied his face for a second, then closed her eyes and rubbed her forehead with a grimace of pain.

"I'll get you water." He shifted toward the exit to the farm. "I'll need to get Lesh, too. Would you wait here for a few minutes?"

She nodded, without opening her eyes.

"While I'm gone, you'll need to wait there." He touched her shoulder, prompting her to look at him, then gestured at the narrow passage that led to the small room with the window. "None of the crew can fit through there. You'll be safe until I come back."

She nodded again, gingerly as not to aggravate her headache, he guessed. She then crawled to the tunnel, without arguing or questioning his request.

He waited until she was safely on the other side before leaving her.

There was no door to lock. The only protection was the smell of the centipedes that overpowered Nadia's scent and the noise of their chitin-covered bodies as they scurried in their cages that drowned out other sounds.

He hoped that would be enough to keep Nadia safe and undetected until he came back.

Chapter 16

THE HEADACHE WAS UNBEARABLE, as if a million jack-hammers rammed against my skull from the inside. The undulating lights of the Anomaly outside the small window didn't help.

With my eyes half-closed, I found some blankets on the floor, wrapped them around myself, and settled down to get some rest, completely exhausted by the effort.

The blankets smelled like Wyck. From him, my thoughts went on to everything that had happened in the past few hours.

Pain and exhaustion weakened whatever hope and resolve I had left. Everything I'd been forced to do here and all the emotions it had caused that I'd tried to burry now rose to the surface. Hiding my face in the blanket, I let the tears out.

The flood didn't last long. I was too tired to even have a proper meltdown. Before the sobbing convulsions had fully subsided, I was asleep.

Brutal thirst woke me. My throat felt like sandpaper. Even my chest and my stomach hurt. In the multi-colored glow cast by the lights outside the window, I spotted a large tumbler of water at the entrance to the passageway between the two rooms. Grabbing it, I drained it in huge, greedy gulps.

The sleep and the water made me feel more like myself again, and I explored the new place a little.

The room was small—just long and wide enough for me to stretch out on the floor in either direction. The ceiling was only high enough for me to stand up on my knees. Initially, it must have been a part of a larger room before a section of the ceiling prolapsed, possibly during the crash, separating it from the rest of the space.

At this point, it was more of a cage or a holding compartment than a livable space. I felt more like a trapped animal here than ever before—a creature kept for entertainment, with absolutely no rights.

I feared this was not the existence I could survive for long without losing my mind. Anguish and sorrow threatened to suffocate me with tears once again.

Crawling to the passageway, I peeked out into the adjacent room.

Wyck lay on his side on the floor there, his back to me. The bulk of his massive body blocked the exit out of the room—even in his sleep, he was protecting me.

Lesh stretched on his feet. The animal raised a head, probably having sensed my movement. Realizing it was me, he relaxed again, lowering the head down and closing his eyes.

The two looked so comfortable out there, despite laying on a bare floor with no bedding. Wyck didn't even have his vest on, his bent arm tucked under his head instead of a pillow.

Dragging a blanket behind me, I crawled through the tunnel to him.

His bare back was warm. I pressed myself to him, drawing the blanket over both of us. His deep, even breathing halted for a fraction of a moment.

"It's safer for you in the other room," he muttered softly, his voice rough from sleep.

"Where are we?"

"Just behind the wall of the *vasai* farm."

"The giant centipedes?"

I've seen *vasai,* the wild creatures that had both an internal and external skeletons, in the movies. On screen, they seemed terrifying.

Wyck must have felt me tense.

"We're safe here," he assured me. "But you should be in that other room."

"Do you want me to go back there, then?" I held my breath, dreading that he would send me away.

"No," he said, after just a moment of hesitation.

I exhaled in relief, snuggling closer.

"Thank you," I whispered, pressing my face to his back, next to the hard, gray ridge over his spine.

I wasn't sure what exactly I was thanking him for—too many things made me feel grateful for having Wyck in my life. His warmth and strength gave me comfort. It melted the shaky wall of defense inside me, making silent tears trickle down my cheeks once again. Then, the sniffles came.

"Nadia." Wyck turned in my arms to face me. "Are you still in pain?"

"No." I shook my head, wiping my tears away only to have the new ones roll down faster.

He gazed at me, his eyes the warm tint of lampshade yellow in the semi-darkness of this room.

"Come here." He draped his large, strong arm around me, pulling me closer.

"I'm so sorry, Wyck. I thought I could change things," I sobbed into his chest. "That I would entice them into accepting a dance instead of..." My words drowned in another bout of tears.

"It's not your fault. I've made a mistake trusting someone more than I should have," he said somberly.

Images of the events in the mess hall came flashing back, like a slideshow of nightmares.

"They could've killed you." A shudder ran through me at the thought of how close I'd come to losing him tonight. "I should've stuck with what worked before...like Svetlana did. Just like you told me to..."

"I don't believe it would've made a difference, to be honest." He stroked my back soothingly. "They always want more, no matter how much you give them."

"How do you know that?" I sniffled, though the tears had slowed down somewhat.

"Because I'm one of them," he said softly into my hair. "I'm just like them, Nadia." He slid his hand up to my nape, his fingers caressing the skin of my neck. "The more I get from you, the more I want. I've just been inside you, and I still want more."

I tilted my head back, finding his eyes with my gaze. There was no threat, no menace in it. The heat of desire simmered in the background, but longing was the overwhelming emotion on his face.

"What is 'more' for you, Wyck?" I asked.

"I want *all* of you, Nadia, my sweet sugar. Every little thing. I want you to come to me whenever you need a hug—only me. I wish all of your kisses to be mine from now on. And I want a *date*, just like in that movie we saw—with a dinner and a movie." He nuzzled the top of my head as I buried my face in his chest.

"I'd love to go on a date with you, Wyck," I confessed, even as sorrow tightened around my heart —so many of the things I used to take for granted weren't possible on the Dark Anomaly.

Freedom. Safety. Going out with a man I liked. Simply walking down a corridor without having to look over my shoulder in fear of an attack was not possible here.

He kept stroking my hair, the tension slowly draining from my heart and my body. Warm and comfy in his arms, I stopped crying. With a long sigh, I drew in another lungful of Wyck's warm, spicy scent. To me, it was now associated with safety. It relaxed me enough to start drifting to sleep again.

Over the course of the past several days, Wyck had become my true safe place, not just on the Dark Anomaly, but in the whole of the Universe.

I WOKE UP TO NOISE outside the room—talking, yelling, the screeching of the rusty cage doors being opened and shut, and the stomping of feet.

"What..." I lifted my head to meet Wyck's eyes directed at me.

He pinched both his lips between his thumb and his forefinger in the Federation's gesture of a call to silence. I made a sign that I understood, without saying a word.

His gesture, however, had led my gaze to his lips, and I let it linger there. The memory of our kiss and his taste on my tongue made my mouth water. I swallowed hard, unable to tear my gaze away.

The expression in his eyes heated. His arm flexed around me, and he shifted closer. Shutting my eyes, I moved forward, searching for his lips with my mouth.

He met me in a kiss with a soft groan.

Warmth and longing flooded through me. The pain, shame, and despair of this place ceased to exist as long as Wyck kept kissing me.

I slid my hand to his face, the short stubble on his cheek tickled my palm. He rolled me to my back, leaning over me. I trailed my fingers down his chest, through the soft dusting of hair there then over his side to his back.

Tentatively, he slid the tip of his tongue past my lips, and I met it with mine. My response seemed to give him reassurance. He was exploring my mouth, diligently and reverently. His movements quickly became more confident and more urgent. Passion started to take over the insecurity and even the caution.

The weight of his body on top of me and the feel of his hard muscles under my palms were invigorating, making me want more of him. Gliding my hands down his back, I slipped my fingers under the waistband of his pants.

He moaned into my mouth as I shoved my hands further down. I trailed my fingers over the hard half-globes of his backside. He jerked his hips, rocking against me with another tortured, muffled moan.

"Nadia..." He tore his mouth from mine. "We can't..."

The noise outside had calmed down, but someone was still moving around out there.

I nodded, reluctantly withdrawing my hands from his pants, but I wouldn't move away. Even as he rolled off me, I scooted closer, snuggling into his chest. The need to be next to him was stronger than anything.

His bicep under my head, he placed his other arm on me. I took his hand in mine, tracing the curved lines of the hard ridges over his knuckles.

"The feeding must be over, now," he whispered as the noise outside our room quieted down.

"You raise the centipedes here?"

"Yes, for meat and eggs." He tipped his head back toward the exit. "They're fed twice during the day. This was the morning feeding."

I would've never considered eating centipede meat back on Earth. Here, however, things were different. Unknowingly, I must've been eating it all along ever since I arrived.

"It should be safe for you to go out soon."

I held on to his hand tighter. Sooner or later, I knew I'd have to go out, to use the bathroom at least. At the moment, however, I was glad to escape the harsh reality of the outside world for just a little bit longer.

I laced my fingers with his, rubbing the tips over his hard knuckles. "These would do some serious damage in a fight," I said thinking about the many times he had used his fists to defend me.

"Mmh," he hummed in response. "Crux used to say that most species have to wear a special brace around their knuckles to match my punch. *Errocks* are born to fight."

"Do you believe that's *all* you were destined to do?"

"What else is there for me?" he glanced down at me.

"The world is so much bigger than this place. Out there, you can be anything you want to be, Wyck, do anything you wish."

He shook his head.

"The world outside of the Dark Anomaly doesn't exist for us, Nadia, just as we don't exist for it."

I rose on my elbow to see his face better.

"What if there was a way out of here?" I said, carefully watching his expression. "Would you consider leaving?"

"There is no way out," he said stubbornly. "Don't even think about it. Escape ideas will drive you mad. Trying to get away will kill you."

I searched his face, gauging whether I could really tell him everything.

"We came here intending to leave once our job was done. Our mission's plan included our departure."

"How?" He sat up.

I trusted him with my life; I decided to trust him with my one chance at regaining my freedom, too.

"Our return capsule is attached to the ship."

"And do you think it'll work?" he asked suspiciously, but I noticed a spark of interest in his eyes. His natural curiosity and the enduring hope of youth challenged his deep-ingrained belief that the Dark Anomaly was inescapable.

"No," I replied honestly, wishing so badly I could give him more than that. "I tried to use it when that ass...when Nocc attacked me, but something is wrong with the capsule. It didn't have enough power for the takeoff. I'm not an engineer or a pilot, though. In fact, I have no technical skills beyond those needed to operate the equipment. My purpose on the mission was to film a movie."

"A movie?" He gaped at me.

Suddenly, my role on our crew seemed as useless and trivial as our entire mission to the Dark Anomaly had proven to be. We didn't come here to rescue Svetlana, she'd been believed long dead. We didn't even come for research or to get any specific data for science, certainly not to give any assistance to the sentient beings stranded in this place—we had no idea about their existence. We came only to get information that would sell well back on Earth. My sole purpose was to preserve and present that information in a nicely done, professionally produced package. Nothing more.

"There has been a big interest—public curiosity—on Earth about the Dark Anomaly," I tried to explain this to Wyck. "Svetlana's disappearance put an end to the government sponsored in-person exploration of it. However, the private sector managed to outfit an expedition of their own..." I heaved a sigh, thinking about my dead team mates again. "Looking back, it was a stupid idea all along. But I was so excited when I got selected to participate in it."

"You *volunteered* to come here?" he asked, his eyes growing bigger with shock.

"I was one of thousands who volunteered." I nodded. "Simply being selected already felt like an achievement. The promise of a huge reward, of course, didn't hurt. I had big plans and needed the money."

"What for?"

I paused, thinking how much I should reveal in my confessions. I'd never told anyone about my plan, it felt too personal. My future family was meant to be all my own, there was no need for anyone to know.

Wyck was no longer just "anyone," though.

"I wanted to start a family," I admitted. "You know, to have a baby..."

"And you need money for that?" His dark eyebrow ridges rose in confusion.

"Out there, you need money for everything once the baby is born. But in my case, I had to pay even for getting pregnant."

"Why?"

"Because I didn't want to waste my life, waiting for the right man to come along. What if he never came? How long would I be waiting? Neither did I want to have sex with a stranger or a casual partner just to get pregnant."

He kept staring at me, clearly confused, so I continued explaining, "My parents had me very late in life. Both were gone before I even reached adulthood. I want to spend as much time with my children as possible, to be there for them when they start their own families, and to meet my grandchildren. With the reward money I was supposed get for this mission, I'd be able to afford a nice place without having to work five days a week. I could stay at home and raise my children. I could have the family time I got so little of with my own parents."

"So, you don't need a man to have a baby on your planet?" Wyck looked shocked by the fact.

"No...I mean yes, technically, there is still a man involved. Except that I've never met him, and I wasn't going to. He anonymously donated his sperm. The clinic kept it until they sold it to me. A doctor would insert it...um, inside me, to get me pregnant."

"There is no joy in that," he stated flatly.

"The procedure is not about joy. It's about having a baby without being involved with the biological father. It's easier that way, you see."

"Maybe, but a family is so much more than just the people you give birth to. You don't even need to share blood to be a family. My brothers and I are not related by blood but—"

He cut himself short. A dark shadow moved over his features, and I wondered if it was from the memory of one of his "brothers" almost killing him last night.

Feeling the need to comfort him somehow, I placed my hand on top of his.

"True. One doesn't need to be related to be close like a family. But what if you don't meet anyone you want to be close to?" I released a long breath. "One has to start somewhere, right? Some people start with a partner. I decided to start with a baby."

He sat in silence for some time.

"Is that why you want to go back to Earth?" he finally asked. "To get pregnant and start a family?"

"Not just because of that, of course. In my world, I have the freedom to lead the life I like. Here, I'm trapped…"

"You said the return capsule doesn't work."

"But it could be fixed. I think. I don't know for sure, but…" What harm could there be in telling him about Val too, now? Maybe he could help me find her? I knew now I could trust him not to hurt her. "There was another woman on my ship when we crashed."

"There was?" He straightened his back quickly. "I knew I saw and smelled someone else."

Smelled.

"Have you caught the same scent anywhere else since?"

"No. Why did you lie about being the only one?"

"Why do you think?" I spread my arms. "By then, most of my crew had been annihilated. I'd been nearly raped by one of you. If Val somehow got a chance to run and hide, I wasn't going to send all of you on a hunt for her."

He regarded me for a moment. "Why are you telling me now?"

I squeezed his hand tight.

"Because I trust you, not just with my own life but with hers, too."

"What do you think happened to her? I haven't heard anyone speak of another female. I'm sure if someone found her, they'd brag about it."

"So, that's a good sign then, right? I hope she hid somewhere and...is still alive."

To survive all this time, Val would need some food and a source of water. With all resources on the Dark Anomaly being controlled to some extent, those things wouldn't be easy to come by.

"Promise me, you won't tell anyone about her," I begged Wyck. Even with his constant protection, I never felt completely safe anywhere on the Dark Anomaly. I dreaded to think what would happen to Val if she were discovered by the crew while on her own.

"It may be a good idea to tell the captain," Wyck suggested. "He would assign her a protector and ensure she is looked after if she is found."

"Is there any man in here who would protect her the way you've protected me?" I challenged.

His expression grew blank.

"Protection" had a different meaning for the rest of the crew. Nocc had made it clear last night that his idea of "not harming" me would be not killing me after a gang rape. That was as much mercy as a woman could count on from him. The rest of them weren't any better.

I doubted that any of them had Wyck's willingness to learn and his ability to change. Being so much older than Wyck, they all had come here as hardened criminals already. Brutality was the only thing they knew. It was also what they chose to live by.

"I can help you look for Val," I offered.

"No." He shook his head resolutely. "You will need to remain here, in safety. I'll search for her myself."

I thought about the cameras I'd installed throughout the living area of our ship. They were to capture the daily routine of the crew on our way to the Dark Anomaly. Now, I wondered if I could use the footage to find out more about Val's fate, provided the captain or the crew hadn't removed the cameras and destroyed or damaged the recordings.

"What happened to our ship?" I asked Wyck. "Is anyone occupying it?"

"No, not yet. Its location is inconvenient, being on the very edge of the habitable sector, away from everything—" he cut himself short, a sudden understanding spreading on his face. "Do you think she would sneak back on it?"

I hadn't thought about that, but it was entirely possible.

"It would make sense." I perked up, feeling hope rising inside me. "The ship has everything for her to survive for weeks if needed, even months."

"All the supplies have been taken from it," Wyck pointed out.

"I doubt *all* have been. One would only take what he *thinks* can be taken."

"What do you mean?"

I shifted to face him fully, eager to explain.

"Until recently, spaceships had to bring all their food and water on the journey with them. The latest technology allowed us to make most of it onboard. We didn't carry canisters of food and water. We have built-in replicators that create them both on demand, from ingredients that take up just a fraction of the space and weigh much less than the final product."

"Are such things even possible?" he gazed at me in wonder.

"They are now." I smiled, patting his knee. "If Val has made it back to the ship, she might be okay. That's where we should start looking."

My excitement was reflected in his eyes.

"I'll go check on my own, first," he said. "But I'll take you to the bathroom first. You'll need to take a shower to wash off your scent."

"That's right. It's been almost twenty-four hours since I showered last. I must be gross and dirty." I winked at him, teasing.

He cupped my chin, bringing our faces closer.

"Not dirty. Sweet." He brushed the tip of his tongue along my bottom lip before taking it in a kiss. "Sweet like sugar," he whispered against my mouth. "And so irresistible to all of us here."

Chapter 17

I LAY ON THE PILE OF Wyck's blankets on the floor of the small room behind the *vasai* farm. He wasn't here, and bouts of worry and terror wracked me.

Tonight would be my third scheduled "performance" at the mess hall. The captain had officially cancelled my appearance days ago. Deprived of their "entertainment," the enraged crew had started a hunt for me. Hundreds of males had been raging through the Dark Anomaly, crushing everything and everyone in their way.

Wyck had forbidden me to leave this room out of fear that the crew would find me. I'd begged him not to go out tonight, either, afraid for his life more than mine.

"I need to know what's going on out there," he'd explained. "I'll lead them away from here if necessary. As soon as it's safe again, we'll go to your ship." He'd kissed me before leaving.

During the past week, Wyck had made a couple of excursions to my ship on his own, sadly finding no trace of Val's presence or scent.

Only I could open the locked doors to our sleeping cabin on the ship where Val still might be hiding. However, Wyck had been reluctant to let me go because I'd have to walk along the entire length of the main corridor of the Dark Anomaly to get there. With the crew actively looking for me for days, it'd been more dangerous than ever.

Wyck's other concern had been the safety of our ship. The cutout that Nocc had made in its hull needed to be repaired. On his last visit to the ship, Wyck had brought along a large slab of metal that he used to block the entrance.

Now that the unrest had finally started to quiet down, we planned my move to the ship.

Wyck wanted to do it early in the morning when most of the crew would be hopefully passed out, exhausted after wreaking havoc all night.

I waited for him to come back soon and, hopefully, confirm that it was safe to finally leave our small hiding place where we'd spent the week.

Afraid to breathe, I was listening carefully to every little noise reaching me from the outside. The now familiar sounds of the centipedes scurrying inside their cages and the clanking of their mandibles against the metal bars didn't scare me. Straining my hearing, I tried to pick out any sound of the rioting crew.

My only defence against them was to remain undiscovered. I had no weapon on me. The large, unmanned cargo ship that had crashed last week ended up completely destroying the glass room, along with Wyck's vest and my knife. Thankfully, to defend himself, Wyck still had the gun and, of course, his fists.

I knew he'd been getting into fights and scuffles, though he wouldn't talk about it when I'd asked. Throughout the past week, I'd spotted blood on his knuckles on more than one occasion. There had also been fresh claw and teeth marks on his arms and back.

The thought of what might be happening to him right now made my stomach churn and my hands shake. I wished to get out of here, to be next to him, but I knew that my presence out there would only make things worse for both of us.

Instead, I was laying here, shaking in my suit, afraid to even get under the blanket in case someone showed up and I'd have to fight for my life. Hiding, I barely breathed, making as little noise as possible.

This had been my existence for the past week—sneaking out to use the bathroom, quickly eating the food Wyck smuggled in for me, lying low, afraid to move, day after day.

Wyck's hugs and occasional kisses were the only things that kept me sane in this nightmarish place. Only in his arms could I get any rest.

Every night, however, I crawled through the short tunnel into the tiny room with the window, leaving him alone to guard the exit. I knew that unless I was safely on the other end of the narrow tunnel, Wyck wouldn't relax enough to fall asleep. My safety had become his mission in life.

Aside from my parents, I'd never had anyone who cared so much about me. In turn, I began to genuinely care about him, too. He meant more and more to me with each passing day. Here, on the Dark Anomaly, Wyck had become my entire world.

Come back to me, please.

I didn't dare say these words out loud, not even in a whisper, for the fear that one of the crew might hear me. But I pleaded for his safe return in my mind.

Come back to me.

The stomping of feet out in the farm made me halt my breath.

Someone crawled into the room on the other side of the tunnel—someone very large by the sound of it.

"Nadia," Wyck's whisper reached me, and I exhaled in relief.

Lesh's soft hissing announced that Wyck's pet had made it back with him, too.

"You're back..." I crawled through the tunnel and into Wyck's arms.

He had a split lip and there was a wide smudge of blood on his temple.

"Wyck, what happened?" I reached back into my room to grab the glass with water. "Are you okay?"

I dipped the end of a blanket in the water then gently dabbed at the blood streak below his lip.

"I'm fine." He attempted to smile then winced instead.

"Hurts?"

"A little." He shrugged.

"How about that one?" I pointed at the smudge on his head.

He brushed his hand along his temple then stared at his bloodied fingers in some confusion.

"That's not my blood."

"Good." I cleaned his face with the wet corner of the blanket while he sat still, gazing at me. "Did you...kill someone?"

"A few." He nodded somberly.

One thing I'd never witnessed in my life before coming to the Dark Anomaly was murder. So many had been killed since. The only thing I was grateful for was that Wyck remained alive.

"Thank God you made it," I said firmly.

"I had help."

Did the other *errocks* finally come to his aid?

"Vrateus helped me get out of there when things got wild at one point."

No *errocks* then. It saddened me because I knew Wyck was hurt when his family had turned against him. And it was all because of me.

"So, the captain was out there, too?"

"If he didn't come, many more would've died. He is the captain, the crew eventually listened to him, for now anyway. It helps that he always carries a lot of guns and shoots fast. As a punishment for the riots, he is making the entire crew scrub the sector clean tomorrow."

"Well, that should keep them busy and out of trouble." I released a short breath.

Wyck's frown didn't ease, however.

"I hope it doesn't cost the captain another mutiny."

"Is there a high chance of that?"

"The crew is a volatile bunch. They're hard to control and quick to get angry. One never knows when an explosion may happen," he replied, rather enigmatically. "We're moving out of here tomorrow night, instead of the morning."

"Why night?"

"It'll be easier to do while everyone is busy cleaning and doing chores."

"While they're all awake and moving about, you mean? How is that easier?"

"Vrateus gave me the code to the lock of the spacesuit storage room. It's the one that's next to the *vasai* farm, very close to here. I'll get a large crate and a dolly from there to transport you to the ship, pretending I'm doing a task for Vrateus like the rest of the crew."

As much as I wished to leave this cage of a room, getting out there felt terrifying. Wyck must have sensed my fear and cupped my face gently.

"We'll be okay, my sweet."

"We'll be fine," I replied, forcing a smile. I was so sick of being scared all the time.

WYCK TOOK A QUICK LOOK inside the ship that had brought me to the Dark Anomaly weeks ago, which seemed like another lifetime, now.

"Come, quickly." He helped me climb out of the crate I'd hidden in while he transported me across almost the entire habitable sector of the Anomaly. "Get in, now." He nudged me toward the cut-out that served as the entrance to the ship.

Despite the late hour, the lights were on. Wyck had told me that the lights were never off on the Dark Anomaly. I wondered if the captain knew that someone was always ready to attack, and he wanted to make it easier for everyone to watch their backs.

"Val?" I called softly as soon as I climbed in.

Wyck had gone through the ship before, finding no trace of anyone occupying it. Yet I still hoped that Val would magically appear when I got here.

No one replied. The place stood bare and desolate. The images of the gruesome murders that had happened here assaulted my memory.

"Vrateus promised to keep the crew away from here." Wyck promptly followed me in, dragging the crate behind him. "But there's always a risk of someone wandering by unexpectedly. We'll need to be careful."

Clinking with his chain, Lesh leaped in through the opening, too, and Wyck leaned a large round slab of metal against the cut-out, blocking the entrance from the inside.

"This is nearly impossible to roll away from the outside," he assured me. "If anyone wants to enter, they'd have to push it in, and we'll hear it crash as it hits the floor."

He stood next to me, turning around to take in the large open space of the common area of the ship—beige walls, the wide control panel far ahead with the six crew seats in front of it; the dining area in the middle; the storage hatch and the medical niche to the left; the wall with the crew cabins behind it to the right. "You said there're places to hide in here?"

"Yes, the sleeping cabins..." I replied distractedly.

The day of our ill-faded arrival kept replaying in my mind. I wandered over to the spot where Nocc had climbed on top of me before Wyck confronted him. The positions of the other members of my crew came to mind. Lee, Jose...all dead.

Val...

"You said you saw Val the day we landed here. Do you remember where she was when you came?"

He rubbed the back of his head.

"I'm not sure, now, if it was her. It could've been just one of your men. Humans are rather puny, male and female."

"Right..." I'd argue with that statement if I weren't so distracted by my thoughts.

I walked over to the main control panel.

"Is something wrong?" Wyck had caught on to my lack of attention.

"I have several cameras installed around this area." I turned on one of the screens on the panel. To my relief, it came to life immediately. "One is between the medical chamber and the space suit storage hatch, two over the dining table next to them, two right here." I pointed at either side of the main control panel. "See those little dark spheres? They've been here all this time. They're off now, but the recording was on during the landing. That was an event I definitely wanted to get on camera. The last time I saw Val, she was lying by the wall near the storage hatch. The camera over there by the cabins should've caught her."

Running my fingers over one of the screens of the control panel, I pulled out the folders containing the footage. It was organized by date and camera number.

"Look." I tapped on the date of our arrival, bringing up the footage from the camera over the cabins.

The echo of that day's horror rushed over me again as the images came to life on the screen. Wyck's back came into view as he stood over me, his shoulders squared, his hands fisted at his sides. I'd been on the floor, too close to the wall, only my legs were in frame. The full frontal of Nocc, however, was visible. The broken body of Lee on the floor behind him. And further back, behind the round table...

"There she is!" I pointed at Val's figure curled on the floor, the bright sponsor logos on her uniform suit glowing in the shadows.

"I knew I saw a woman!" Wyck exclaimed triumphantly.

The two *errocks* on the screen threw punches at each other, and the small figure by the wall stirred. Slowly, she crawled under the table, then behind one of the chairs, and out of camera range.

"She was alive! There must be more videos. There has to be..." I opened every single folder marked with that date, closely examining the images taken by each of the cameras.

Unfortunately, I had no camera pointed on the exit from the ship. Back then, before Nocc cut the hole in the hull, it was just a boring wall with some storage cabinets. There had been nothing to film at that angle until that day.

"No..." I groaned, disheartened. "What happened to her?"

Val had been injured during the landing. Even perfectly healthy, a woman had a slim chance of surviving this place for long.

"I hope she's okay, that she's still alive, somehow." I bit my lip as it began to tremble. Tears prickled behind my eyelids.

Wyck hugged me from behind. "If the worst has happened to her, sugar, we would've found something by now. A body part, some of her clothing, blood—something." He kissed the side of my face. "No one has seen anything. That has to be a good sign."

That had to be because I refused to lose hope of finding Val alive one day.

"We're here now," he continued. "We'll be here if she comes back."

I nodded, drawing in a shuddered breath. "Maybe we could figure out a way to put a camera outside the entrance, in the corridor? That way we'd see her even if she can't push the slab away to get in."

"Good idea. It'd be helpful to see who comes to the door. Now..." He released me from his arms, turning around to face the room again. "I need to hide you better than this. Where did you say those cabins were?"

"Right here." I walked over to the wall covered with beige, textured paneling, the same as the rest of the ship's interior. The two vertical slits running up from floor to ceiling could easily be mistaken for seams between two pieces of the wall material. However, a small square screen at my eye level lit up when I waved my hand in front of it. I pressed my palm to it, and a wall panel slid aside, revealing our cabin inside.

"That's sleek." Wyck clicked his tongue with appreciation, following me in.

The cabin was large enough to comfortably accommodate Val and me on our nearly two-month-long journey to this part of the Galaxy.

Unlike the main area, this room hadn't been raided—all my things remained intact. Which must mean that neither the captain nor the crew knew about the cabins.

I promptly closed the doors behind Wyck. Here, we were safer than anywhere else on the ship, right now.

"This is where I lived on our way here." I swept the place with my arm.

The entrance was right in the middle, with the room divided in two equal parts on each side. My area was on the left, Val's on the right, with the common space in the middle. A narrow bunk bed folded out of the wall in each personal area. We each had a desk and a chair, too.

I walked over to Val's part of the room and pressed the button on the wall. The grey, solid privacy partition lowered from the ceiling, hiding from view what used to be Val's personal sleeping and working space.

"This is Val's," I muttered, rubbing my upper arms with my hands. "We shouldn't go there."

The sitting area in the middle of the cabin had a small breakfast table, a couple of chairs and a very comfy couch. Here, we used to have our meals on those days when we didn't feel like going out into the common area to eat. The two of us would watch movies while sitting on this couch. When Val had to work elsewhere on the ship, I used to like reading here.

On the wall to the right of the entrance was a wall-mounted food station with a narrow counter below it and a small sink. To the left was the bathroom with a toilet and a shower.

"As I said, it's self-contained." I brushed my fingers over the food station screen with lit-up pictures. "There should still be enough supplies to create food for two human females for at least two more months—the duration of our journey home if we had managed to take off in the ship. Though, the escape capsule was considered to be our most likely means of return."

There was another food station in the common area, but I had no idea how long the supplies there were supposed to last.

Wyck walked around the space, inspecting the equipment and the furniture.

"This will do for now." He gave me a smile, visibly relieved. "You can take the bed, I'll sleep on the floor." With a long exhale, he brushed his hand over his face, his slumping shoulders evidence of his exhaustion.

"Um..." I followed his gaze from the bunk bed to the floor next to it.

I'd spent way too many nights alone, listening to him breathing in the other room and wishing he were holding me while I slept.

Here, we were in relative safety. There was no need for us to sleep separately. Yet it didn't feel entirely right for me to demand that we sleep together.

Wyck had been doing so much for me, and it'd cost him. The job of looking after me had damaged his relationship with the rest of the crew, including his family.

I'd been taking so much from him—his time, his attention, his support, and protection. Demanding his presence in my bed, now, would be like asking for more of all of that when I felt I had nothing to give him back.

Wyck deserved so much better. He deserved everything.

He noticed my hesitation. "Is something wrong?"

"No… It's just that…" I clasped my hands in front of me. "I can sleep on the floor, too."

He tilted his head, giving me an inquisitive look.

"With me? Or alone?"

Now that he'd asked me directly, I couldn't pretend.

"With you." I dropped my gaze down. "If you don't mind, of course."

He stepped closer. So close, I could feel the warmth of his body, but he wouldn't touch me. Instead, he drew in a long inhale.

"You should take a shower, then." He took a bar of soap out of his pant pocket.

"Okay." The relief that he'd agreed to sleep together made me ridiculously happy. "Let's just make the bed first," I offered, not giving him a chance to change his mind.

I took the mattress pad off my bunk bed. The two of us then stretched it to more than double its original width.

"That's amazing how you can simply change its size," Wyck mused, pushing with both hands on the thick and comfy pad.

"It's made from the same material that's currently used to make mattresses on Earth. It goes from single to double size and even bigger. Which is much more practical than the old way of manufacturing and storing all possible sizes of mattresses," I chatted, grateful for the distraction.

There was a certain tension in the air, the awkwardness I hadn't experienced in Wyck's presence lately, and I didn't know how to deal with it.

We put the sheets on the mattress on the floor then spread the blankets we had brought with us. At the end, it turned out to be a perfect bed, much more comfortable than anything I'd been sleeping on since the day I got to the Dark Anomaly.

A corner of the top blanket happened to be bent over, and we both reached for it to straightened it out. Our hands touched. A spark of sensation, hot and intense like lightning, shot up my arm. I jerked my hand away quickly, darting my gaze to Wyck's face.

He was crouching next to me, his thigh touching mine. His expression mirrored my confusion.

We'd touched many times before. We'd kissed. Never before, however, had we been in a place that felt this comfortable for both of us. With no immediate danger to worry about, my attraction to him bloomed brighter. The hunger in his eyes burned hotter than ever.

Since he'd lost his vest, Wyck had been wearing nothing but the gun holster on his torso. The wide, ornately embossed leather belt crossed his massive chest. I balled my hand into a fist to stop myself from reaching out to touch it.

"I better go have that shower," I mumbled.

Quickly rising to my feet, I escaped to the bathroom.

I slid the door panel closed behind me and yanked the closure of my suit down. Usually barely noticeable, the material of the suit seemed extremely irritating right now, too hot and confining. I couldn't wait to get rid of it, peeling it off quickly.

Naked, I drew in a long breath. The air in the room seemed to be hot and heavy, too. It stroked along my bare arms and breasts like a caress, making my skin tingle. Leaning over the shower control panel on the wall, I started to program the water temperature and flow.

Judging by my body's reaction, I needed a cool shower tonight, especially if I wanted to share a bed with Wyck—an ice-cold shower.

Suddenly, the bathroom door slid open.

"You forgot the soap." Wyck stood in the doorway.

His gaze roamed greedily over my naked body. He squeezed his fists so hard, the bar of soap cracked in his hand. Yet he wouldn't cross the threshold.

My heart thundered in my chest but not from fear, for once. With Wyck, I didn't need to be afraid. The streams of warm water rushed down from the ceiling, caressing my skin. I wished it was Wyck's rough hands instead.

"Bring it here," I said, stepping back to make space for him.

The shower area was just enough for one person. As Wyck entered the bathroom, his huge body nearly filled the entire room.

Pressing the buttons on the control screen, I made the toilet slide into the floor. The sink folded into the wall, and the streams of water rushed from the openings along the entire surface of the ceiling. The whole bathroom had now become one much larger shower with smooth, metallic walls and a fine mesh over the floor.

Water sluiced over Wyck, drenching the material of his pants and running into his boots. His pronounced eyebrow ridges kept the water out of his eyes, diverting it around his face. Wyck wiped it off with his forearm.

"Soap?" He handed me the bar.

I placed the soap on top of a dispenser nearby and took his hand in mine. There was no blood on his knuckles this time, but the size of his hand and the fierce hardness of the ridges on it left no doubt, this hand could be and had been used as a weapon.

"Do you still believe that *errocks* are born to fight? Do you think you're inherently brutal by nature?" I lifted my gaze to his. "Do you want to hurt me, Wyck?"

He stepped to me, leaving his hand in mine. There was but a hairbreadth of space between us, yet he wouldn't close it, ravaging me with his gaze alone.

"I want to fuck you hard," he growled. "I want to see your hair tangle and your skin drip with sweat. I want to hear you gasping for air as I pound into you. But I don't want to hurt you, Nadia. I want you to enjoy it all as much as I would."

The warmth of the water seeped through my skin into my muscles. The heat in his gaze reached all the way through to my core.

Wyck towered over me. He was so much bigger and stronger than me. Yet I felt *I* had the power over what would happen here, now. He'd given it to me freely.

An overwhelming sense of gratitude for this man flooded me. He had been my one and only ray of sunshine for so long. No one and nothing could spoil this for us.

"We will make it right," I whispered as a mantra, closing the distance between us.

Everything about him felt *right*, even his wrongs.

I slid my hand around his back, unbuckling the gun holster from around his chest.

Sinking his fingers into the wet hair on the back of my head, he kissed me, deep and hard. The familiar taste of his kiss thrilled and relaxed me at the same time.

"Does it hurt?" I asked when he let me come up for air. I hovered the tip of my finger over the cut on his lip.

"The pain is worth the pleasure I always feel when I kiss you." He gave me a happy smile. "Do you like kissing me, Nadia?"

His kisses had been like shots of medicine against the festering sickness of my mind during the darkest time of my life. I'd been using Wyck to help me cope and now, he had become the addiction I could no longer quit. I didn't want to quit. But I wished to try giving something back to him.

If he felt pleasure from kissing me, I wanted to make him feel more.

"Let's get you out of these wet pants," I murmured, clicking the front closures of his waistband open.

The smile slipped off his face when I reached inside, my fingers sliding along his hard-as-rock erection—one of them.

"Do you really want this, Nadia?" His tone sounded almost like a threat, a warning. "Because once I start, I won't be able to stop."

The sound of his deep, low voice made my skin tingle with anticipation. I wished to give him pleasure, but I sensed I'd enjoy doing it. Wyck deserved it all. We both had earned this moment of time together, away from everyone else.

Instead of an answer, I resolutely shoved his pants down his legs. I sank to my knees in front of him. Opening the heavy buckles on his boots, I made him kick them off.

"You're all mine now," I whispered, sliding my hands up his long, muscular legs.

His two enormous dicks were positioned about an inch or two apart, one over the other. Both were so hard, the higher one pointed straight up, nearly touching his stomach.

I'd never seen a naked *errock* before, not even in a picture. I knew of the scientific and cultural exchange between our species. To my knowledge, however, there'd been no collaborations in terms of reproduction yet.

There was no point in asking Wyck about the *errocks'* cultural norms in terms of sex. All he knew would be mostly the customs of the group of *errocks* on the Dark Anomaly. Whatever little information he got had been filtered for him by those who had raised him.

He and I would have to discover our own ways.

"Tell me if you don't like something I'm doing," I told him, gliding my hands up the insides of his bulging thighs, thick with ropes of muscles.

His hard abs rippled when I took both of his massive dicks in my hands. He hissed, spreading his arms to grab onto the walls.

"Are you okay?" I asked, trailing my fingers along both his lengths.

He nodded quickly, sucking in another breath.

His girth—either of the two—was too thick for one hand. I let go of the top one and focused my attention on the lower one for now. Wrapping the fingers of both hands around it, I slid my hands up and down. When I squeezed my hands tighter, it got thinner, the clear, shimmering moisture beading along the entire surface. The moment I loosened my grip, he slowly grew bigger again.

It felt like having a thick roll of dense clay in my hands, and I couldn't resist playing with it. I squeezed, patted, and rolled.

"Do you like this?" I slid my hands up and down once more, then leaned in and flicked my tongue over the tip. The slick liquid seeping from his skin had a taste, I discovered. The flavor reminded me of cloves and nutmeg, a bit spicy and unexpectantly pleasant.

He threw his head back with a long, guttural groan.

"Tell me if you want me to stop." I wrapped my lips around the tip then slid my mouth along his length, taking more of it.

"Don't..." he rasped. "Do whatever you want to me, but do *not* stop."

I hummed in agreement, flexing my lips and pumping my hand along what I couldn't fit into my mouth. I swirled my tongue around the tip.

His abs flexed and his thighs shook.

"I—" he managed before his hard, throbbing length spasmed in my mouth. A hot, spicy stream hit the back of my throat.

Not expecting so much of it and so soon, I gagged, coughing. He slipped out of my mouth. Spurts of vivid green with a pearly sheen, kept shooting out as I pumped him with my hands. Mixed with water, they swirled around my legs before being sucked into the floor.

I took my hands off only when he stopped coming. He swayed then dropped to his knees in front of me.

I cupped his face. "Was it good?" I searched his eyes. His expression was a confusing mix of torture and bliss. "Better than the last time?" I asked with hope.

"Every time with you is simply amazing," he groaned, wrapping his arms around my waist.

He lowered his mouth to mine, sliding me into his lap.

My core connected with another hard thickness between us. His second penis remained as erect as ever, throbbing urgently between us.

"I never got to learn what *you* like," Wyck said softly, placing a kiss on my shoulder next.

"Generally, it takes time for human women." I felt the need to warn him after having witnessed, twice now, how quickly he came himself. "Our bodies need some... um, longer stimulation to reach an orgasm."

"I've got time," he murmured against my skin, moving his kisses up to my neck. "I don't have to be anywhere until breakfast, which is in about eight hours. Would that be enough? Or shall we forget about breakfast tomorrow?"

The stubble on his chin tickled against the skin on my collar bone, making me giggle.

"It shouldn't take *that* long," I said. "If we do it right, we may even have some time left for sleep, out of those eight hours."

Judging by the way my body already buzzed with desire, it might not even take long at all.

"Remember I don't know what I'm doing." He slid his hands up my back then slipped one between us to cup my breast. "You'll have to teach me."

His thumb grazed my nipple, and I inhaled sharply as ripples of pleasure fluttered through my chest to my lower belly.

"You liked that?" He took my other breast in his other hand, rolling the tip under his thumb. "Does this feel good?"

"You're... an excellent student," I breathed out.

Sweet pressure swelled hot between my legs, and I rocked my hips against him, needing to move.

"I want to taste you," he whispered, catching my mouth with his once again. His tongue found mine quickly as he kissed me with passion and confidence.

The taste of him still lingered in my mouth—spicy, pleasant, and clean. He released my breasts, and I pressed myself closer to him.

"I want you inside me," I begged, grasping for the erection between us.

He was so huge, and I was too impatient in my desperate desire for him. Sliding my hand just once or twice along his length, I didn't make him much smaller before impaling myself on him.

A deep roar vibrated deep inside his throat as I lowered my hips into his lap. Despite the intense urge to have him in me, I had to do it slowly. Tightly stretched around him, I inched down, each tiny slide shooting sparks of pleasure through my entire body.

"Nadia, you look—" Wyck gazed at me intensely. "Am I hurting you?"

"No, sweetheart..." I rose over his thighs, letting him out a little, then lowered my hips again, taking him deeper. "This is *everything*. Having you inside me is...wonderful."

Wrapping my arms tightly around his neck, I kissed him, putting everything I couldn't express in words into that kiss.

Wyck had been my survival. He'd always made me feel safe. But for the first time since I came here, the joy of life was seeping back into my heart. He didn't just help me survive, he was bringing me back to life.

"Take me, darling." I slid all the way down into his lap, taking all of him.

With a groan, he rose to his feet, lifting me up, too. His expression turned from tortured to wild as he pressed my back to the wall.

"I'm *taking* you," he growled, thrusting his hips into me. "You're mine." He pumped harder, rubbing just the right spot in this position. "*My* woman."

His speed increased. He rutted wildly, violently. I felt his power with each brutal thrust. It spread through me with ache and pleasure, claiming me for him.

He came, just as fiercely, with a growl and gritting of teeth.

The moment his cock slipped out of me, his hand was between my legs.

"How?" He cupped me there, sliding a finger in and out of me and trailing it around my opening. "How do I make you come? Show me where?" he demanded.

Pleasure skirted and pulsed around my core from his touch. I rocked my hips against his hand, needing all of it and more.

I found his finger with my hand and pressed it to that one spot where I needed him most. "Right here."

"This here?" He circled the tight, throbbing bud, and I gasped as my hips bucked. "So small?" he muttered in amazement. He pressed harder, watching me writhe in ecstasy against his hand. "And so very powerful."

I hooked my arm around his neck. He rubbed, caressed, and rolled, playing with me the way I'd played with him just a little while ago. Each movement of his exploring fingers was taking me higher. With another press of his hand, the orgasm finally hit me.

I gasped with a moan, hugging him tighter. My hips jerked as an intense pleasure spasmed inside me, blinding me to the rest of the world.

"There you go," Wyck murmured, his voice thick with satisfaction. He lightened his touch, gently stroking the last ripples of the orgasm out of me. "It didn't take long at all."

I smiled against his neck, slowly drifting down from the crest.

"I guess you're right." I sighed, relaxing in his arms under the warm streams of water rushing over us.

It'd been a while since I'd had sex, but that wasn't what had made it so incredibly amazing this time.

"It's because I really like you, Wyck. I like you so much."

Chapter 18

I WOKE UP TO THE CARESS of lips and to the slight prickle of stubble along my skin.

Wyck trailed soft, tender kisses up my shoulder.

I stretched with a moan. The achy feeling through my body reminded me of everything Wyck and his two glorious dicks had done to me last night.

"How does it happen for you?" he asked, his warm breath fanning along my chest as he moved on to my left breast. "When do you start feeling desire?" He licked my nipple then sucked on it. "What are you feeling right now?"

He was learning, I realized. Everything he'd ever been taught about sex he needed to re-learn because all of that knowledge was warped.

"You care about what I feel?" He obviously did, but I wanted him to express it in words. I needed to hear it. "Why?"

"It brings me joy to know you feel what I'm feeling," he replied simply. "My pleasure is not complete without yours."

I trailed my fingers down the familiar dips and elevations of the three ridges on his head. Between them, the skin of his scalp was completely smooth, unlike the stubble he had on his cheeks and chin. The stubble never grew into a beard, though. I'd never seen him shave. It was always the same length, just like the slightly longer and softer hair on his chest.

"Sex really is like dancing, then." I smiled. "A couple dance works the best when both partners are equally into it. For me personally, the desire starts like a fire. It begins with a spark from a touch, a word, or even a thought. Then it grows with more touching until it bursts with release. How does it happen for you?"

He exhaled a laugh, resting his head between my breasts.

"For me, it's always there, my sweet sugar. Pain and pleasure—both urgent and intense. The real challenge is to wrestle it under control, to hold it back long enough to be able to think and function. Every day."

I cradled his head to me with one arm, wrapping the other one around his massive shoulders. "Thank you for wrestling it and for holding it back until I was ready."

He raised his head to catch my gaze.

"I want *your* desire for me to match *mine* for you, as wild and crazy as it is. Do you think it's possible?"

I could see it all in his eyes—the raging desire he spoke about, the desperate struggle he led to contain it, the intense hope in anticipation of my answer.

"I believe it is possible for me to want you as desperately as you want me, Wyck. In every way. You're firmly in my heart already, and apparently it doesn't take long for my body to catch up with my heart. We saw it last night." I smiled wider.

"Your body likes being touched," he stated it as a fact.

"By *you*," I clarified. "The person who is doing the touching makes all the difference."

He seemed to contemplate my words, gliding his hand over my ribs to cup my breast then back down again. He repeated the motion a few times, as if lost in thought. The sensation of his palm against my skin spread warm tiny ripples through me. On his next slide up, his thumb slightly brushed over my nipple, making me gasp softly. The sound seemed to bring him back into the moment.

He slid a gaze down my body, all the way to the blanket that was covering me up to my waist.

"I want to learn all the places you like me to touch you, Nadia. Here?" He kissed my shoulder again.

A shoulder wouldn't be considered one of the most exciting erogenous zones. But Wyck had often kissed me there. By now, it had become a sign of his affection to me. His caress now fanned my anticipation.

"Do you like it when I do this?" he asked, trailing his mouth further along my collar bone.

The warmth and softness of his lips, along with the prickle of the short stubble along his jawline, created a unique sensation inside me. A series of tingles scattered down my bare arms.

"I do," I admitted. "I like it very much."

"How about here?" He kissed my throat, and I tilted my head back, giving him more room to keep kissing.

"Definitely," I agreed. Feather-light pleasure stroked my skin at his caress, and I hummed in delight.

He continued to tantalize me with his touch, kissing up my neck.

"I know for a fact you like this," he murmured before sliding his lips over mine and taking my mouth in a deep, ravenous kiss.

His alternating between gentle and passionate teased and ignited me. I had no idea if he'd ever had a chance to build a fire while living on the Dark Anomaly, but he sure knew how to stoke the flames inside me.

Arching my back, I squeezed my right breast, pinching the nipple, and he immediately followed my gesture, replacing my hand with his. The sensation of his hands felt so much better than that of my own. My breast all but drowned in his large hand, his rough palm rubbing against the tip in a most delightful way.

I moaned into his mouth through the waves of growing pleasure.

"More," he exhaled, tearing his mouth away from mine. "I want to taste more of you."

Sliding down my body, he sucked the tip of my right breast into his mouth. All the pinching and rubbing had made my nipples hard, hot, and highly sensitive. The heat of his mouth and the smooth glide of his tongue now sent a new charge of desire through my body.

The building pressure between my legs throbbed with heat. I kicked off the blankets, spreading my legs open. The cool stroke of air against my heated folds felt more thrilling than soothing. My need flared higher.

I reached down, between my legs. My gesture served as another guiding sign to Wyck in his exploratory journey along my body. Before I could touch myself, he beat me to it.

His thick finger slipped inside me, probing, swirling, exploring in and out.

"Oh yes, Wyck…" I pressed my legs together, trapping his hand between them.

He rubbed his hand against my most sensitive spot, and I moaned, rocking my hips against him.

Pumping his finger in and out of me, he rested his head on my chest.

"I wonder if you taste as deliciously sweet as you smell, sugar," he said with a crooked smile and a glimmer of heat in his gold-yellow eyes.

I was not in a position to reply, moaning wildly from the onslaught of intense pleasure with his hand on me and with his finger inside me.

Thankfully, he didn't wait for a reply. Shifting smoothly down my body, he threw my legs over his shoulders and fitted his head between my thighs. The hot slide of his tongue between my folds made me buck my hips.

"Hmm," he hummed, his mouth hovering over my sensitive flesh. "More delicious than I could've ever imagined."

The puff of his breath felt simultaneously hot and cold, the need for him spiked higher. I fisted my hands into the bedding, pressing myself against his tongue as he lapped at me.

"How much do you want this, Nadia?" he asked between the brief nibbles and long sucks that drove me wild with lust. "How much do you want *me*?"

"More than anything, Wyck..." I panted. "More than anything in the world."

"As much as I want you, then," he said softly before sucking at me again.

One firm swirl of his tongue set it off. I grabbed on to his head with both hands, riding the most intense orgasm of my life. His mouth turned from relentless to gentle, tenderly guiding me down from the crest.

I let my hands fall away as the last tremors of bliss had subsided. My legs dropped to the mattress, my body heavy and warm.

"How are you feeling right now?" Wyck shifted back up to me.

His mouth glistened wet and enticing, and I couldn't resist placing a small kiss on his bottom lip.

"Happy," I replied honestly. "This very moment, I feel completely happy, Wyck." I threw my arms around his neck. Happiness inside the Dark Anomaly was nothing short of a miracle, and I had no one but Wyck to thank for that. "I want to make you feel happy, too."

"I'm already—" he started.

"You're in pain, aren't you?" I cut him off.

The slight furrowing of his brow, the barely contained lust in his eyes, the way he held his lower body angled away from me—all told me that I was right in my assumption. He was highly aroused and...hurting.

"Pain is a part of desire," he said calmly. "It always hurts when I'm hard. And I'm hard more often than I'm not."

I wondered if having two erections at once only made it twice as painful for him.

"Doesn't it get better when you come?" It was an easy solution in my mind.

"Usually," he replied evasively.

"Why not always?"

The idea of Wyck hurting in any way while he made me feel so blissfully happy pained me.

"My pleasure is not complete without yours."

His words from earlier made even more sense now because I also didn't feel completely satisfied without him feeling the same.

I slid my hand down and wrapped my fingers around one of his hard-ons. He tensed next to me, a shudder running through his body.

"Do you like this?" I asked softly, sliding my hand up and down along his slick length.

He closed his eyes, thrusting his hips into my hand. Yet his expression remained tortured.

"What is it, Wyck? What am I doing wrong?" I was doing the same thing I'd done last night. He'd seemed to fully enjoy himself, then. But had it been truly *fully*? "Does this feel good?"

"It does," he groaned, rolling onto his back. I shifted after him, not letting go unless he told me to. "The cock you're holding feels amazing beyond belief. The other one, however..." He groaned again, but this time it was filled with agony.

"The other one?" I moved aside the one I held in my hands, bringing the one under it into view. Thick and swollen to almost twice the size of the one in my fingers, his lower cock visibly pulsed with tension, a bluish tint mixed into the warm earthy tones of its skin. "It looks like it's ripping at the seams," I muttered with concern.

"It feels that way, too." Wyck heaved a long, shuddered breath. "Like it's about to explode, and not in a good way."

"What can I do?" I asked, gently stroking along his second length. It jerked under my fingers.

Wyck gritted his teeth.

"Was that better or worse?"

"Better," he croaked. "More. Please."

I circled both of them, one in each hand, even though my fingers on either hand were way too far from meeting the thumbs.

"Last night, you came from both. Was it not enough?" I asked, sliding my hands up and down simultaneously and making sure I was giving an equal attention to both of his huge members.

He stretched, spreading his arms, his expression relaxing somewhat.

"One at a time doesn't work as well," he explained, his eyes closed and his voice a bit dreamy. "When I come from one only, the other one gets harder. And hurts more."

"So for you, the orgasm from one penis is never a complete orgasm?" I said, not slowing down the glide of my hands on him. "I've heard that *errock* women have two birth canals."

"Two vaginas? Yes."

"Hm." I pursed my lips. It made sense for the males to have two penises, then. Combined, the double amount of semen must be intended by nature to increase the chances of conception.

In my case, however...

"There is something we could still try," I said tentatively, fully realizing the risk of potential mortification in what I was about to offer. "I've never done this before, to be completely honest."

With Wyck, I was willing to try anything. I trusted him fully and completely. I'd even risk the potential embarrassment because I believed he would not make me feel bad if my attempt failed.

"What are you talking about?" He opened his eyes and rose on his elbows.

"Do you trust me?" I asked, straddling his thighs.

He watched me closely for a moment as I increased the pressure of my left hand, the one that was wrapped around his lower erection. The tighter I squeezed, the thinner it got.

"I do, my sweet. I trust you." His voice was soft and breathy, his expression intrigued, and his eyes full of anticipation.

I blew out a breath, calming my nerves. I cared about this man, and I knew he cared about me. This was worth a try.

Kneading and rolling, I shaped his lower penis as thin as possible. I only managed to shorten it to about the length of a hotdog, though.

"Stay on your back," I instructed, rising on my knees and positioning myself over his pelvic area. "Ready?" I asked more for my benefit than his. Panting hard, the blankets twisted in his fists, Wyck had appeared very *ready* for a while now.

"Here we go," I said in an exaggeratedly cheery voice as my heart pounded and the skin on my arms prickled with nerves. Positioning each of his cocks against both of my openings, one in the front, the other—the tighter one—at the back, I slowly lowered my hips down.

Even though I'd made the lower penis so much thinner, I felt the invasion from the back more acutely. The deeper I took him, the more the sensation of being filled thoroughly and completely overwhelmed me.

"Oh God..." I swayed, sinking onto the top of his thighs and fully taking him inside me.

He sat up promptly, catching me in his arms.

"How... how is it possible?" he asked, his eyes open wide in wonder. "I thought human females only had one vagina."

I wished he wouldn't speak about it, at all. Even hearing the word "vagina" right now made me cringe inside. But he was learning, and I needed to teach. As far as human women went—or any women, really—Wyck still knew so little.

"The vagina is at the front." I wrapped my arms around his neck and whispered straight into his ear, hiding my blushing face. "And at the back... Well, the opening there is not used for procreation purposes, at all. Though, humans still use it during sex, sometimes."

"Do some human males also have two penises, then?" he asked innocently.

"No. If a woman wants two penises on Earth, she has to, you know, be with two men at once."

Leaning back, he regarded me for a moment. "Have you ever been with two men at once?"

"No!" I slapped him lightly on his shoulder. "I told you I haven't done any of this before..." Having this conversation, with both of my orifices filled, started to feel rather awkward. "You know what, let's just get on with this, okay? Before I completely freak out and bail on you."

"Don't bail," he pleaded with a soft kiss on my temple. "Tell me what to do."

"Lie back down."

Pushing against his shoulders, I made him sink back to the mattress. Hands pressed into his hard chest, I lifted my hips off his lap. His long moan of pure pleasure rewarded me for my efforts. The slick sliding of him inside me sent warm ripples through my body.

He rolled his head on the pillow.

"I want you to enjoy this, too." His voice sounded slightly delirious after another pump of my hips.

"You know what? I just might," I murmured as another wave of pleasurable shivers rolled though me.

The sensation of being filled to the limit, combined with the tingling pressure from being stretched so very tight, fanned my arousal brighter every time I moved over him. The fact that I had a complete control in this position gave me confidence. Gradually increasing the pace, I moved faster.

I slightly shifted my hips, finding the perfect angle and hitting just the right spot with each glide against him.

Pleasure rippled and ebbed, flooding my lower body with heat. Just a little bit longer... I could already sense the first tantalizing wisps of the approaching orgasm.

Wyck's long, pained groan reached me. I snapped my gaze to his.

He sank his teeth into his bottom lip, his expression strained, his thighs trembling under me.

"Come for me, Wyck," I whispered.

"Not without you," he gritted through his teeth.

Sitting up, he grabbed my hips. Bringing me closer, he made the contact between our bodies tighter. The increased pressure released my climax. The pleasure unfurled like a tightly wound spring, shooting through me in spasms of ecstasy.

I gripped his shoulders, the bumps of his ridges there digging into my palms. My gasps and moans mingled with his roars and grunts as he joined me, our bodies rocking together through our orgasms. Swept into the hurricane of pleasure, I clung to him. My own climax felt that much more intense because Wyck shared it with me.

He breathed hard, drawing in air in big, hungry gulps. His arms tight around me, he buried his face in the place between my neck and my shoulder.

I stroked his nape, tracing the dips and protrusions along his spine, and wishing I never had to let go. If there was a way for me to ever leave this place, I vowed then and there to beg Wyck to come with me. The world outside, my carefully planned life on Earth—none of that would be complete without him anymore.

"Nadia?" he asked softly, not lifting his head from my shoulder. "Is love a good or a bad thing to a woman?"

Love?

Hearing that word from him made my heart skip a beat. It then resumed its beating in loud thuds.

"Generally," I started tentatively, my fingers hovering over his back motionlessly. "Being loved is considered a good thing, both by men and women. A *very* good thing."

I leaned back a little, making him lift his head. I needed to see his eyes.

"Why do you ask, Wyck?"

His expression was serious when he met my gaze straight on.

"In that dancing movie we watched together," he said. "When the man told his woman he loved her at the end, she cried."

"Those were happy tears." I smiled, stroking the side of his face. "After everything the two of them had been through together, she was so happy to hear those words from him, the feeling overwhelmed her to the point of tears."

He seemed to mull my words over for a moment.

"The man didn't cry, though, when she said it to him."

"He probably was already expecting her to say it back and had been better prepared?" I gave him a small shrug. "Why are you asking?"

"It's just...confusing." He rubbed his chest then pulled me into a firm hug. "All of this. The emotions..."

There was so much in what he and I shared. The wide array of feelings I held for Wyck had confused me too, at times. Lately, however, it all appeared to make more sense—my own emotions merged into something strong and bright for him, giving me some clarity.

"You'll sort it all out, darling." I gently stroked his cheek. "With time."

And time was all we had in here, on the Dark Anomaly.

Chapter 19

THE CRASHING NOISE of the metal slab blocking the entrance to the ship made me jump in my seat inside our cabin. It wasn't Wyck returning. He had enough strength to roll the slab aside quietly.

Everything inside me immediately froze with dread. My fingers tightened on the frame of the tablet I held in my hands, and I felt momentarily paralyzed with fear.

Wyck had gone out right after breakfast that morning. In addition to taking care of me, he had other tasks to do on the Dark Anomaly, like everyone else on the crew.

It'd been a week since we moved to the new place—a blissfully uneventful week. We'd spent it talking, making love, reading, and watching movies together—getting to know each other in every way.

Together, we'd also managed to move a camera outside and mounted it over the entrance. However, I was still trying to figure out how to transfer the feed to a tablet in the cabin. For now, all footage was transmitted to the control panel in the main area.

Today would be the time of my next "session" in the mess hall had the captain not cancelled the "entertainment." I knew the crew had been severely upset by the cancellation. Their mutiny had more or less been suppressed by now. But what if the crew had managed to find me here, after all?

Wyck had taken Lesh along, but he left his gun with me, for my protection.

It appeared I might have to use it.

The sound of someone moving around in the common area of the ship filtered through the wall. The person must be smaller than

Wyck, their footfalls sounded lighter. That didn't mean much, everyone here was smaller than Wyck. They might still be able to cause a lot of harm to me if they found me here.

Setting the tablet aside, I got up from the couch as noiselessly as I could. Drawing the gun out of its holster loosely draped over my shoulder, I pointed it at the door panel.

Chances were the intruder would leave soon. No one had discovered the cabins so far. Most likely, all I had to do was remain quiet and wait for them to go.

The footsteps moved closer, then stopped. It appeared the person now stood right at the door, on the other side of the wall.

I held my breath, half-expecting the dreadfully familiar spray of sparks from a cutting tool to shoot through the wall any minute. Raising my gun higher, I tightened my grip on it, ready to fire. I was not going to let them catch me off guard. Nocc was not going to touch me ever again.

Instead of the sparks, the beeping noise of the lock screen came. No one could open the doors, not even Wyck. The lock had been programmed with my and Val's palm prints only. The cabin was our private area.

The door slid open, revealing a woman standing behind it. To my disappointment, it wasn't Val, though she looked eerily familiar. Shock flashed on her face when she saw me. She leaped back, training her own gun at me.

"Svetlana? Svetlana Kostyk?" I mumbled, lowering my weapon.

She was exactly the same as in the pictures taken of her over fifty years ago—completely unchanged by time. Goosebumps rushed down my arms.

"You?" She stepped inside, quickly tucking her gun back into the holster at her belt. "So, that's where he's been hiding you?"

"You know of me?" I gaped at her, flabbergasted.

With a wide smile, she came up to me promptly and unexpectedly enclosed me in a hug.

"I can't believe I've found you," she muttered, holding me close, as if I were her long-lost relative. "I can't believe you crashed here."

She leaned back, holding me by my shoulders, and gave me a once-over, friendly excitement on her face.

I stared at her, too. Upon closer look, there actually were many differences between the woman who now stood in front of me and the official pictures of Svetlana Kostyk that I'd seen back on Earth.

Just like in the pictures, she had her long, wavy, chestnut hair pulled back into a ponytail. However, it wasn't the sleek, tight, high ponytail in her official portrait. Now, it was low and loose, with tendrils of fly-away hair framing her lovely face.

Instead of the white uniform suit, she was dressed in a knee-length, flowery tunic with long sleeves and a pair of black pants.

The smile on her face smoothed out the severe wrinkle of focus and concentration she had on her brow in all the pictures I'd seen back on Earth.

"I did not expect to see another human here any time soon!" she gushed in a very girly way. Then, the excitement on her face dimmed. "I mean I'm sorry about the accident that brought you here."

"It was no accident." I shook my head. "The expedition was planned."

"It was, wasn't it?" She nodded slowly, not appearing surprised by my statement. "I wondered about that."

"Why?"

"I've analyzed all available data of the past crashes. The one from your ship didn't follow the usual pattern. At least not until the very end."

"That's when we lost control." I sighed.

"So I thought."

"Listen..." I took a nervous look at the door she'd left open. The sight of the gaping entrance filled me with anxiety. "We should lock it. And block the entrance to the ship, too."

She followed my gaze then nodded with understanding. "Right."

Together, we managed to prop the metal block against the entrance to the ship again. Then, Svetlana lifted the opaque cover of the electronic lock from the floor by my cabin.

"Did you break it?" I stared at it in alarm. Broken things scared me, I had no clue how to fix them. In this place, a broken lock was more than an inconvenience, it could be a matter of life and death.

"I've disabled it. Temporarily." She deftly adjusted something inside the lock panel then fixed the cover back in place. To my relief, the soft glow immediately returned to the screen. "I've finally figured out how to reprogram palm readers, but not this one. The technology has sure advanced. Is it programmed with your handprint?"

"Mine and another woman's who used to live here with me."

She tilted her head, regarding me with interest. "Where did she go?"

"Disappeared. Shortly after our landing here."

She stared at me for a bit longer. "You need to tell me everything."

"WHAT'S YOUR NAME?" Svetlana asked, sitting on one end of the couch in our cabin.

I took two cups of freshly brewed coffee out of the food station compartment. "Nadia."

"Are you Russian?" she asked, switching from English to Russian.

"My parents were," I kept speaking Universal.

I hadn't spoken the language of my parents since they'd passed away. Generally, when talking about work, using Universal was so much easier for me. It didn't matter what language either of us spoke anyway, since we both had our translator implants.

I handed her the cup, and her dark-brown eyes lit up with delight.

"Mmm." Through her nose, she drew in some of the steam that was rising from the cup. "Coffee... How I missed you!" She took a small sip then closed her eyes, a blissful expression spreading across her face. "This must be the most amazing invention of the past fifty years—the food replicator."

"Um..." I rubbed the back of my neck, trying to recall all technological advancements of the past half century. "There have been quite a few more."

"I'm sure there have." With a sigh, she swept the cabin with her gaze. "How long did it take you to get here?"

"Two months. Approximately."

"Fast. It took my team nearly a year." She took another sip of her coffee.

I tried to imagine what it would feel like for Svetlana to have the world as she knew it gone.

"Did you leave a family behind?" I asked softly. "Friends?"

"Not many." She heaved a sigh. "Colleagues, mostly. I suppose all of them would be gone by now. Their work surely contributed to the progress of the past fifty years." She glanced up at me. "That was what mattered most to many of my team—to leave our mark on the scientific world."

Talking with this woman, who was born many decades before me yet looked just a few years older, made me feel like time travel was possible. Though, it remained unclear who exactly had time travelled in our case. Had Svetlana moved ahead into the future? Or had I slid back into the past.

Probably both. Time hung suspended inside the Dark Anomaly, allowing for the meeting of the future and the past.

I took a seat on the opposite end of the couch.

"Are you with the Earth Space Coalition, too?" she asked, regarding my suit with interest.

The colorful patches of sponsor logos shimmered with a metallic sheen all over my arms, legs, and torso. Compared to the old plain-white Coalition uniforms, my outfit was more decorated than a Nascar driver's racing suit.

"No." I fingered one of the patches that had been molded into the fabric on my sleeve. "After your disappearance, the Coalition stopped their exploration of this part of the Galaxy. All countries' governments refused to finance it. Our expedition was sponsored and outfitted by the private sector."

She frowned. "Did it have any scientific purpose at all?"

"Mostly commercial," I admitted.

"Then you are..."

"*Not* a scientist." I took a long drink of my coffee. It had cooled off a bit by now, warm enough without scalding. I inhaled the pleasant aroma, savoring it. "My mission was to produce a movie. Except that I haven't filmed much while being here," I huffed a short laugh.

There were no regrets in me for not collecting any footage at all other than whatever had been recorded automatically by the on-board cameras of the ship. Most of what I'd seen here so far would be horror-movie worthy. I wouldn't wish to relive any of it other than the moments with Wyck, and those were too private for others to see.

"A movie?" She gazed at me, confused. "For entertainment?"

"A documentary, of sorts." More like a reality TV of the past, if I were to be entirely honest with myself. "Something of commercial value for our sponsors."

"And how were you supposed to get the movie to them?" She tilted her head. "You're aware that no signal travels past the force field of the Anomaly?"

I inhaled deeply.

"The plan was for us to leave here."

"I see." She pressed her lips into a slim line.

"Our landing was harder than expected," I hurried to explain. "Some of the equipment might've gotten damaged. I don't have the necessary knowledge to accurately assess the damage. However, I believe the escape capsule is salvageable."

"Is it the one with the hole cut in the door?"

"Right." I nodded. "Nocc did that..."

Svetlana sat quiet for a moment, gazing at me with compassion.

"Vrateus told me about the murders of your crew. I'm really sorry about your friends and colleagues." She frowned again. "What else did Nocc do?"

"Nothing good," I said, my reply clipped.

She waited for a second or two, but I didn't elaborate. Recounting the details of that day felt like it would release too much hurt at once. I wasn't sure I could deal with all that pain yet.

She nodded somberly, as if she understood even without me saying anything.

"I'm really sorry about all of it, Nadia." Her chest rose with a sigh. "Vrateus didn't tell me about you right away. He means well and strives to do the right thing, but his understanding of what's *right* is still a bit skewed. He thought he was protecting me by keeping your arrival a secret from me. On your landing day, he didn't tell me that your ship had a crew on board or that it came from Earth. I had no idea there was another woman on the Anomaly until I saw you with Wyck."

"When?" I had no memory of ever seeing her until today.

"A week ago. You seemed to be asleep or unconscious. Wyck took you away before I could stop him."

"That must've happened when the newest crash destroyed the glass room where I'd been kept," I explained. "I passed out from lack of oxygen."

"I made Vrateus tell me everything, right then and there. He didn't know where Wyck took you, but he assured me you were safe. I've been searching for you ever since." She gave me a long look. "Are you okay, Nadia? Have you been hurt? Is there anything I can do?"

Nothing about this place had been okay. However, Wyck had managed to keep the worst of it away from me.

"I'm fine," I said. "I haven't been hurt. Thanks to Wyck."

"Wyck?" A note of surprise rang in her voice. "He's been difficult for me to figure out. However, as a protector, he'd be my first choice over the rest. Not that the rest are any good at all. I believe Wyck severely dislikes me, though. Has he been treating you well?"

"Yes." I quickly lowered my gaze to the coffee cup in my hands, hoping she wouldn't notice the blush that heated my cheeks. "Wyck has been very nice to me," I mumbled, before raising my eyes back to hers. "He's a good man. Why do you think he doesn't like you?"

"He has good reason to dislike me. I killed one of his kind," she said simply. "I shot an *errock*—Crux."

"You did?" I stared at her in shock.

"It was self-defence, but I'm afraid that's not how Wyck sees it."

"Crux was the closest Wyck had to a father growing up," I said softly.

Her slim dark eyebrows knotted into a deep frown. "I didn't know that."

"From what I've learned, Crux sucked at parenting," I pointed out.

"That doesn't surprise me. The Dark Anomaly is not a nice place. It's filled with brutal people. The fact that Wyck has managed to grow into a 'good man,' as you say, is a miracle."

It was a miracle. If nurture were a hundred percent responsible for the kind of a person he'd become, he wouldn't be what he was. From what I'd heard, Wyck's biological father hadn't been much different than Crux. I wondered if everything that was good and wholesome in Wyck had come from his mother. He didn't talk about her, and I believed it might be because he didn't remember much of her and didn't want to repeat what the others had told him about her.

"It definitely is not the best place to grow up," I agreed then added tentatively, "Would you consider leaving here?"

She nearly spilled her coffee at the question.

"Consider?" she laughed. "I'd die for a chance to get off the Dark Anomaly. In fact, if it wasn't for Vrateus, I would've died already, trying to leave."

"The captain wouldn't let you?"

"He saved my life by stopping me. The force field that had brought all of us here would've crushed me against the hull of a ship along the edge of the Anomaly disk."

I set my empty mug on the table and leaned a little closer toward her. "What if there was a way to fix the capsule? Some of the best minds of our century have been involved in the planning of this expedition. They believed the departure from here *was* possible."

"No one," she lifted an eyebrow, leaning closer to me, too. "No one in the Universe knows the Dark Anomaly better than I do now. And, I'll tell you that there is no sure way to leave it. Any attempt would carry some risk, to an extent even I cannot predict."

Hope was evaporating from my heart with her every word.

"Yet I would still try," she added unexpectedly.

"You would? Even knowing you'd be risking your life?"

She nodded with an easy smile.

"There is little I wouldn't do to solve the mystery of the Dark Anomaly. I've dedicated my life to this research. I've risked it before, and I'd do it again in a heartbeat if the results gave humanity answers to the many questions I have." She paused, taking a long breath in. "However, I would *not* risk Vrateus's life for any of that."

"Vrateus? The captain?" I asked, wondering what exactly she meant by that.

The warm expression lingering on her face explained it all—Svetlana loved Vrateus. She hadn't become "the captain's woman" out of the need to survive. She truly cared for him, so much that she was prepared to spend the rest of her life in the place she despised—because of him.

"If there is the slightest possibility of harm coming to Vrateus, I'd rather spend the rest of my life here than search for a way out," she confirmed my assumption. "You see, I love him and would never leave without him. He loves me, too, and he trusts me enough to follow me anywhere I choose to go. It places an enormous responsibility on me. I'm in charge of his safety in this case, and I can't bear the thought of hurting him in any way."

"So, you'd stay here, just because leaving may carry some risk? Not to you, but to him?"

"Exactly."

I leaned back against the couch, trying to make sense of it. Svetlana was sacrificing her chance at a better life because of a risk to another person? She appeared to have made that choice all by herself. Vrateus hadn't coerced her.

Then, my thoughts drifted to Wyck. At this point, I wouldn't want to leave him behind, either. Would I choose to stay in this hell forever because of that, though?

Svetlana straightened in her seat.

"Well, that doesn't mean I don't want to explore any new opportunities presented by the technology of your ship and its equipment. All of it is new and exciting. I do want to get that capsule fixed, even if just to run an unmanned test. Would you like to help?"

"Of course. I'll do my best. 'My best' isn't much, though, I have to warn you. Val would've been much better help here than me. She was... She *is* a pilot."

Is or *was*? That was the scary question.

"Val? Is it short for Valya? The full name—Valentina?"

"Yes. It's the name of the woman who disappeared."

"So far, without a trace," Svetlana said slowly, her expression contemplative.

I didn't want to think about what the phrase "without a trace" could mean in a place with a recent history of cannibalism.

"Yeah. Wyck has searched for her, but so far without any luck."

"I'll talk to Vrateus about her. He knows the habitable sector much better than I do. He knows his crew, too. He might be able to figure out what has happened to her."

She released a breath and pushed up to her feet.

"I should go. Vrateus dropped me off at the gardens, to work with Malahki. He'd freak out if he came to pick me up and didn't find me there. Would you mind if I told him I've found you? I hate keeping secrets from him, even though he kept you a secret from me. I need to teach him by setting a good example. I want to be completely honest with him."

"I suppose there wouldn't be any harm in him knowing—"

The slamming noise of the entrance block crashing to the ground made my words stick in my throat. Svetlana's face turned as pale as a bedsheet. She yanked her gun out of its holster, spinning to face the closed door to the cabin.

Panic spiked high inside me, and I fumbled for my gun, too.

"Nadia!" Wyck's voice bellowed from the main room.

"It's Wyck!" I rushed to the door of the cabin.

Svetlana touched my shoulder in a gesture of caution.

"Be careful. You don't know who might be with him."

Wyck pushing the slab in was unusual. Normally, he'd roll it away, making little noise.

"Nadia! Are you there?" He slammed a hand into the panelling outside the cabin. The worry reverberating in his tone made my heart melt.

"He can smell you," I said, moving to the door past Svetlana. "And he's concerned for me."

Svetlana stepped aside and got into a position, aiming her gun at the entrance. I placed my right hand on the screen to unlock it, holding the gun in my left hand, just in case.

The door slid open, and Wyck barged in.

"You okay?" he exhaled, grabbing me in a one-armed hug, his other hand balled into a fist, ready to strike. His roaming gaze fell on Svetlana, sliding to the gun she had trained on him. "What is *she* doing here?"

Chain rattling, Lesh leaped into the cabin, too, making Svetlana stagger out of his way. I pressed my hand to the screen of the lock again, sliding the door closed—leaving it open even for a few seconds unsettled me.

"Why is she here?" Wyck glowered at Svetlana, drawing me closer to his side.

She lowered her gun.

"I mean no harm to you or Nadia."

"That remains to be seen," he snapped reproachfully.

I jumped to her defence, "Svetlana learned about me and searched for me. She wanted to meet me. We're from the same planet, Wyck. The only women here. We have a lot in common."

"Your own kind can betray you, too," he said gloomily.

My heart pinched with compassion. Family loyalty meant so much to Wyck. Yet I'd seen the *errocks* turn against him, because of me.

"I didn't come to betray, to fight, or to argue." Svetlana holstered her gun. Only then did Wyck unfold his fists. "I wanted to make sure Nadia was well and alive."

"Keeping her well and alive is my job, not yours." He glanced my way. "She is safe with me."

Svetlana followed his eyes, carefully regarding both of us for a moment or two.

"I'm glad to hear that. Wyck..." She turned to face him fully. "I know you don't like me much—"

"Don't like?" he scoffed. "I *hate* you." He put so much emphasis on that one word, it made me wonder if he did it as much for his own benefit as for hers. "Had I done the right thing as I was supposed to, you would've been long dead."

"Wyck..." I took one of his large hands in mine. His body ridged with tension so strong it appeared to bleed into the air and vibrate between the three of us.

"Do you truly believe that killing me is the right thing to do?" Svetlana challenged him.

"That's what the honor demands from me."

"What honor would there be in murdering a woman who stood up for herself against her attacker? You know that the only reason Crux didn't kill me first that day was because he wanted to use my life as a bargaining chip against Vrateus."

"It doesn't matter—"

"But it does. It makes all the difference, and you know it. You know there is a dissonance between what you've been taught and the way you really feel. That's the reason why I'm still alive, why Vrateus believed that Nadia would be safe with you, and that's why she *is* safe. Anyone else from your 'family' would've done to her the same horrible things that Crux wanted to do to me. Wouldn't they?"

His chest heaving, Wyck flexed his arm tighter around my shoulders and remained silent.

Svetlana stepped closer and carefully placed her hand on his forearm.

"You're not like them," she said softly. "And that's *not* a bad thing, Wyck."

WE SAID GOODBYE TO Svetlana at the exit to the main corridor.

She glanced at the heavy slab that Wyck and I used to block the opening in the wall. The floor panels by the entrance had shattered and cracked from the impact of the slab when Wyck had shoved it forcefully on his way in.

"This could be done better," Svetlana muttered. "We should make a sliding door here, with a proper lock or two."

"How long would that take?" Wyck asked. His tone remained guarded when speaking to her. However, the open hostility had disappeared from his voice and his glare.

"It depends if Vrateus finds some time to help us. He's been busy searching for a new room for us."

"You're moving?"

She nodded. "We have to. Vrateus is getting increasingly worried that our room may be destroyed with another ship crashing on the Dark Anomaly. It's always just a matter of time. But since the latest crash, he fears time is running out."

I worried my lip with my teeth, moving my gaze from Wyck to Svetlana then back again. I liked them both, but would inviting her to live under the same roof be asking for trouble?

"You can move here if you want," I suggested after a little consideration. "This way, we can fix the door, the capsule, and whatever else needs to be fixed here much quicker."

"Here?" Svetlana glanced around the main area of the ship.

"*Where* exactly?" Wyck frowned.

"There is another cabin right next to ours."

"There is?" Both of them turned to stare at the wall with the door to our cabin. Another narrow slit ran along it, a short distance to the right.

"That's the one where the male part of our crew used to live," I explained. "Their cabin is even bigger than the one where Wyck and I are because it was made to house four people instead of two. I can't open their door, the panel is not programmed for my palm print, but since you know how to disable them…" I turned to Svetlana.

"This might work," she muttered under her breath, taking a closer look at the wall and the panel.

"It has its own bathroom and a food station. If we make a proper main door, the whole ship would be safer, too." I glanced up at Wyck, feeling his worry and suspicion. "It may be better for the four of us to stick together. Don't you think?"

"Vrateus living here would give away your location to the rest of the crew," Wyck pointed out. "There is already a risk of someone tracking me to this place, no matter how careful I am. With two—" He glanced at Svetlana. "With *three* people coming and going as they please, someone would figure it out quickly."

"They would," Svetlana agreed. "Two women being in the same place will make this an appealing target for everyone."

"We may need to fortify it even better, then. Maybe all of us could limit our trips outside? This ship is entirely self-contained. We can make enough food and water to sustain all of us for a while, even if we lose access to the food supply of the Dark Anomaly for any reason."

"And, there is coffee." Svetlana smiled with a wink at me.

"Exactly." I grinned back. I really could use a friend in this place. The idea of her and the captain moving in appealed to me more and more.

"I'll talk to Vrateus," she assured me then turned to face Wyck. "Trust me we don't want to jeopardize Nadia's safety, but it's just a matter of time until the crew finds out about her whereabouts. In which case, it's best to be prepared. Together, we'll be stronger."

Chapter 20

"I HAVE SOMETHING FOR you." Svetlana hopped off her seat at the table and rushed to the men's cabin, which was now her and Vrateus's room.

Vrateus and Svetlana had officially moved in last night, less than a week after she'd first found me here.

After Svetlana had left that day, Wyck and I talked for a while about the four of us living on the ship. His main concern was safety. Though, he agreed that he would feel better having someone with me while he was gone, even if the someone would be Svetlana.

She had her tasks on the Dark Anomaly, but Vrateus had been cutting them down lately, reducing the amount of time she spent outside of their room. The captain was obviously concerned about the unstable situation with his rebellious crew.

"Are you sure you'll be okay sharing the ship with more people?" I'd asked Wyck. "It's not that much space around here."

He'd only laughed at that. "Sugar, I've had nothing but a bunk bed and a curtain to my name, my entire life. And even that I had to share with one pretty large *mahdi*. Despite my size, I don't need that much space to be comfortable."

During their move, Wyck had been civil to Svetlana and even carried a few things from their old room over to our ship for her when Vrateus happened to be busy elsewhere. I still sensed some tension on Wyck's part toward her, though to my relief, there was no obvious resentment in his behaviour.

I watched him shoot a brief glance her way as she left the table now. He then calmly returned to eating his breakfast—*vasai* eggs and dark bread rolls Svetlana had brought from the kitchen.

Vrateus laid his food utensil down the moment Svetlana moved away, his eyes focused on the door behind which she'd disappeared.

Overall, the captain had exchanged only a handful of sentences with me since the move. He always appeared to be lost in thought, an expression of severe concentration on his face. I could almost hear the wheels spinning in his head, whirring and humming as daily plans constantly rolled through his mind. Running the life of hundreds of people on the Dark Anomaly couldn't be easy. As focused as he seemed to be on that, though, he also appeared to be aware of Svetlana's whereabouts at all times.

"Here." She came back into the room, carrying a large bejewelled pot.

It looked like a kettle, with four ornately curved spouts spread out equally around it. Made from gold-tone metal, it was decorated with swirls of green and blue enamel, the intricate designs inlaid with shimmering crystals.

"A housewarming gift, kind of." She smiled setting the kettle on the table in front of me. "Thank you for having us here."

"Wow, thank you. It looks so pretty." I trailed my finger along the relief of the design on its surface. "What is it?"

"According to an article I found, it's a family tea pot. I'm sure you could use it for coffee, too. It works like this."

She lifted the kettle by its ornate handle then placed all of our mugs under it, on the table. Rotating each of the four spouts to point down, she positioned the kettle so that each spout ended up directly over one of the cups.

"See? You can pour a cup of coffee for all of us at the same time, and it all comes from the same source. It eliminates a chance of poisoning each other," she added abruptly.

"Poisoning?" I asked, confused.

She winced and scratched her ear.

"Sorry, that last part has absolutely nothing to do with the four of us. I'm not even sure why I said it. Vrateus has been poisoned once, but it has nothing to do with this gift, of course." She awkwardly thrust the kettle to me. "Anyway. I'm not good at this social...um, friends and family stuff. Vrateus found this pot in one of the storage rooms a while back. I thought about you and the coffee as I was packing things for the move. I looked it up. It comes from the planet Hexol, the *errocks'* world. It seemed a fitting gift..."

She cast a quick glance at Wyck, who stared at the pot in my arms with a new interest.

"It belonged to the Roohala dynasty, which ruled around the same time your ship crashed here," Svetlana said to him.

"It came from my planet?" He took the kettle from me, turning it in his hands. "An *errock* made this?"

"Probably more than one *errock*." Svetlana stepped closer. "After the metal had been forged and shaped, a more delicate hand would've been required to paint all these designs, you see?" She leaned over his shoulder, tracing the delicate curve of one of the lines with her fingers. "And to lay these tiny crystals, too. Your nation has always excelled at producing items that require high precision and craftmanship."

"All of this was made by hand?" Wyck asked, continuing to inspect the ornate surface of the piece.

"Most of it. The Roohala dynasty era marks a unique time in Hexol's history when space travel on some parts of the planet happened alongside a relatively simple lifestyle of manual labor and low-technology in the others. I can give you the slate with the article I read about it," she offered. "It's written in Universal. Can you read in that language?"

"Yes, I can." Wyck met her gaze.

I simply loved the confidence and the pride in his voice when he said that. I felt so proud of him, too.

Vrateus lifted one of his thick eyebrows.

"Really? You can read Universal?" he asked. "A while back, Crux told me not to give you any written instructions. He said it wasn't possible to teach you anything, including reading."

Wyck's jaw tightened. Blood rushed hot to my face with a stab of indignation for him through my heart.

"Crux just didn't want to bother with teaching Wyck anything good or useful," I snapped. "Wyck is an incredibly capable student. He is smart and quick, with an amazing memory and perseverance. He works hard. And he *can* read."

The captain stared at me, his eyebrow arched even higher. My passionate defence of Wyck must've amused him, especially since no one was actually attacking Wyck at the moment. I had jumped into a fight that wasn't there, punching the air instead of an opponent.

"Looks like I got you a good defender," Vrateus said with a spark of humour in his orange cat-eyes.

"Yes. He is good at defending too," I said earnestly.

"I was talking to Wyck, this time." The captain's firm lips twitched, his severe expression melting into a smile. "You're *his* defender. A very passionate one, too."

"Oh..." I shifted in my seat.

A ramble of laughter suddenly erupted next to me. I spun in my chair to find Wyck laughing heartily. Svetlana's soft chuckle joined the roaring sound. She leaned over Vrateus's shoulder, hugging him from behind.

"Come here, my vicious defender." Wyck dragged me out of my chair and into his lap. "Thank you for standing up for me, sugar." He said with a warm kiss on my lips.

The merry mood at the table caught on like a wild fire. I let out a burst of happy laughter, too, hugging Wyck's neck.

"You're worth fighting for, darling."

He leaned back, catching my gaze. "I've never heard you laugh before. And now I never want to stop hearing the sound of it."

Chapter 21

APPARENTLY, A HUMAN being could get used to anything, even life on the Dark Anomaly. Or at least, I could. It helped that the four of us had managed to create a pretty decent life for ourselves here.

After a week of living with Wyck, Vrateus, and Svetlana on the ship, we all fell into a routine.

The thick slab of metal that blocked the entrance had been mounted on tracks and fitted with several locks. This way, it made for a sturdy, secure sliding door. Vrateus also made sure to bring on board all tools that could be used to cut through it, making our living here that much safer.

Vrateus, Wyck, and Lesh left the ship right after breakfast. By now, Wyck had become not just the head of the captain's guard, he was also the only *errock* guard Vrateus fully trusted. Together, they did what needed to be done to keep the Dark Anomaly running and all of us inside it alive.

Both men were firmly against Svetlana and me going out on our own, even if the two of us were armed and went together. They were convinced that two women would present a doubly attractive target for the crew—too tempting not to attack.

With Wyck and Lesh for escort, Svetlana would leave for the kitchen in the afternoon, to cook enough food for the crew to last for the next twenty-four hours. I stayed behind with not much to do.

I ended up rearranging the remaining cameras in the living area. Then, I set them up to record at certain times of the day. Taking videos of some of our mealtimes or conversations felt like making a family movie. I didn't do it for sponsors or for anyone else out there. I simply had more happy moments in my life that I wished to keep a record of.

Before their move, Svetlana also used to work in the gardens in the mornings, helping Malahki, the *damirian* gardener. However, Vrateus had cancelled that task. He said Malahki had informed him that her help was no longer necessary, and I knew the captain was relieved she now spent most of her time securely locked on the ship with me.

I liked having Svetlana to keep me company. I waited with excitement for Wyck and Vrateus to come home in the evening. All four of us often had dinner together.

There was a feeling of normalcy in this routine. Sometimes, I had to remind myself that nothing about this situation was normal. I wasn't spending my time behind the closed doors because I liked it that way. I kept hiding from what awaited me outside if I stuck my head out.

Every night after dinner, all of us had been working on the escape capsule. We had managed to patch up the door to our satisfaction. However, Svetlana had some upsetting news after reviewing the data of the capsule's system.

"This one is more sophisticated than the one on my suit was," she muttered under her breath, scrolling through pages and pages of data on the console inside the capsule. "This system measures the fluctuations of the gravity field around the Dark Anomaly. It calculated that the engines didn't have enough power to break free from it after take-off. So, it didn't even launch."

"Is that what the error message meant?"

Not enough power...

It'd flashed on the screen as I desperately tried to escape Nocc's clutches the day of our arrival.

Svetlana rested her hand on my shoulder. "The capsule's system saved your life, Nadia. If it took off, you would've crashed and possibly died."

"So, the escape capsule can never be our *escape*?"

"I'm afraid not."

My heart dropped as our last hope disappeared. Was I destined to spend my life here, on the Dark Anomaly? The thought chilled me with dread. My carefully planned future had disappeared into the dark fog of fear and uncertainty.

Wyck came up silently and enclosed me in a tight embrace.

I cried into his chest, and he made sweet love to me that night. He masterfully used everything he'd learned about my body. Each tender touch of his soothed the pain a little, as if he tried to prove that not everything about being stranded on the Dark Anomaly was horrible.

In that, he was right. Wyck coming into my life had turned out to be the best thing that had ever happened to me. He was my safe place, the one bright ray of light that pierced through the dark, scary gloom of the future.

As calm as our life on the ship had been in the past week, the rest of the Dark Anomaly was far from stable. From the brief conversations between Vrateus and Wyck, I'd gathered that the situation outside of our sanctuary was heating up.

Although the captain had been able to control the outbreaks of mutiny so far, the crew hadn't forgotten or forgiven my sudden disappearance, and they blamed Wyck for it. Their hostility had spread to include the captain and Svetlana, too.

Living in the confinement of the ship might not be the best. However, there was no safer place for me anywhere else. The times I'd been forced to spend with the crew were still giving me nightmares. For now, I was happy to remain behind locked doors.

"WELL, I BETTER GO." Svetlana took the last long drink of her tea after we'd finished lunch. "Are you sure you're okay doing the dishes?"

"Yes." I got up to take our empty lunch plates over to the cleaning unit. "It's not like I have much else to do around here."

"I'll try to finish early in the kitchen today." She followed me, carrying her mug to the unit. "You and I can cook something fun for dinner tonight. The crew sure loves their stew. Their tastes don't leave me much room for experimenting."

"I'd love that. Let's do a dessert, too. I've been craving a cake—a simple vanilla cake. Can we come up with something like that? Even if it ends up looking tar-black?"

"I guarantee it will turn out looking black." She laughed. "The bark flour is black, remember?"

She smoothed the long skirt of the red-and-gray dress she wore over a pair of pants. I'd noticed she always wore several layers of clothing when leaving the ship. The captain kept the air temperature mildly warm on the Dark Anomaly for the comfort of the majority of the species here. Svetlana didn't dress in layers to keep warm, I suspected, but to add any extra barrier in case of an attack.

I liked the colorful dresses she wore but decided to stick with my suit for the time being—its material was nearly impossible to tear. My clothes' most important value to me was in how difficult they'd be to rip off me—a sad and scary fact.

Svetlana walked over to the main control panel in the front of the ship. She turned on the screen with the feed from the camera mounted in the corridor over the entrance to our ship.

"Is Wyck there?" I asked.

"Nope. Not yet."

It was unusual for Wyck to be late for picking up Svetlana to escort her to the kitchen each afternoon. Vrateus maintained a strict schedule, running our daily routine like clockwork. Wyck barely had time to give me a long kiss before rushing off when picking her up every day.

"Why would he be late?"

I tried not to worry. Things happened; people got delayed. Except that the things that happened in this place were never good.

"And there he is!" Svetlana pointed at the screen then hurried to the door. "Since he's late, make your kiss quick this time," she said with a wink as she passed me.

A blush warmed my cheeks. When we were alone, Wyck never held back on his displays of affection. He'd quickly grown comfortable with having Vrateus and Svetlana around, too, hugging and kissing me in their presence whenever he felt like it. Not that I fought him on that. The closer to him I was, the happier I felt.

Svetlana threw the locks open. I slid the heavy door aside, eager to see his handsome face again.

A muscular arm with the familiar bony gray ridge along it quickly reached in from the corridor. It hooked around Svetlana's neck and roughly yanked her out.

"Wyck?" I frowned, leaning out of the door. "What are you d—"

The question stuck in my throat as I came face to face with Nocc. He was wearing Wyck's leather holster and was holding Wyck's gun as he dragged Svetlana out and into the corridor.

She managed to twist out of his grip, and he lunged for her. She gritted her teeth, reaching for the gun at her hip. "Run, Nadia!"

"Get that one, Krakhil," Nocc barked out the order, tipping his head my way.

A huge *dimo* stomped around them, heading in my direction.

I leaped back into the ship with a squeak of terror and quickly rolled the door shut. With trembling fingers, I threw a lock on before my legs gave out and I slid down to the floor. My knees shook, and my heart beat so hard, I felt it all the way up in my throat.

The old, sickening fear washed over me, making it hard to breathe or think. Panic urged me to run and hide, like I had done all this time. Hiding and waiting it out had always been the wisest choice for me. The safest one.

Except that Svetlana was getting murdered out there while I sat in here.

Not even trying to get up, I scurried on all fours to the holster with the gun that Vrateus had brought specifically for me. He'd showed me how to use it, and it'd been hanging on the back of my chair at our dining table, ever since. I hadn't used it, not even once. Until now, I'd been relying on everyone else to keep me safe.

Now, it was my turn to help someone. Svetlana needed me. And Wyck...

I tried not to think about what could've happened to him and how Nocc had come into the possession of Wyck's things. Grabbing my gun, I finally scrambled to my feet.

There were two choices before me now—to stay here and hide or to open that door. And there was only one choice I could live with without being ashamed of myself for the rest of my life.

Heaving a bracing breath, I opened the door.

Nocc and Krakhil had been joined by at least two dozen more of the crew members, now. Even more of them were rushing down the corridor, like a rolling wave of menace.

To my surprise and relief, Svetlana was far from defeated.

Her back to the wall, she fired her gun at whoever came the closest, a pile of dead bodies forming on the floor around her. In the space constraints of the corridor, only a few of the males could advance on her at once. It limited the number of her immediate attackers, allowing her to singlehandedly hold defence.

Holding Wyck's gun in his hand, Nocc stood back. Hiding behind the others from Svetlana's fire, he wouldn't shoot at her, possibly hoping to capture her alive or maybe having difficulty getting a clear shot in the scuffle.

"You! Get here!" Enkail, another *dimo*, launched for me, shoving others out of his way. His elbow knocked the gun out of Nocc's hand, but the *dimo* didn't seem to notice it.

Raising my gun in my shaking hand, I pressed the rounded trigger in the handle, just like Vrateus had showed me. A blast of blueish light shot out, scorching a black line across Enkail's armoured shoulder.

"You..." he gritted through his teeth, stomping inside the ship after me.

The laser ray hadn't caused him much harm.

"Press and hold, Nadia!" Svetlana's voice rang high from the corridor. "Press and hold to burn through his armor!"

"Good advice," Enkail smirked, stalking my way. "Not that it'll help you."

I shot again, aiming at his face.

He charged me, moving faster than could've been expected from someone that large with limbs enclosed into hard shell.

I jumped back, out of his reach, but tripped over my own feet in fear and panic and fell backwards. Landing on my ass, I scurried away, crab-walking.

"Where do you think you're going?" he scoffed, advancing on me.

Where *was* I going?

Panic had deprived me of logic. I kept moving further inside the ship, leaving Svetlana to fight for her life out in the corridor.

My goal should be getting Enkail out of here and helping Svetlana to get back in.

Enkail out, Svetlana in.

Gathering my legs under me, I jumped up and aside. "Come and get me, tough guy!"

Holding the gun in my hand, I ran around the table and back to the exit.

With a grunt, Enkail followed.

Someone, a *yourlu*, poked his head into the ship. His tentacles snaked in, trying to block my way. I pointed my gun at his narrow forehead, right under the purple tuft of hair on the top of his head and fired. A smoldering hole formed in his bluish skin, then he crashed to the ground.

"I just killed a person!"

The thought shot through me, not unlike the laser blast. Only I had no time to freak out or even comprehend the full meaning of it. Someone else took the *yourlu's* place, and I shot again, then again, blasting my way out of the ship.

"Nadia!" A deep roar reverberated through the corridor.

Wyck!

Far down the corridor, his massive figure towered behind the crowd. Lesh's chain was wound around Wyck's torso, binding his arms to his sides. A group of *errocks* held him back as he fought against them, shoving at them with his wide shoulders.

Having no slack in the chain, Lesh tangled at his master's legs. Leshy and Leshic snapped at the ankles of his attackers. Nearly strangled by his collar on a shortened chain, Lesher seemed to be fighting for air.

I'd just taken the shortest glance at them, but it cost me a split second of concentration. Enkail gained on me. Grabbing my foot, he knocked me to the ground.

Wyck's roar shook the corridor, spreading through the bowels of the Dark Anomaly. Pure horror distorted his beloved features.

"Get off her!" He thundered.

His huge body strained. Blood rushed to his face, turning his skin from the warm color of reddish clay to flaming red, like a volcano ready to erupt. Veins in his thick neck swelled, and the muscles in his arms bulged. A link in the chain gave in under his enormous physical power. It bent and snapped, sending two ends of the chain flying open.

Enkail crawled over me, pressing my hips into the floor and reaching for the gun in my hand. Twisting aside, I held the gun with both hands and fired straight into his face, between his eyes.

"Press and hold," Svetlana's words rang in my head as I kept the trigger pressed.

Enkrail roared in pain and jerked aside. I moved my arms, aiming the laser ray at the exact same spot on his face. The laser burned through the plating between his eyes. The wound got deeper and wider, the nauseating stench of burnt flesh filling the air. The *dimo's* hard, heavy body slacked, still partially on top of me, yet I kept pressing—my finger froze in place as terror paralyzed me.

"He's dead." Svetlana yanked on my arm. The ray had made its way through the *dimo's* skull, leaving a scorch mark on the opposite wall. "Let go, Nadia."

I drew in a gasping breath, filling my lungs with the smell of the burning flesh of the male I'd just killed. My arms shook and my teeth chattered.

"Come." Svetlana helped me up. Tugging me up with one hand, she held her gun in the other, shooting at anyone who dared to approach us. Raising my gun in my shaking hand, I shot, too.

Wyck was working through the crowd to us. Pieces of the chain dangled off him. He swung his fists left and right like a pair of maces, crushing the bone and skulls of those in his way.

"Wyck!" Nocc leaped in front of him and thrust a long piece of a thick metal rod at him. "Stop this right now, boy."

"Get out of my way." Wyck kept moving ahead, ignoring Nocc and his makeshift weapon. "Nadia!"

"Is that your choice, boy?" Nocc yelled, pressing the jagged end of the rod into Wyck's chest so hard, a trickle of blood formed where it dug into Wyck's skin. "You choose some pathetic female over us, your family? You're betraying your own kind!"

"*My kind* is larger than you, Nocc," Wyck growled wildly. "There're billions of *errocks* out there, and they're better than any of you."

"What's *there* doesn't mean shit when you're *here*. Your father—"

"I'm *not* like my father!" Wyck shoved Nocc aside. "I *choose* not to be like him."

"Then you're no good to me, boy," Nocc spat through his teeth, charging Wyck.

The rod entered through Wyck's chest, like a spear.

A scream of horror lodged in my throat, blocking my next inhale.

Shock registered on Wyck's face—an utter disbelief at the betrayal. He clamped his large hands around the rod then yanked it out of his flesh and from Nocc's grip. Dark blood gushed in pulsing spurts from his chest. In one powerful movement, he speared the rod through Nocc's throat, then collapsed to his knees.

Everything inside me froze in terror. The world around me seemed to slow down, shrouded in thick fog.

I was only half aware of Svetlana holding back the feral crowd of males, drunk on blood, lust, and violence.

Of Nocc writhing on the floor in the last convulsions before stilling for good in the puddle of dark blood.

Of Vrateus suddenly rushing down the corridor, his guns drawn and firing.

Of the only *damirian* on the Dark Anomaly, Malahki, running with the captain, then skidding to a stop at the entrance to the gardens.

My vision shrunk, obscuring the view of all of them completely. My mind, my thoughts, the focus of my entire being at that moment narrowed on the hulking figure of my beloved giant tipping over to the floor. Cut down and crashed, like a hundred-year-old oak tree, he lay on his side. Without Wyck, existence on the Dark Anomaly suddenly made no sense to me. The entire world turned cold and lonely without him.

"Wyck!" Climbing over Nocc's motionless body, I scurried to Wyck's side.

I pressed both my hands against the deep wound in his chest. The stream of his hot blood pulsed through my fingers, uncontainable.

"My sweetness..." he whispered. His golden eyes glossed over before closing completely.

Svetlana's slender hand came into view as she pressed it to the side of his neck then to his chest over his heart.

"Let's go, Nadia." She tried to drag me away.

"No." I clung to his arm, my hands bathed in his blood.

"He is...dead, sweetie." Her voice broke, and my heart shuttered. "We can't help him."

"No..." I doubled over in horror, pressing his hand to my forehead. The hard ridges of his knuckles dug into my skin. The pain of that was nothing compared to the burning agony of loss in my chest.

"Quickly!" Vrateus rushed to us, urging both of us toward the ship. "There're more coming, and they're armed."

"Armed?" Svetlana gasped, her voice brittle with fear. "With guns, you mean?"

"Krakhil discovered the storage in our old room. They took the weapons that I'd left there. Come, Nadia. Or we'll all die."

"No!" I shifted closer to Wyck. My hands under his arms, I tried to drag him to the ship. "I'm not leaving him here."

It was like trying to move a mountain. Wyck's massive body wouldn't budge.

"We don't have much time," Vrateus's voice rang with urgency.

I dug my heels into the floor and kept trying to pull, afraid he would make me leave Wyck out here, in the corridor, at the mercy of the wild beings who could hardly be called "people" at all.

Nervously glancing down the corridor, Svetlana lifted Wyck's legs. "Nadia is right. We can't leave his body for them to desecrate."

Dragging the remainder of the broken chain behind him, Lesh limped our way. He whistled and hissed wistfully at Wyck's side then got hold of his master's pants on the side, helping us pull him along.

"Quickly then." Stepping over a few dead aliens, Vrateus came to my side and grabbed on to Wyck with me.

My vision blurred as we dragged Wyck over to the opening to our ship. Tears dripped down onto my arms, washing paths through the layer of blood—Wyck's blood. There was so much of it...

"Close the door," Vrateus told Svetlana as soon as all of us were finally inside the ship.

She dropped Wyck's legs and slid the heavy door back into place. Vrateus rushed to help her engage all the locks.

"Nadia, sweetie..." Svetlana returned to my side, compassion warming her voice.

I wouldn't have it, though. Evading her embrace, I stumbled to the niche in the wall opposite of our cabins and activated the flat screen mounted there. A long, padded panel slid out of the wall.

"What's that?" Both Svetlana and Vrateus stared at it in confusion.

"Medical capsule," I sniffed, whipping the tears out of my eyes with my shoulder. "Help me get him up here."

I punched commands into the screen, lowering the padded bunk to the ground.

"Nadia," Vrateus said carefully as he helped me heave Wyck's body onto the padded surface. "He has no pulse, no detectable breathing."

"It may be too late," Svetlana added softly.

I realized that. My brain—the logical part of it—understood it all, but my heart wouldn't accept it.

"Well, let's hurry then," I mumbled stubbornly, swiping the commands on the screen.

The bunk-gurney slid back up along the wall, lifting Wyck with it. A clear rounded canopy descended over him, its edges fusing with the perimeter of the gurney.

"*A patient detected. Species* errock. *Male. Please confirm,*" a metallic voice demanded impassively.

"Yes!" I yelled. "Help him!"

"*Assessing...*" the voice continued. "*The patient is clinically dead.*"

Blinking the rushing tears away, I frantically swiped though more commands, trying to remember everything I'd been taught during training. The medical capsule was Lee's area of expertise. The rest of us had only gone through the basic steps of operating it in case of an emergency. No one could've imagined back then what exactly the *emergency* would be.

"Select 'resuscitate,'" Svetlana came to my assistance, reading the commands for me as the words and letters on the panel merged into a blur in front of my eyes—the fog of tears obstructing my vision. "Then 'life support.'"

"Right." I wiped at the tears with my sleeve, entering the series of commands as she kept reading them to me.

Tubes and probes launched into motion inside the capsule, prodding and sliding along Wyck's body. Two slim tubes snaked into his nostrils. One slipped between his lips and into his mouth.

"Tissue and organ damage detected," came from the machine. *"Recommendation—repair the physical damage while on full life support, before the following functions of the body can be fully restored."*

A list scrolled down the screen, and I glanced at Svetlana, unable to focus enough to read it.

"Yes." She nodded. "Repair the damage."

"Please confirm the voice command," the machine demanded.

"Do it!" I punched the screen buttons to confirm. "Just do it, dammit!"

Svetlana gripped my shoulders from behind as I sobbed, my hands splayed on the glass of the capsule.

The metal tools hovered in a cluster over Wyck's gaping chest wound. Some clamped onto the rugged edges of it, holding it open, while hair-thin wires descended inside.

Several agonising moments that felt more like centuries passed while the robotics did their work. I moved my gaze from them to Wyck's face.

The warm glow had disappeared from his skin, making it look dull and ashen. Droplets of blood dried on his cheeks, a few clinging to the lips I loved kissing so much.

"Please, please, please..." I prayed to every deity out there. *"Don't take him from me. He's all I've got. He is my everything."*

Most of the tools withdrew. A few were still working on the skin around the wound. The muscles underneath it had been fused together. A dozen tiny pincers pulled the cleaned edges of the skin to each other. Then, a healing ray sealed the wound, the sides of it knitting together into a flat, pale scar.

Wyck's chest rose with an inhale but I kept the hope at bay. In full life-support mode, the machine was doing the breathing for him, as it did everything else at the moment.

"How is he?" I croaked, my throat dry and painful.

"What's the patient's status?" Svetlana asked in a much stronger, clearer voice than mine.

"The patient has been resuscitated and stabilized," the life-saving machine replied impassively.

"What is his prognosis?" She squeezed my shoulders in a reassuring gesture.

"Undetermined."

"Why?" I cried out.

Wrapping her arms around me, Svetlana held me closer.

"How long until you can *determine* it?" she asked the machine.

"Approximately twenty-four to forty-eight hours."

Svetlana's chest rose with a sigh, pushing against my back as she kept hugging me from behind.

"All we can do is wait," Vrateus said somberly, standing next to us.

Svetlana rubbed my arms gently.

"He'll be okay."

I nodded, drawing in a tight breath.

Wyck had to be okay. He needed to get better. Because without him, my life had no meaning on the Dark Anomaly or beyond.

Chapter 22

"DID YOU SLEEP OUT HERE again?" Svetlana asked, entering the common area with a mug of coffee in her hand.

I hadn't moved our mattress back to Wyck's and my cabin yet. The evidence of my spending yet another night on the floor under the medical capsule was right there for her to see.

"I don't want to miss any changes," I mumbled, drawing circles with my finger on the smooth surface of the glass canopy.

It was the second day of Wyck being enclosed there. And every day, the system kept repeating the same thing about the "twenty-four to forty-eight hours." It was driving me mad with worry. I didn't trust the machine. There was no way for me to tell if it even was functioning properly or if it'd suffered some damage during the landing. I'd run the diagnostics on the main control panel; however, no damages had been reported. Yet there'd been no progress and no updates on Wyck during these two long days.

"Come have some breakfast with me," Svetlana said, her voice warm and caring.

From the food replicator, she carried a second cup of coffee for me and two pieces of plain toast, one for each of us.

The atmosphere outside our ship remained volatile, forcing all of us to stay inside since the last attack. Cut off from the resources of the Dark Anomaly for the time being, we'd begun to ration the food supply available from the replicators on board. There were no more lavish meals for us.

"Come, Nadia." She set our modest breakfast on the table.

"I'll need to get my bed out of here, first." I toed my mattress with my bare foot. I'd slept in my suit, but I'd taken my boots off for the night and didn't bother putting them back on yet.

"I'll help you move it back after breakfast," she said. "You'll need to eat something. Please?"

I took a seat next to her at the table and bit into the toast. The smell of coffee was oddly nauseating, so I didn't touch the mug. I felt ravenously hungry, though, and polished off the toast in a few huge bites.

"Is Vrateus still asleep?" I asked, attempting to converse, even as all my thoughts remained on that capsule.

"Yes." Svetlana glanced at the door to their cabin and lowered her voice. "He stayed up late last night, analyzing the situation."

"And?"

She inhaled deeply, hugging her coffee mug with both hands.

"It's not the first time that Vrateus has had to deal with mutiny on the Dark Anomaly."

I nodded. Judging by the wild nature of his crew, it didn't surprise me they'd proven difficult to control. I'd heard of other mutiny attempts before.

"He'd been able to make them submit, every time," she continued. "But now, he's doubting if it's worth the price."

"What do you mean?

"Every time there is a power struggle, a lot of people die. And Vrateus has grown to care about some of the people here too much to risk their lives." She smiled. "I'm talking about you, me, and Wyck, of course. He wonders if he should even bother fighting for power at all."

"He doesn't want to be the captain anymore?"

"His main goal, now, is to keep the four of us safe and well. And it's getting harder and harder to do so out there." She gestured at the entrance to the corridor. "The life out there carries a constant risk, and it's not just about surviving hardships. The crew are actively killing each other. Nothing would stop them from killing us, too."

I understood the problem. The solution remained vague, however.

"What does Vrateus want to do?"

She bit her lip.

"There aren't that many options, sadly. We could start a smaller community with just the four of us and whoever else would want to join on the condition that everyone works hard and respects each other. That would mean of course that the rest of the crew would be left to their own devices. It pains Vrateus to abandon them. He's cared for their wellbeing for so long."

"While they've been trying to overthrow and murder him, constantly." I scoffed.

"True." She scraped her hand over her face. "Anyway, we'll have to discuss it together when Wyck gets better..."

We both turned to the medical capsule at her words.

A soft-yellow light lit up on its control screen. It hadn't been there before. Shoving my chair back, I got up quickly, worry spiking in me.

"Something's happening." I hurried to the capsule, yelling at it, "Patient's status update!"

"The life support is no longer necessary for the following functions and systems..."

A long list scrolled down the screen as the robotic voice read it out loud.

"Breathing, heartbeat, blood production..." The list went on and on.

"What exactly does it mean?" I demanded. "Is he getting better? When is he going to be well again?"

"Initiating the sequence of returning the patient to full consciousness," the system announced instead of replying to my questions.

"He'll be waking up, now." Svetlana stood next to me as we both gazed at Wyck lying under the glass.

I sucked in a breath and gripped her hand.

"What is the patient's prognosis, now?" she asked.

"Full recovery," the mechanical voice replied with zero emotion.

A wall of feelings rushed through me, I swayed on my feet, nearly knocked over by relief, hope, and worry. All tubes were removed from him and disappeared back into the wall.

Wyck's chest rose with a breath he took all on his own. His eyelids fluttered, then his eyes opened.

A loud sob tore from my throat at the sight of his luminous eyes—bright yellow with calming specs of green.

The transparent canopy lifted.

"Go to him." Svetlana softly nudged me.

By "go to him" she might have meant a hug, hand holding, or maybe a kiss.

None of those seemed sufficient at the moment. I needed all of that and more. I wanted all of him, at once.

Sobbing, I climbed on the bed to him as Svetlana left the room, going to tell Vrateus the news.

A knee on each side of Wyck's hips, I braced my legs to keep my weight entirely off him. I leaned over him, cupping his face.

"Wyck..." I gently kissed his lips. "My love..."

I couldn't stop kissing his face, every touch of my lips against his warm skin being another reassurance of him finally coming back to me.

"Love?" He blinked in the bright light of the room and slid his hands up my hips to my waist. "I know exactly what that means, my sweet sugar. I love you."

Tears streamed anew, and I didn't bother to wipe them away. They dropped on his chin, getting lost in his stubble.

He lifted a finger to my face, tracing a tear from my eye down my cheek.

"Are those happy tears?" he asked.

"A new patient detected..." the system suddenly announced.

I paid it no attention, lost in the moment with Wyck.

"Happy tears," I whispered, staring into his eyes. "Those are very happy tears, Wyck. *My* Wyck. I love you, too."

He slid his hand behind my neck, then lowered my head down to his mouth for a kiss.

"Human female..." the system kept talking.

I raised my hand, blindly searching along the wall for the screen to shut it up. I was not going to break our kiss even if...

"Gestational age of the fetus is estimated at five weeks..."

I dropped my hand down, sitting upright abruptly.

"What is it saying?" I gaped at Wyck as if he had an explanation.

"Mixed species— errock *and human. Gender male. Development normal for this stage of pregnancy..."*

Shock rolled through me.

"A fetus?" Wyck sat up, too, shifting me into his lap.

"A baby?" I mumbled, and we both stared at my stomach area.

"Is that possible?" he asked me. "Are there babies of mixed species out there?"

"A few. To my knowledge, all of them have been created by artificial insemination. In a lab. Not like...this. And no human-*errock* ones yet."

"Five weeks?" He looked just as utterly confused as I must have.

"They calculate the gestational age in a weird way. The fetus..." I touched my belly, with trembling fingers. "The baby has actually been there only for two or three weeks of that time."

It must've been conceived shortly after Wyck and I moved here over three weeks ago.

"There is..." He covered my hand with his. "There is a baby in there?"

"That's what the medical capsule says, and I have no other way of confirming it." Other than my rather sudden aversion to the smell of coffee. "Could the system be malfunctioning?"

"Is it the same system that has just patched me up?"

I nodded, shaken and overwhelmed.

He rubbed the faint scar on his chest. "Seems to be functioning pretty good. I feel great." He splayed one hand on my stomach, sinking the fingers of the other into the hair on the back of my head. "Are we starting our very own family, then?"

"I guess we are," I breathed out, staring at his golden eyes full of life and love. "How do you feel about it?"

"Nadia." He leaned his forehead to mine. "You are *my kind*. You and...he, the baby. I'd die for you."

"You already have." I took his face in my hands, finding his eyes with mine again. "You've already died once. You've just come back from the dead. No more dying, my darling. We need to live, now. All of us."

His eyes shimmered, glistening brighter than ever. Then a tear rolled out, trembling on the end of an eyelash. I leaned closer, kissing it off. "Don't cry, sweetheart," I whispered, my heart overflowing with tenderness and love.

"These are all happy tears, promise," he laughed and cried, holding me closer. "Sugar, I've never been happier in my life."

EPILOGUE

"Hmm," Nadia hummed softly, rolling his cock between her palms while straddling his thighs. "What shall we do this time?"

He didn't know what she had in mind, and that made the whole thing so much more exciting.

"There are so many variations with you, you know," she giggled quietly. He loved that happy sound of hers. He loved every little thing about her.

The way her golden-brown hair, mussed from sleep, was framing her lovely face.

The way her green eyes glistened mischievously from under the few tangled tresses hanging over her face.

The way her lips curved with a teasing smile, just begging for him to kiss them.

The way her breasts swayed enticingly as she rolled and kneaded his cock between her hot, little palms...

He strained, pulsing with need. The thought of her tight channels made him ready to beg or charge forward and take. He knew, she'd welcome either action from him. Nadia liked it both ways, either rough or gentle.

He chose to go with gentle this time. His body shaking with anticipation, he caught her breasts in his hands and stroked her nipples. He wished for her to feel the desperation that was torturing him. He was going to make *her* beg him.

Bending his knees, he made her slide down his thighs, until her slick core pressed hot against his bottom erection.

She inhaled sharply, rubbing herself against him.

"On second thought..." she rasped, her voice breathy. "Forget searching for variations. I want you, right now." She leaned over him, sliding his bottom cock inside her. "I want you, Wyck," she groaned softly as he plunged deeper. "So, so much."

The top cock got trapped between them as she slid up and down along his body. The tandem pleasure in both was driving him wild.

"You feel so good, my sweet," he moaned with a rumble vibrating deep inside his chest. He'd chosen to be gentle, and he strained his muscles to restrain himself.

Slow meant he could savour every glide of their bodies against each other.

She leaned closer to his chest, grinding her hips against him. "This is...*perfect*," she exhaled, pressing her forehead to his shoulder.

And...he was done with being gentle. Holding her in his arms, he rolled them over, taking control.

She squeaked with surprise and delight.

He angled his hips, aiming for that spot he knew would drive her mad with desire and pleasure. Rising over her, he pounded hard as the approaching climax rolled closer. A surge of pleasure tightened the muscles in his thighs and lower belly, ready to explode if he let it.

His eyes on her, he watched for the familiar signs of her orgasm nearing. He'd learned to read her expressions as well as a book.

Her eyes closed tight, her lips parted, her brows drew into a frown of both torture and rapture.

He thrust one more time, both of his cocks strained to the limit and ready to erupt. His skin gliding smoothly against hers.

She tilted her head back, her neck flexed, and a shuddering wave of orgasm rocked her body. Her climax set his off. His release exploded, flooding him with ecstasy and blissful relief.

"Your pleasure is mine..." she muttered, with her eyes still closed, her hips undulating under him. She couldn't see him, but he knew she felt him with every cell of her body, because that's how he felt her.

"And yours is mine." He kissed her deeply—his sweet, delicious woman.

She was his home, his one true family.

Next to her was the only place where he belonged.

WYCK

A gun in each hand, he walked along the corridor, trying to step as noiselessly as his size and weight would allow.

Vrateus and he had been taking turns patrolling this portion of the corridor and the adjacent hallways next to the human ship.

While staying on the ship, the four of them were safe. They had their own water, air, and light, separate from the grid on the Dark Anomaly. The food supply, however, was limited. The occasional trips off the ship remained necessary.

Every now and then, one of them would sneak out to get some supplies from a storage room that hadn't been fully raided by the crew yet, or to hunt an occasional *vasai* centipede for meat.

The added purpose of these expeditions was to assess the current state of the Dark Anomaly.

Judging by the many signs he had passed, the situation wasn't great. Bare bones of *vasai* centipedes littered the floor, mixed with debris and an occasional mangled body part of one of the crew.

The order Vrateus had maintained on the Dark Anomaly was gone within hours once the crew had taken over. Complete and utter anarchy had reigned ever since.

Wyck snuck into the gardens—a desolate and abandoned place, now that Malahki was no longer there. The *damirian* had been last seen the day Krakhil had locked the captain in a storage room while

Nocc and the others overpowered Wyck and tied him with Lesh's chain. The rogue *errock* and the *dimo* then tricked and attacked the two women.

Malahki had helped the captain escape that day, alerting him to the attack on the human ship. The *damirian* disappeared shortly after that. Wyck hoped for its sake that Malahki had managed to hide somewhere. Though chances were, it'd been attacked and eaten sometime during the past weeks of anarchy.

Vrateus was concerned about Malahki's fate. He'd instructed Wyck to watch for any trace of the *damirian* whenever possible.

Neglected, the gardens had been slowly deteriorating. Some parts had been growing out of control, wild and unkept. In the others, the plants withered and died—the planters here stood almost bare of green already and overhung with dead foliage.

Walking between them, Wyck collected some of the fruit that had survived, then ripped off an entire vine of edible leaves, withered but still green. Not finding any signs of the *damirian* here, he headed back.

A small nook behind a planter by the entrance caught his attention when a faint whiff of an old scent reached him.

He snuck around a large planter, staying close to the wall. Clicking a flashlight on, he shone its ray into the nook.

A rusty smear on the floor must be what had left the scent. Someone appeared to have bled here. Considering the state of things lately, it could've been any one of the crew.

He turned to leave. Then the ray of the flashlight illuminated a short string of characters on the wall, just above the spilled blood on the floor.

It wasn't written in Universal because Wyck couldn't read it. Though, he believed that the characters had a meaning. They reminded him of letters forming words. The lines and swirls had an order and had been drawn in that deliberate way he'd come to expect from written language.

Back at the entrance to the human ship, he tilted his head back to clearly display his face to the camera above the door then knocked.

The door slid open, revealing Nadia's beautiful face, a gun in her hand pointed at his chest.

"Come in." She stepped aside promptly, aiming the gun behind him.

As soon as the door was closed and locked, he hugged her to him. The feeling of her warm, soft body in his arms and her sweet familiar scent made everything right with the world, even in the middle of the chaos they called the Dark Anomaly.

"I got some fruit," he said, when he'd gathered enough willpower to tear himself away from her.

"Fruit?" Her eyes lit up.

She'd had a healthy appetite lately, which pleased him greatly. However, she'd also been craving odd things. Most were from her home planet, Earth. He didn't always know what they were, but he wished to get them all for her. Nadia was his family, the future mother of his son. She deserved to have anything she desired. It frustrated him that he couldn't get everything she wished for her.

"Do you want some?" he asked, happy to fulfill this one wish of hers.

"Yes, please." She smiled, and he couldn't resist stealing another kiss from her.

Svetlana took the mesh bag out of his hand. "I'll get it washed and peeled. You just keep kissing there." She waved her hand at them.

Wyck thought about the letters on the wall, breaking the kiss.

"What is it?" Nadia frowned, sensing his concern.

"Nothing to worry about, my sweet." He kissed the tiny wrinkle that had formed between her slim eyebrows. "I just need to ask you something.'

He walked over to the table where Svetlana had already unpacked the fruit.

"How are things?" Vrateus asked, setting the tablet he'd been reading aside.

"Wild." Wyck leaned over the table, propping his hands against it. "I've found something."

He picked up Vrateus's tablet. Recalling the characters he'd seen, he recreated them on the tablet's screen from memory, by gliding his finger over the lit surface of the slate.

"Do you know what this means?" He turned the screen to the captain.

"No." Vrateus stared at it closely. "What language is it?"

"Let me see?" Nadia peeked around his arm.

Svetlana was plucking the leaves off the vine, placing them into a wide dish. She took a glance at the screen, too, from across the table.

Both women's faces paled.

"Do you know this language?" he asked, now absolutely certain this was a language, and the characters represented words or letters.

Svetlana nodded.

"It's English, one of Earth's languages. Do you think it's from Val?" She turned to Nadia.

Nadia kept staring at the screen, her green eyes larger than ever.

"It must be from her. And it could only be meant for me. She didn't know about you being alive. And she didn't want anyone from the crew to understand it, that's why she wrote it in English, not Universal."

"What does it mean, sugar?" he asked. "What does it say?"

"It says 'Help Me.'"

THE END

EXPLOSION, book 3 of Dark Anomaly, is coming soon.

Please see www.marinasimcoe.com for updates.

EXPERIMENT

CHAPTER 1

"Isabella Bruno." The man in a dark suit wasn't asking. Staring at me from the other side of the front entrance as I held the door open, he stated my name confidently, as if he already knew it was me.

"How can I help you?" I asked cautiously, glancing at the two others behind him. The large, black vehicles parked at the curb in front of our house did not put my mind at ease either.

"Michael Trevin." He offered me his hand. "May we come in?"

"Trevin?" I stared at him in shock, ignoring his hand. "The Michael Trevin?" I asked, dumbfounded, even as I had already recognized the face of one of the three North American representatives in the coalition of Earth Governments. "You're here? In Deer Rock?"

The fact that someone so high up in the government personally visited our small town—far up North on the territory that used to be Canada before the three countries of the continent had been merged into one—should be a huge event.

Had his visit been made public? How had I missed the news? And why was he at my house?

"Can we come in?" he asked more persistently, moving forward, which forced me to step back.

"Um, sure," I mumbled, as if my permission meant anything at that point—all three had entered our small hallway.

I smoothed my hair quickly and brushed my palms down my t-shirt, feeling painfully underdressed in my pajama pants. It was mid-morning on a weekday, but I had an evening shift at the store today and hadn't changed yet. Luckily, I had at least put a bra on.

"Who is it, Bella?" Mom came out of the kitchen, bouncing Lily, one of my sister's twins, on her hip. "Mister Trevin . . ." She stared at the representative, her eyes opened wide, her mouth agape. "In my house?"

"Mrs Bruno." He shook her hand energetically. "Where would be the best place for us to have a quick talk?" Without waiting for an answer, he shoved past her and into our kitchen. His escort followed.

"Um . . . About what?" Mom hurried after them. "Would you like anything? Tea? Water?"

"We don't have much time." Trevin pulled a chair from the table and sat down. "Secretary Carter. Agent Miller." He gestured at the two men accompanying him as they took seats at the table too.

"What is it all about?" Mom moved her gaze from one man to another. Both her and I remained standing.

"We are here to collect Isabella Bruno," Miller blurted out, earning a stern glare from Trevin.

"Me?" I stepped into the kitchen from the entrance where I had been standing.

Surely this was some kind of misunderstanding.

"What did she do?" Mom sent me a questioning stare.

"Before I explain," Trevin raised a hand in a calming gesture, "allow me to remind you that although our coalition is the main human governing body on the planet, it has been under the jurisdiction of the planet Keala for the past nine years. The extraterrestrials have left us to administer our population, but the Kealan laws take precedence over ours."

The aliens had come to Earth suddenly one day. Several giant flying saucers had hovered over a few major cities, and it didn't take long for them to make it clear they did not come in peace.

All military attempts by the coalition to attack the spaceships resulted in the immediate annihilation of our aircraft and missiles.

Then they attacked us. Entire populations of several towns and small cities around the world were eradicated within minutes when bright rays of light had descended from the ships. All structures, machines, and animals were left intact. However, the people in those places were turned to dust in seconds—white ash all that remained.

Human capitulation came right after the aliens threatened to annihilate the entire population of Earth in the same fashion if we didn't surrender.

As Trevin pointed out, the Kealans left the coalition in charge of Earth's administration, not getting involved much in our politics or our way of life. They built two facilities, one on each of Earth's poles, and implemented mandatory annual medical evaluations for all humans aged eighteen to sixty.

Other than that, it was easy to forget with time that Earth had been conquered at all.

"Please take a seat, Isabella." Trevin's stare carried a power I found myself unable to disobey. I sat at the table across from him, folding my hands over the large red strawberries printed on the plastic tablecloth. "About a week ago, the coalition received a request from the Kealans. They demanded you be handed over to them."

"Me?" I repeated, stunned, a fog of confusion and denial settled over my brain. "There must be some mistake . . ."

"No mistake. They want you," Miller bit off.

Trevin leaned in, resting his hands on the table. "We were able to negotiate some time to discuss the situation last week. However, this morning, their request was made urgent—" A sudden thought appeared to flash through his mind. "When was your last medical examination?"

"Yesterday," I replied, clutching my hands tight. "What do they want with me?"

The exams were done by the local doctor, for free and with no known health consequences observed. Alien robot-drones delivered the test kits and collected the data obtained. After nine years, the global medical exams had become the norm. By now, hardly anyone questioned it, begrudgingly accepting having to go see the doctor once a year as something that had to be done—kind of like renewing one's driver's licence, or filing taxes.

"You had one done yesterday?" Trevin exchanged a knowing look with the other men at the table. "That may explain the urgency."

"How?" Even more perplexed, I moved my gaze from one face to another. "What do they want?" I asked again, since no one had answered me the first time.

"Well." Trevin leaned against the back of his chair, stretching his neck and obviously stalling his answer.

"Your current physical state may be of some importance to them," Carter joined in.

"What do you mean? When will I be able to come home?"

Carter glanced at Trevin. Something in the expressions of the two sent a chill of trepidation down my spine.

"I will come back, won't I?" I insisted, louder.

"The extraterrestrials offered you Kealan citizenship. Through marriage." Trevin shifted in his chair, making it squeak. "To that extent, they also agreed to honour our traditions and have a proper wedding ceremony—"

"What wedding?" both Mom and I said at once.

Rolling his eyes to the ceiling, Miller leaned back in his chair and crossed his arms over his chest. "Yours," he explained, with a dramatic sigh of exasperation. "The aliens want one of them to marry you."

"Which is a good thing when you think about it," Carter rushed in. "It could be presented as a gesture of good will—"

"Presented to whom?" I jumped from my seat. All of it stopped making any sense whatsoever. "What are you all talking about? I'm not going anywhere. I'm perfectly fine where I am. Why would the aliens want me anyway? I've never met them and don't want to."

I'd watched the news broadcast of the few official visits of the Kealans with the coalition. The images of their tall figures, draped in black cloaks, hoods drawn low over their faces, left an unpleasant impression on me, bringing the Grim Reaper to mind.

"And . . . a wedding? Really?" I wrung my hands, pacing in front of the table, as if moving could help me wrap my mind around all of this.

"Miss Bruno . . ." Carter jumped out of his seat, too.

"This is just stupid!" Skipping down the stairs, my sister, Mary, barged into the room, her son Luca under her arm. "His diaper is changed." She handed Luca to my mom, who put him on her other hip, opposite to his twin. "Honestly, guys." Hands propped on the tabletop, Mary stared down Trevin and his escort. Less than two years younger than me, she had always been the more assertive and outspoken one. "Just listen to you! An alien wedding? What the hell are you talking about? Is this some kind of a joke for reality TV or something?"

"It will be televised," Carter announced, brightly. "The preparations for the event have been in full swing since the initial demand was received."

"Even before I was notified?" I muttered, wishing I could just wake up and stop this nightmare.

"And who are you?" Mary threw at Carter sarcastically, one corner of her mouth lifting up. "The wedding planner?"

"Ma'am." Miller rose from the table and moved on to my sister. "It's imperative we deliver Isabella Bruno—"

"What do you mean by 'deliver?'" Mary scoffed. "Bella is a free woman, she has rights—"

"Exactly," Mom stepped in, balancing the twins on each hip. "You can't just come in here and take her—"

"You're forgetting that none of us are free, miss." Trevin got up, shoving the chair back with a screeching noise, his jaw muscles flexed. "Not since the capitulation to the Kealans nine years ago."

"We have orders to take your sister." Miller crossed his arms over his chest. "Your permission is not required."

"I don't want to go." Dread slithered up my spine, cold and sticky. "My home is here. My job. I have a life . . . I—"

"Isabella." Trevin took a step my way.

"No." I glared at him.

"She is not going anywhere," Mary insisted stubbornly.

"This is all definitely way too fast." Moving her gaze across the room, Mom appeared completely lost. "Why all this rush? Who is this man . . . um, this alien, who wants to marry her? Why? Does he like her? They've never met . . ."

"Like?" Miller grimaced. "What does that have to do with anything?"

The front door opened with a knock.

"Bell? Are you home?" I heard the familiar voice of Johnny, my boyfriend of four years.

Mom bounced on her heels to calm the twins who started fussing. "What I'm saying is that this is not a proper way to ask someone to marry you," she argued with Miller.

Trevin pinched the bridge of his nose. "You're missing the point, ma'am. We are not the ones who make demands here."

"Who is getting married?" Johnny walked in, tossing back his shoulder-length blond hair, some of which perpetually hung over his face.

"The freaking aliens are planning a wedding with Bella!" Mary blurted out, gesturing at Miller and Trevin, as if they were the aliens in question.

"Mary . . ." I exhaled, feeling like my knees were about to give out, a pounding headache threatened to set in.

Johnny moved a confused glance from her to Miller then finally to me. "Is that true?"

"We don't have much time." Trevin ignored him. "The flight to Capital City will take at least two hours. With the ceremony scheduled for tonight, the team will have to start getting you ready soon."

Ready...

Ready for what? The wedding?

Tonight?

My heart skipped at the realization that all of this was real after all. Fear settled heavily in my chest, threatening to turn into panic.

"How will you ever get anyone ready to marry some alien dude?" Mary yelled at the three. "No matter how much time you have. Who the hell is he anyway?"

"We have not been given the groom's identity," Trevin replied coolly.

"Mary is right, though." Mom shook her head. "This is insane."

"Your family will be well compensated, of course," Carter started.

"This is not about money!" Mary snapped.

"Her dad is in the hospital," my mom muttered softly, shifting her pleading gaze from one of the men to another. "At the very least, you need to let her say goodbye... Why this rush?" she groaned.

"Johnny..." I grabbed my boyfriend by the arm and shoved him into the hallway, desperate to get away from it all, to shut the noise out, to get some time to do something... Anything.

"Is it true what they're saying, Bell?" Johnny asked as I dragged him around the corner and out of everyone's sight. "Are those SUV's outside theirs? And is that Michael Trevin, for real?"

"Miss Bruno!" Miller's voice thundered behind me.

"A minute, please. Give me one freaking minute!" I yelled back. "Johnny." I whispered quickly, panic vibrating through me. "This can't be happening..."

"Do they really want you to marry an alien?"

"Apparently, it's the aliens who want this. Johnny." Gripping his shoulders, I gave him a shake. "Please, help me. Let's run."

There was no way I was going to return to that kitchen where they all waited for me.

Until this morning, I'd been a regular small-town girl, working in a convenience store since I graduated high school eight years ago. With my oldest brother in and out of jail for the past several years and my father in and out of hospitals with his ailing heart and lungs, I had been helping my mom with my four younger brothers who were still in grade school and more recently, with Mary's ten-month-old twins.

My plans for the future had mostly included marrying Johnny—whenever he saved up enough money to buy me a ring and asked me to be his wife—and eventually starting a family.

It was not a glorious life, but it was my life, and I was content, living right here in Deer Rock, where I knew everybody and everyone knew me from the day I was born.

This whole thing now felt surreal and terrifying.

"Get me out of here, please," I whispered, not sure myself how that could be accomplished or where I could run to. I just needed to be far away from here. "I'm not going with them. I need to hide."

"Bell." His hesitant expression broke my heart. "You know their drones can find you by your DNA?"

I knew—that was how the Kealans traced those who tried to evade the medical testing—but I couldn't think rationally at that point.

"We'll hide in a cave, somewhere, where the drones can't fly?" My voice dropped, however, as did the hope in my heart. "I can't do this, Johnny . . ."

"Maybe just for a little while?" he suggested.

"What?" I stared at him in disbelief. "You actually want me to go with them?"

"Tony should be out next month," he spoke quickly. "I'm sure your brother will think of something."

Tony—my oldest brother and Johnny's idol since we were little—always came up with something. I wished he were here. Unfortunately, Tony's ingenuity had been wasted on raiding gas stations and convenience stores, which had put him in jail for the second time in his twenty-nine years.

"Together, we will find a way to get you out later," Johnny promised.

"It means I'll have to go with them now," I whispered, every fibre of my being refusing to accept the idea of that.

"Listen," he said soothingly, stroking my arms, but his gaze flickered to the wall behind me as he refused to meet my eyes. "If they want you . . ."

"Then you don't?" I snapped.

"No, it's not that. Just, you know, they always get their way . . ."

"Johnny. Are you afraid of them, too?" I stepped back, not wanting to believe the obvious, but feeling completely alone already. "Are you breaking up with me?"

"There is going to be a wedding, Bell," he sounded apologetic. "I don't want you to end up feeling guilty over what may come afterwards."

"Are you kidding me?" My throat tightened painfully, and I brought my hand to it.

"I just want to make it easier for you," he continued in a rush. "No matter what, I won't see it as cheating on your part. Okay?"

"I can't believe it!" With a sob, I shrunk further away from him, feeling both ashamed and disgusted.

He reached for me. "You know we don't have a choice—"

"Isabella, it's time." Trevin walked out of the kitchen, his voice firm.

Breathing hard, I backed away from both of them, moving to the front door.

"Miss Bruno . . ." Miller came from around Trevin, but I was no longer listening to whatever either of them had to say.

Twisting around, I dashed for the exit.

"You go, sis!" Mary cheered from the kitchen just as one of the twins started crying.

Shoving at the front door with my shoulder, I ran outside, without having any idea where I was going. Panic overtook me, propelling me to sprint as far away from this place as possible, away from the men in suits.

"Miss Bruno!" The doors of one of the black vehicles in front of our house flew open, and two men in black uniforms leaped out. They cut me off and tackled me to the ground in our front yard.

"Quickly, in the van with her," Miller bit out the command, catching up with us.

"Let me go!" I screamed, fighting against the hands lifting me off the ground. "I don't want this! I'm not going!"

The last I saw before they shoved me in and shut the doors were the pale faces of my family standing in the doorway of the house where I grew up.

My sister, comforting Lily in her arms. My mom, her hand over her mouth, Luca crawling at her feet. The thought of Tony and my dad flashed through my brain. The images of my little brothers who would come home from school that afternoon and find me gone.

I never got a chance to say a proper goodbye to any of them.

⎯⎯✕⎯⎯

EXPERIMENT by Marina Simcoe is available now at all major book retailers.

More by Marina Simcoe

PARANORMAL ROMANCE

Madame Tan's Freakshow
Call of Water
Madness of the Moon
Power of Rage

Demons, Complete Series
Demon Mine
The Forgotten
Grand Master
The Last Unforgiven - Cursed
The Last Unforgiven - Freed

Stand Alone Novels Set in Demons World
The Real Thing
To Love A Monster

Midnight Coven Author Group
Wicked Warlock (Cursed Coven)

SCIENCE-FICTION ROMANCE

Dark Anomaly Trilogy
Gravity
Power
Explosion

My Holiday Tails
Married To Krampus
My Tiny Giant – January 2021

Standalone Novels
Experiment
Enduring (Valos Of Sonhadra)

About the Author

MARINA SIMCOE LIKES to write love stories with characters, who may or may not be entirely human, because she firmly believes that our contemporary world could always use a little bit of the extraordinary.

She has lots of fun exploring how her out-of-this-world characters with their own beliefs, values, and aspirations fit into our everyday life.

She lives in Canada with her very own captain, their three little offsprings, and a cat, who is definitely out of this world.

For updates on her books please visit Marina Simcoe Author page on Facebook or www.marinasimcoe.com.

Please Stay in Touch

Newsletter signup: http://eepurl.com/c__RGn
Facebook Readers' Group: Marina's Reading Cave
www.instagram.com/marinasimcoeauthor
www.marinasimcoe.com
www.facebook.com/MarinaSimcoeAuthor/
www.amazon.com/author/marinasimcoe
www.bookbub.com/profile/marina-simcoe
www.goodreads.com/MarinaSimcoe